Flight From
Deathrow

Flight From Deathrow

HARRY HILL

sphere

SPHERE

First published in Great Britain in 2002 by Time Warner Books
This revised edition published in 2009 by Sphere

Copyright © 2002, 2009 by Harry Hill

The moral right of the author has been asserted.

The author gratefully acknowledges permission to quote from the following:
'Rockin' All Over The World' © John Fogerty. Reproduced by permission of
Hornall Brothers Music Ltd/Wenaha Music Company.
'Star Trekkin'' © G. Lister, J. O'Connor and R. Kehoe. Reproduced by permission of
Bushranger Music/Bark Music.
'Down Down' © Francis Rossi and Bob Young, 1974. Reproduced by permission of
EMI Music Publishing Ltd/MCA Music Publishing, London WC2H 0QY.

Every effort has been made to trace the copyright holders and to clear
permissions for the following: 'Caroline', 'These Boots Are Made For Walkin'',
'Thank U', 'Touch Me (I Want To Feel Your Body)', 'Shaddup You Face'.
If notified, the publisher will be pleased to rectify any omission in future editions.

A CIP catalogue record for this book
is available from the British Library.

ISBN 978-0-7515-4234-9

Typeset in Palatino by M Rules
Printed and bound in Great Britain by
Clays Ltd, St Ives plc

Papers used by Sphere are natural, renewable and
recyclable products sourced from well-managed forests and certified in
accordance with the rules of the Forest Stewardship Council.

Mixed Sources
Product group from well-managed
forests and other controlled sources
www.fsc.org Cert no. SGS-COC-004081
© 1996 Forest Stewardship Council

FSC

Sphere
An imprint of
Little, Brown Book Group
100 Victoria Embankment
London EC4Y 0DY

An Hachette UK Company
www.hachette.co.uk

www.littlebrown.co.uk

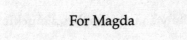

For Magda

'Many a mickle makes a muckle'

Alice Botting, 1973

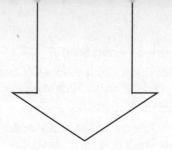

Contents

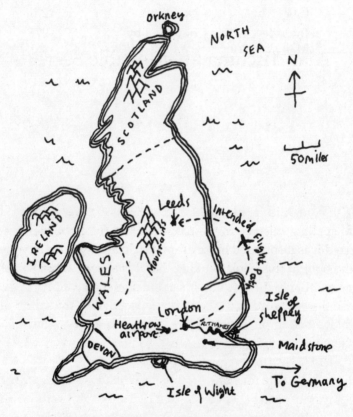

Map of U.K. to show main points

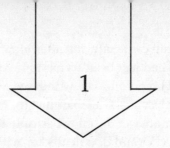

Alan Titchmarsh's Terrible Secret

That should read *Flight From Heathrow*. There was a spelling mistake in the first draft but the publisher preferred it as it sounded more dramatic. So apologies to anyone who bought this book thinking that it is a story about someone waiting to die. It's not. It's about someone waiting to fly. Also the last word in the book is supposed to be the sound of a plane taking off – just so you know and are not confused when you get to it. Right, let's get stuck in . . .

I had lived there for twelve years, so when I got the booking I jumped at the chance to go back to Leeds. Oh Leeds! With your cobbled streets and quaint Tudor architecture leading as it does to the cathedral – or is that York? Oh Leeds! With your rolling river, and tower of Big Ben. Oh Leeds, with your Bull Ring shopping centre and . . . I've just realised I've never been to Leeds. Fortunately that doesn't really affect the story because it's more about a call to go to Leeds than any particular Leeds-based memories I might have; although that would have been a nice way to pad out the start of the book.

No matter, the call came late one afternoon. I remember that much because I had just been trying to invent a new biscuit. Ever try that? Have you ever wondered why there isn't a wider variety of biscuits available? Just try inventing one and you'll have your answer. Biscuits basically fall into two categories: single decker and double decker with fondant centre. Okay, you get some coated with chocolate, or sprinkled with sugar, or with bits in, but basically these are the main two types. The problem for inventors is that as soon as you take the biscuit out of its two dimensions and build it up, it becomes a cake. There are still a few lone biscuit inventors, like myself, who strive for the elusive third way, but we're pretty much dismissed as crackpots.

That morning I thought I'd got close. I'd got one half of a Bourbon and built up two Custard Creams at either end into a kind of pyramidal structure. This enabled me to work out that the cream in the Bourbon is equal to the Custard Cream on the two remaining sides, but the Bourbon side was too long and protruded and, as I say, I was rounding it down with a power tool when the phone rang. I didn't recognise it at first as no one had phoned me for so long; there was just this sort of ringing sound, which seemed to be coming from the table. I lifted up the table and said, 'Hello?'

As I did so, the telephone receiver fell on to the floor. Thus the ringing sound gave way to a tiny voice, which sounded like my agent Zevon saying, 'Hello?' but as if he was extremely small or a long way away.

I got down on my hands and knees and started looking for a tiny man who was maybe related to Zevon and so had a similar timbre to his voice. In my mind this soon became a forgotten withered twin. Yes, that was it, a housebound withered twin who Zevon normally kept hidden away in a room, only this time Zevon had gone out and forgotten to lock the door properly. The withered twin, seeing his chance, had broken free from the shackles that had held him loosely chained to the radiator (you can knock it, but at winter time it's lovely and warm) and started to claw his way over to the door, his fingernails scraping on the rough matting that had served as his bed for the last thirty-six years. Summoning all his strength – which wasn't huge because he was so withered and being locked up all those years hadn't exactly helped; in fact he had never been more withered in his life – he'd managed to push the door open. The light flooded in and blinded him, burning his pallid skin. And look!

'Oh no!' he exclaimed. 'Stairs!'

There was a long staircase, all carpeted in beige shag pile, and he thought, 'I'll never get down there', and had started to turn back when he saw the phone and decided to ring me.

As I thought this theory through I realised it couldn't possibly be the case as assuming my agent had a withered twin – let's call him Evo – if Evo even existed why would he phone me? He has, as far as I can remember, never met me – and believe me, when someone introduces you to their withered twin you don't forget that kinda thing too easy. I remember when TV horticulturalist Alan Titchmarsh introduced me to his withered twin Eddie, he did so in a very dramatic – if not *over*-dramatic, some would say *unkind* – way.

He'd had him hidden. We were all at a dinner party round at his house and had all been wondering what was on the raised podium, under the sheet throughout the main course, but it was as the coffees were served that Alan, by now rather drunk, staggered over to it and called, at the top of his voice, 'Ladies and gentlemen, what you are about to see is an affront to all that is holy . . . my withered twin – Eddie!' And with that he gave the sheet a tug and there was Eddie. Exactly like Alan, only withered. I still have nightmares about it.

Then he served Eddie his dinner, which he'd been keeping warm in the oven all this time; what had been lovely moist

3

slices of turkey roast, croquet potatoes and peas was now a dry mass, glued fast to the plate by congealed gravy. Eddie set about devouring the lot.

As the evening wore on, it turned out that Eddie was really great fun – bright, witty and interesting, full of stories of his life in Alan's shadow – and we all thought that had he not been withered it might well have been Eddie who was the more successful of the two brothers. I know what you're dying to ask: was he any good at gardening? Poor Eddie! He could barely hold a trowel let alone wield it to improve the garden of an unsuspecting-member-of-the-public-who-has-been-set-up-by-a-close-friend-or-relative. So Alan employed him as his agent.

Oh, I can see it from Alan's point of view – at least Eddie was doing something constructive; but Eddie wasn't great at brokering the big deals because halfway through the negotiations he'd come over all withered and weak, and settle for less. That's how Alan had only made some four hundred pounds out of the whole *Ground Force* phenomenon. That and Eddie's whopping 40 per cent commission. Still, I admire Alan's loyalty.

I knocked about with the Titchmarsh Twins for a while, until they got bored of me and discarded me like so many chaffinches into a council tip. That's how I found out all about the behind-the-scenes scandals of *Ground Force*. If you never saw it, three professionals – Alan, Tommy and Charlie – as a surprise, do up the garden of someone who has no interest in gardening, or time to maintain a garden. They've only got a couple of days to complete the 'makeover' and so they have to rush it. Then when it's done and the person whose garden it is discovers them, they celebrate with champagne.

It's not widely known but when the cameras stop rolling, it's common for the team to continue drinking bottle after bottle of champagne and get so unruly that they start to

4

vandalise parts of the garden that they've just fixed up. The three of them will stand there, stripped to the waist, covered in potting compost and hurling abuse at passers-by, until a *Ground Force* minder bundles them into the back of a limousine and takes them on to the Fingers Bar at the Royal Horticultural Society, whilst a man in dark glasses pays off the now distraught victims with large wads of cash, plus cassette tapes of Alan's novels.

As the post-makeover months pass by, their hapless victims are confused: they never liked gardening – that's how the garden got in such a mess in the first place – but now people expect it to look good. They're well known around the area as 'the people who had that gardening programme in' but now they've got a champagne habit they can't afford to maintain and the new water feature has been wrecked by squirrels. Many of the victims of *Ground Force* spend years in therapy trying to work the whole thing out. The suicide rate for these people is some 4 per cent higher than the national average,[1] and that is why now they all get a follow-up call from Victim Support; a fact they don't mention in the programmes.

Having been delivered to the Fingers Bar Titchmarsh, Tommy Walsh and Charlie Dimmock would writhe around singing ribald gardening songs: 'Show Me Your Privets', 'She Let Me Trim Her Gorse But Her Dwarf Rhododendron . . . Was Out Of My Reach' and 'Place The Clematis Up Against The Wall But Be Careful When Handling The Root Ball As Damage May Occur'.

Withered Eddie Titchmarsh would look on in disgust, slumped down in a crack between the seats, unable to move and unable to join in. Why did Alan let this go on? he thought. What would Mum have said? She was a proud lady, Ma Titchmarsh, and would take in washing to help make

1 Almost as high as for *60 Minute Makeover*.

ends meet. She never made much money at it because people expected it to be washed as well as being just 'taken in' but she had her pride. Her husband was long gone; himself a gardener, he'd spent years perfecting the seedless walnut, hoping to make his fortune, but since this was essentially just an empty shell he'd got very little interest and very short shrift on *Dragon's Den* series one, particularly from Deborah Meaden.[2] Basically, with the lack of any nutritional value to the nut he'd shot himself in the foot.

That was the Titchmarsh family's chosen punishment. 'You'll tidy your room, Alan, or I'll shoot you in the foot!' his father would bellow from the stairwell, rocking back on his two Durban[3] artificial feet.

'Yes, Father,' said the young Alan, determined to escape this old house just as soon as he reached forty-two.

The Fingers Bar was always rockin' on a Monday night, and do you know there were absolutely no plants there? Hard to believe, I know, but they didn't even stock crisps or nuts behind the bar as these were classed as plants. No, you could only get pork scratchings because to these gardeners plants were work, and when 'we're down the Fingers, that is play'.

Kim Wilde staggered up on to an old wooden pallet at one end of the bar, which they used as a stage, and did a mickey-take of her hit 'Kids in America'. Stefan Buczacki from *Gardeners' Question Time* grabbed the microphone off her and yodelled along to the All Saints hit 'Never Ever'. This is how these top gardeners unwind.

2 'There is no nut, and for that reason, I'm afraid, I'm out,' she'd said but had also run at him and kicked him in both shins with flick knives that protruded from the front of her shoes.
3 Durban were the market leaders in artificial feet and sponsors of the orginal West End run of *Footloose*, the show that was sort of about dancing.

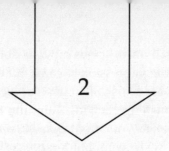

Author Knocked Unconscious

for a Year

Maybe Zevon had it on one of his presets. Maybe 'Evo' inadvertently pressed the preset button on Zevon's phone with my number on it. Maybe that's how it could have happened.

It was then I saw the telephone handset and realised that the voice was coming from there.

'Hello? Ouch!' I said, bumping my head on the underside of the table.

'It's Zevon,' he said.

That problem solved, then.

'I've got you a booking,' he said. I jumped for joy, banging my head again on the underside of the table and this time knocking myself unconscious. I have no memory of the events of the ensuing year.

It was 1987 and so, even to this day, whenever I hear Sam Fox singing 'Touch Me' or 'Star Trekkin'' by The Firm, I have no feelings of nostalgia and, tragically, anything by Amazulu still leaves me cold.

A little tip for you if you're going to fall unconscious: try not, as I did, to fall unconscious on your door key because it takes weeks for the impression to come out of your face, and all that time you are at risk of an unscrupulous felon using it as a mould by pushing chewing gum into it and creating a chewing-gum key to your front door. Clever, the chewing-gum key – hard when cold, but as soon as you are through the front door just pop it into your mouth and start chewing. There's no flavour to it by now though, so pop a couple of Tic Tacs in if that bothers you.[1]

So I was in this coma for all of '87, and it was odd – if you've ever been in a coma you'll know what I mean. You might be in one now for all I know. What's it like? Well, your life appears to go on but the events are essentially made up. So while in the conscious world on 12 January 1987 Richard Eyre took over from Sir Peter Hall as director of the National Theatre, in my coma year 1987 Normski took over. Remember Normski? The BBC's black youth presenter with the crazy carrot-top haircut, who went out with Janet Street-Porter? Got him? Yes, well he took over the National Theatre and his first move was to book Aswad in for six weeks solid in the Cottesloe. They got rave reviews from even the most hard-bitten theatre critics:

'A theatrical tour de force, loved it' – Sheridan Morley in *The Times*.

'All my doubts cast aside in a single smile from their charismatic lead singer . . .' – Nicholas de Jongh writing in the *London Evening Standard*.[2]

1 You might like to coat the Tic Tacs with the chewed-up gum using your tongue, thus increasing your glossal dexterity index.
2 Admittedly Baz Bamigboye from the *Daily Mail* was a little non-committal saying, 'It was quite good.'

With a canny piece of programming Normski had booked *Waiting For Godot* in the Olivier to mop up the Aswad over-spill. People were clamouring for tickets. Ordinary people were being converted to Beckett overnight. There were queues stretching from the box office as far as Waterloo Bridge. Suddenly it truly was becoming the people's theatre.

Sir Peter Hall was stark staring angry about his consider-able loss of face. How dare they! he thought as he sat in the front row with his posse on press night, heckling the band mercilessly and was eventually escorted from the premises.

Meanwhile in the bar, Esther Rantzen, relaxing with a drink after playing to a packed house at the Old Vic with *That's Live!*, her tales of botched building works, 'jobsworths' and slides of hilariously shaped vegetables (neither Doc nor Cyril Fletcher saw a penny of the box-office money because they had stupidly agreed to a wage), had got into an argu-ment with Janet Street-Porter, down to support her beau. A 'TV presenter stand-off' ensued, during which their teeth became locked. The two dames shuffled about the bar area, grunting expletives and overturning tables as they went. In the end a net was dropped over them, a sedative dart fired into each of their fleshy rumps and a dentist, using a hacksaw, did what we've all been itching to do for years, and just sawed the teeth down flat to the gums. Rather a sad end to an otherwise great night's entertainment.

With two massive sell-outs Normski was on a roll, and fol-lowed through with a live game show: *PIG 3-2-1*. He had the revolving stage at the Olivier filled with 2,000 litres of mud and manure, and installed three families of six pigs on it. Then every evening Ted Rogers, Chris Emmett and the team would turn up and give the pigs the chance of winning a hol-iday, a car or go home to their sties empty-handed with a ceramic 'Dusty bin'.

At the same time Judi Dench and Siân Phillips held court in

the Cottesloe with Sondheim's finest, *A Little Night Music*. Well, the queues stretched down the Thames as far as Wapping. Fat-arsed builders on scaffolding up and down the country could be plainly heard whistling 'Send In The Clowns'.

The individual pigs became celebrities in their own right, making personal appearances for massive fees. One hectic day for a pig called 'Wise Estrakhan' involved opening a supermarket in Poole, taking a fast car to visit an intensive care unit in Edgbaston, then a chopper ride to the BBC TV Centre just in time to record three episodes of *Blankety Blank*.

Then it all went wrong. A story appeared in the *Mirror* saying that it was fixed – that Estrakhan the wise pig was being slipped the cryptic clues beforehand. It was true that if you went every night (though no one could – tickets by now had been rationed to just two per household) you could plainly see that Estrakhan was on an uncannily lucky winning streak: so far he'd banked a music centre, a fondue set, a portable television with remote control, a set of carvers, a hat, an atom bomb and the holiday – twice! There was uproar. The public rebelled, ticket sales plummeted, the pigs were slaughtered and eaten and Normski was forced to resign.

Who tipped off the *Mirror*? Well, the call was traced to a phone box in Hampstead. When the police looked for evidence they discovered belly and love-handle prints that they were 90 per cent certain (from photographs taken of him on holiday) belonged to Sir Peter Hall. However, he had been clever and worn a cummerbund, so there wasn't enough evidence to prosecute.

Normski's successor, Simon Groom from *Blue Peter*, in a silly lapse of judgement booked a series of pro-literary boxing matches. The first week saw Harold Pinter knocked out in the first round by Alan Minter (the commentary: 'Pinter . . . Minter . . . Pinter . . . Minter . . . Pinter . . . Minter . . . Oh, he's down! Pinter's down!') with Alan Bennett suffering a similar fate in the matinee. It was all pretty much the same story except for Arthur Miller who somehow managed to beat Joe Bugner on points. The fact was, people just didn't want to see their favourite playwrights being bashed around the ring. The shows folded and the building was sold to contractors who knocked it into one and just used it as a marquee show-room (well, you need somewhere big to show off marquees properly).

So imagine my surprise: when waking from my coma in 1988, I discovered that Richard Eyre was in charge, not Groom, and 'The National' was very much still there at the forefront of exciting new theatre in this country.

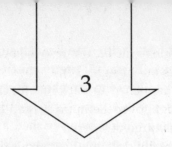

3

An Exciting Engagement in Leeds

As I stirred from my year-long coma the phone rang again. I picked up the receiver. It was Zevon – he'd had it on 'ring back'.

'Hello?' said Zevon. 'What took you?'

'I was unconscious,' I said.

'There's this gig in Leeds,' he ploughed on.

'Yes?' I said, stifling my excitement but very aware of the tabletop above me. I couldn't afford to lose another year.

He explained that the booking was for a corporate event for the moulded-plastic-toy industry.

'Do they make Postman Pat?' I asked.

'No, no, I'm afraid they don't,' Zevon replied.

I burst into tears. To this day I don't know why, just the call out of the blue, the year unconscious, the key impression on my forehead making me feel vulnerable to burglary; all these things suddenly compounded by me mentioning Postman Pat.

'He's great, isn't he?' said Zevon, himself choking back tears.

'Yes,' said I. 'I love the bit where he comes over the hill in the van and goes out of sight. For a split second you worry, has something happened to Pat? Has he crashed the van? Then, sure enough, over the humpbacked bridge he comes with his precious cargo of letters.'[1]

They should really do something about that blind corner, though. I'd been writing letters for years to try to get them to award it a black spot, or at least cut back some of the foliage there. You may mock but it was only tireless campaigning by me that got proper street lighting in Trumpton, with the result that violent crime dropped by 40 per cent.

'Who do they do then?' I asked.

'Uh?'

'The toy factory; who do they do?'

'Gonks,'[2] said Zevon.

'Hmm.' It was a booking for a meet-and-greet at a Gonk factory. The good news was that it was in Leeds and that during my year's absence, Zevon had managed to negotiate the fee up by some seven pounds in my favour. I was thrilled; it would be nice to see the old Gonks and it sounded like it wasn't going to be too much like hard work. I was expected merely to hang around looking like me, chatting to the staff, being nice, that sort of thing – no actual performance. These corporate engagements were low prestige and degrading, but the money was good, and I agreed to the deal with the usual provisos: Club Class seats to Leeds for myself and Zevon,

1 Unlike the rest of *Postman Pat*, which is recorded, Pat insists on doing this title sequence live every episode as he says it helps him maintain his edge. During the recording of episode 6, series 4, he crashed the van off the bridge and suffered a gash under his nose and did the rest of the series with a moustache which was 'painted out' in post-production.

2 Gonk – a largely felt-based creature popular in the seventies, killed off by the mumps epidemic of '89 where their faces swelled, the felt burst and their brains leaked, making them vulnerable to flies.

postcards of the local area and the added proviso that I would be met personally from the airport by the person on their staff who looked the most like Postman Pat.

I'd started collecting Polaroids of me with people who are thought by their workmates to most resemble Postman Pat some years previously, and had built up a collection of some four hundred. My favourite was Graham Hallam who had Pat's nose and moustache from series 4 but sadly was let down by his steeply sloping forehead – the legacy of a clash with a hole punch at the Basingstoke Belt Factory where I was booked to appear at their Christmas party. Colin Stewart (of Sheerness Shin Pads – Bespoke Pads for All Occasions) was pretty convincing but unlike Postman Pat had no eyes, which was inevitably very distracting, no matter where he positioned the glasses.

The other small caveat was that people should act towards me as if I'm important. In this game, forget money; the wheels turn by what I call 'ego-puff points'. Here's an example: you get an invitation to the BAFTAs – that's one ego-puff point. At the BAFTAs the controller of a TV station approaches for a chat – award yourself two more ego-puff points. He blanks you – subtract three ego-puff points. He is seen to blank you by another act – subtract four ego-puff points. He is seen to blank you by that same act's agent – subtract five ego-puff points. Sir Alan Sugar asks for a photo with you for one of his daughters, add 8 ego-puff points, and so on. You add up the total at the end of the week, divide by seven and that's your daily ego-puff value.[3]

You can't just sit at home and do nothing either. Avoiding situations where you may lose or gain points doesn't work as there is a daily loss of three puff points automatically. If you take a holiday it depends where you go; if it's somewhere

3 The highest I ever got was 16 during Euro 96.

like Mustique give yourself four puff points a day for the first four days, then three, then two and so on. Take a British seaside holiday and you haemorrhage an unsustainable four points a day unless it's your second home, in which case take one, or it's with Cliff Richard. These days unless you're scoring twelve ego-puff points a day, you're on your way out. At this point – 1988 – after a year in a coma, I'm struggling to make two.

'I'll do it,' I said to Zevon.

'Great, I'll make the necessary orang-utans,' said Zevon. Inserting the name of a monkey where it sort of sounded like the actual word he should have used was something he did from time to time.

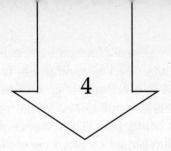

4

Dale Make Me Normal Again!

I remember that BAFTA trip. I'd waited in the executive car for ten minutes (awarding myself one ego-puff point), peeking at the celebrities as they arrived. Carol Vorderman started up the red carpet in that dress. I say 'dress'; it was a child's toy-dinghy sail attached to her privates with double-sided sticky tape. I snuck in behind her, using her as cover. She chose to zigzag up the carpet, prolonging media exposure, and I was committed to tacking up beside her.[1]

In front of Carol, Vanessa Feltz, wearing only a tiny piece of insulation tape, had opted for the 'tiny steps' approach: taking steps measuring just two inches at a time. Her ploy backfired on her: the photographers, thinking they had plenty of time to snap her, were lulled into a false sense of security, then got distracted by Amanda Holden. No photographs exist of Vanessa's visit; just a large hole in all of our scrapbooks.

---

1 As she meandered she lost tiny amounts of the dark foundation she uses to colour her body and I ended up at the top of the red carpet looking like I'd just been on holiday.

There was a low squeal, my nostrils filled with the smell of pure, uncut manure and I spun round to see Estrakhan the wise pig and his family. I was momentarily floored. But surely they're dead, I thought, then I remembered: that all happened in my coma year. In actual fact Estrakhan had been appearing regularly in *Pig Brother*, where six pigs are placed in a big sty and observed twenty-four hours a day by closed-circuit TV. Every two days one is selected by viewers' votes, killed and eaten. These animal reality shows were getting really big now, as most of the general public had already appeared on television and were bored of it. So the TV execs had turned to animals. So far there had been *Pig Brother*, *Pony Fortunes*, *Beeflebrity Squares* and *Who Wants to be a Millionaire Sheep*. The problem was that nine times out of ten it ended up with the losers being killed and eaten, and the TV top brass needed new twists if they were to keep pulling in the ratings.

'I need new formats!' bellowed Kevil Garment,[2] the new controller of ITV, from his office on the tenth floor of the ITV building. He'd just got the overnight ratings through on his new Saturday evening show *Make Your Mumma Puke With Pride* fronted by Kylie Minogue. The format was simple enough: members of the public got up on stage and sang a ballad with their mother in the audience, and the viewers at home voted on who was the best. They then announced the winner, keeping the camera on the mother, while the winner strutted about, talking movingly about their mum before reprising the ballad. The object was to make your mum so proud that she threw up. In week one a young black girl

2 The son of legendary impressario Acton Garment and nephew of Fadro Garment the founder of Garment and Garment, the first TV broadcaster to show people in corduroy trousers. Kevil had been given the job of ITV Controller as an eighteenth birthday present.

from Manchester had managed to elicit only a weak gagging response from her mother, so the show really lacked a climax. The producer had tried to get Kylie to stick her fingers down the contestant's throat in the ad break but everyone else thought this was going too far and to give the mum a chance.

Kevil already regretted commissioning it but couldn't move it until he had a better alternative. Then, what should flop on to his desk but an outline for a show called *Dale Make Me Normal Again!*, a format so simple and yet so perfect that Kevil kicked his leg out, put his hand behind his back and up between his legs and did a little wave at his secretary, Pauline who stood watching, slightly disgusted.

Pauline had been working for Kevil now for six months and still felt she didn't really know him. Most of the time he'd be fine, then he'd do something like this through-the-legs wave, and she'd be back to square one. How was she supposed to react? She had tried mimicking the manoeuvre back to him, but his face had turned sour and he'd ordered her out of the room. What was the protocol with this thing? She'd phoned his previous secretary, Joan Marsh, who had been with him for some ten years.

'Oh God, has it got worse? He used to do it a bit towards the end of my time with him. I shouldn't have just ignored it; I should have stamped it out early on. If he knows he can get away with something he will.'

'What should I do?' asked Pauline.

'I don't know, love, it may be too late.'

So she'd taken to ignoring the move when he did it and instead rewarding him with a Kit Kat or laughter when he didn't. She hoped he was slowly coming round. He hadn't done it now for three weeks. She knew because she kept a diary. For instance, 12th May's entry: 'Done it'; 13th May: 'Didn't do it'; 20th May: 'Done it', etc.

'No!' she said firmly to Kevil. His face collapsed into tears. She hadn't meant to be so crushing, but if she didn't react firmly, how was he going to learn? What if he did it to someone important? Like a client, a dentist or, even worse, to the Queen at the Royal Command Performance?

'Here,' she said, proffering a hanky and a Lion Bar. 'Dry your eyes.'

Kevil took her floral hanky, dabbed at his big eyes and nose, took a bite from the Lion Bar and looked at the proposal before him. *Dale Make Me Normal Again!*

Dale Winton and his team of makeover experts cruise around three major cities in a van looking for down and outs. They jump out and surprise the tramps with the question, 'Do you want it all back?' to which they have to reply (it's written on a card), 'Dale make me normal again!' They are then whisked off to a TV studio, interviewed and followed over the weeks as they are groomed, weaned off Special Brew, interviewed for jobs, given new teeth, taken to dating agencies and given money to buy a flat. Then, when all six of the down and outs are considered to be 'normal' (married with jobs, watching *EastEnders*, fantasising about meeting Jordan, etc), they are brought together to form the pop group Tramps, who release a single, a tie-in coffee-table book and a hilarious out-takes video for Christmas. The format is then sold round the world and is rounded off with a massive play-off at which Tramps from all round the world compete – via satellite – to do the most accurate Chris de Burgh impression.

It was dynamite! Kevil jumped to his feet and was about to do the through-the-legs wave when he saw Pauline and checked himself.

'Get Dale Winton's agent on the phone, Pauline, would you?'

'Yes, sir!' she said, thinking that she was finally getting somewhere with his antisocial behaviour.

Estrakhan the wise pig nodded to me in greeting and continued along the red carpet, trampling an overenthusiastic local radio presenter underfoot. His cries of pain mixed with Estrakhan's piggy snorts were broadcast live to several hundred homes in the Chilterns.[3]

Suddenly there was a blinding white light as the journos spotted Miss Kelly Brook. She'd topped them all: she was wearing a red, blue, green and yellow outfit fashioned from three one-centimetre lengths of the rubber coating you get on the wires of a plug – live, neutral and earth. Then to maximise coverage she pulled this out of the bag: she lay down and rocked from side to side; three rocks and then she rolled over on to her front; three more rocks and she was over on to her back. In this way she rolled slowly up the red carpet achieving maximum press coverage, ego-puff points and corporate feed foods.

Finally we got to the top of the carpet; me and Carol V. 'I'm going back round again!' she shrilled, and darted into the hotel, out the front and back round.

I wasn't up for a BAFTA; I was merely asked along to boost morale. It had been a tough year for the British Artificial Foot Trade, and this sort of high-profile event would help to put British artificial feet firmly back on the map. Recent years had seen marked losses to the Chinese artificial-foot industry. Their feet – modelled as they were on bound Chinese feet – were cheaper and much smaller, so

3 A tape of it would later turn up on the internet prompting Estrakhan to donate several hundred pounds to a trust fund to help local radio DJs be less chirpy.

they were able to accommodate children's shoes, which meant, of course, that you didn't pay the VAT.

BAFT had countered by placing a compass in the heel of their feet, just in case you got lost, but a lot of people said this was just a cheap gimmick, and several of them had fallen over while trying to consult it. This was why BAFT was lobbying the government for a full Chinese artificial foot embargo.

It was Manny Durban who had thrown a British artificial foot at President Deng Xiaoping when he'd come over on a state visit. Manny was the head of Durban Feet, an old family-run bespoke-artificial-foot firm. They'd been making artificial feet since the eighteenth century, and he was damned if he was going to see the company disappear because of some cheap Far Eastern interlopers.

As Deng Xiaoping had got out of his presidential limousine, Manny had let fly with a size-twelve Caucasian foot and it had clocked the hapless premier on the head. Manny then started to sing, paraphrasing the old Nancy Sinatra hit: 'Our feet are made for walking, and that's just what they'll do . . .!'

David Yip was in charge of security that day and immediately detailed four coppers to grab Manny and bundle him into the back of a Black Maria.[4]

---

4 The story was suppressed and to this day if you go on Wikipedia you'll find no mention of it.

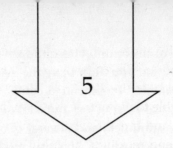

5

Now Available on Sock

'One of these days these feet are gonna walk all over you!' sang Manny as the doors closed, but he'd adjusted the key of the song down so low to enable him to sing the first bit, that it rendered the last line virtually inaudible. Deng Xiaoping, a bruise already forming between his eyebrows, looked round towards the sound.

'The low rumble of a tube train, Mr Ping,' offered Mrs Thatcher, her own forehead wet with a salty fluid where she'd got it wet passing under a low, damp bush and then got it salty by wiping a hand on it that had just dipped into a packet of plain crisps. 'Yes,' she went on, 'the tube trains run directly under our feet, Mr Ping.'[1]

Deng nodded politely. He hadn't understood a single word that had been spoken to him since arriving in the country they called 'Yookay', and he was just going along with everything for the time being, hoping that he would be able to slip away to Tower Records later.

---

1 It's true that for some reason Margaret Thatcher's feet did attract tube trains and it would cause chaos if she ever went walkabout at rush hour.

Deng had really gotten into Status Quo when they'd come over and played in China, and was interested to know whether he could get 'In The Army Now' on twelve-inch. Maybe he'd be able to nip into Tower later on when they got back to the bed and breakfast. Mrs Lamb was a very strict landlady but Deng reckoned he could squeeze out of the window and on to the flat roof extension, jump into the baobab tree below, and get a late train from Walthamstow into Liverpool Street. It would then be just a case of catching a rickshaw to Piccadilly Circus. He was annoyed with his Foreign Secretary-cum-brother-in-law, Tokwan Ping, who had assured him that Walthamstow was right in the centre of London, and 'just across from Tower Records'. Oh well, he would probably kill him when he got back. Not personally, he'd get someone else to do it.

Apart from Mrs Lamb's strict curfew, the Tower Records Bed and Breakfast[2] was one of the best Deng had stayed in, and he'd stayed in a lot all over the world. Clean, satellite TV in the room, no en suite facility but then he always got first shout at the bathroom because of Tokwan's fear of being killed. Mrs Lamb wasn't too strict about them being out the whole time; yesterday it had been raining and she'd let them sit in the lounge and watch the golf on TV.

It was almost like a holiday. He couldn't let Mrs Xiaoping know that, of course; no, he would phone her back in China and tell her what hard work it was. Otherwise she would resent his trips abroad. He'd make it up to her by popping into Sock Shop on Regent Street – conveniently just round the corner from Tower Records – and get her something nice; maybe a pair of those musical socks, she liked those. Other people liked CDs or vinyl or MP3s, but sock was Mrs

2 It's still there and is a major landmark on the many *Flight from Deathrow* walking tours.

Xiaoping's musical format of choice; she liked to listen to tunes coming from ankle level. The last pair he bought her, she wouldn't take off. It was 'Like A Virgin', the Madonna hit on Argyll. She played them non-stop and the batteries had only lasted a week (and they're so difficult to replace; you're supposed to be able to get them from the chemist, but they never seem to have quite the right ones, and okay, you can threaten to kill the staff, but most of the time they genuinely couldn't find this type of battery in the catalogue). Even though she knew the batteries were way past it, Mrs Xiaoping still refused to take the socks off and subsequently suffered battery-acid burns to her calves.

'. . . isn't that right, President?' said Mrs Margaret Thatcher, snapping Deng out of his Tower Records daydream. To him, of course, it sounded like 'Wagwahwang wicky wangy tappytap tap.'

Deng nodded; he couldn't work this guy out. How old was he? Forty-something? Then how come he looked so weird? Was he a sex change who'd run out of money for the operation halfway through? That walk he did, was it supposed to be funny? The tall thin guy too – Tebbit. Where did he find these guys?

'What are you running here? A freak show?' blurted Deng. Tokwan gasped, but it was okay; the tall man in the blue dress and bow didn't understand him.

Thatcher nodded. 'Yes, yes, slitty-eyed midget,' she said smiling, and Deng nodded back.

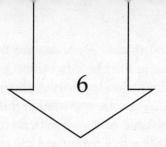

6

Hennessy's Return from Flanders

The awards ceremony itself was pretty dispiriting. The artificial-foot tradespeople mainly work from home and thus have pale, milky skins, and wispy, vitamin-deficient beards that break off easily. Their clothes, mainly by George – Asda's own brand – have been snatched whilst food shopping, and as they lay in the bottom of the shopping trolley, they garner stains: a leaking boil-in-the-bag dinner, a thawed choc-ice, or a burst yoghurt. The smell of these stains mixes with the smell of the powerful resins they use to seal the artificial feet and form a heady mixture, so the men wear cotton-wool balls up their nose to prevent them from gagging. Many also wear 'Free The Guildford Size-Twelve One' stickers, a reference to Manny Durban who was languishing in Ford Open Prison.

But these were still men with powerful testosterone coursing through their veins, and their faces lit up as they glimpsed Amanda Holden. Holden was pretty good with them; she had two or three round her and she hugged them up to her chest, breaking their beards off as she did so. She winked at Vorderman who was doing similar.

'Go to Carol now!' said Amanda, and the foot craftsmen trundled off leaving their beards behind them glued to her semi-nude body by static electricity. A photograph of her covered in these wispy beards appeared in the fashion pages of the *Daily Telegraph* the next day with the caption, Amanda Holden In Something By Alexander McQueen.[1]

Feltz, meanwhile, was cautioned to relax her grip as one man's face had gone blue.

Estrakhan and family guzzled from a giant trough full of crushed vol-au-vents mixed with Red Bull.

Someone somewhere tapped an artificial foot against a brass bell and the men broke free from their hosts and took up their dinner places.

'The award for best domestic foot goes to . . . Manny Durban!'

A huge cheer went up; he was a popular choice. Most commentators had predicted Durban walking off with the prize but it still somehow caught his wife Jenny by surprise, partly because the feet Manny had been making that year had not, she felt, been up to his usual standard, but also because at the moment the award was announced she was staring into the eyes of her new beau Bradley Hennessy, who had just returned from a business trip to Flanders. Bradley was heir to Hennessy's Feet, the Scottish artificial-foot-making conglomerate, and though he was a full twenty years younger than Manny, she admired Bradley for his spirit, and even more for the workmanship in his artificial feet.

Disapproved of by many (and Manny in particular) in the trade, Bradley Hennessy had been campaigning for modernisation. It had been he who had suggested designer feet – artificial feet with a Nike or Adidas logo. It had been he who had okayed the use of the instep for use as advertising space

[1] These beards, when boiled, make excellent stock.

and suggested phasing out the little toe as an unnecessary appendage in today's cut-and-thrust world.

'We must play the Chinese at their own game,' Bradley had announced at the trade's annual conference in Sheppey, and had gone straight from the meeting to organise a whole series of table-tennis tournaments with his Chinese counterparts. The UK artificial-foot trade never stood a chance and were thrashed fourteen games to one, which left morale even lower. To cap it all, the Chinese had resisted an invitation for a return tournament, this time of our own game – darts.

Bradley was a regular on the artificial-foot trade-fair circuit, and since Manny's arrest Jenny Durban had increasingly been bumping into him. The Durban stand had been next to the Hennessy's at the Ideal Foot Exhibition in Earls Court and inevitably they'd started chatting.

Virtually bald except for a narrow hedge of wiry black hairs at the front of his head, placed there by a Swedish trichologist, and with tiny eyes framed by heavy black glasses, Bradley was classically good-looking. His seduction technique had always been to just jump girls and wrestle them to the floor.

'Dnnn!' said Jenny, one minute busy with a customer, extolling the virtues of the naked foot over the one that looks like you've got a shoe on ('Feet never go out of fashion – shoes do'), then suddenly she was on the floor with Bradley Hennessy on top of her, her stubby nose forced into an artificial foot, her blond bun unravelled. She swung her legs up over his back, but he was quicker and grabbed both her ankles in his left hand, pinning them to the floor. She countered by grabbing his wiry fringe of hair and forced his head back on its neck. He momentarily relaxed his grip on her ankles; this was just the chance she needed, and she brought her left foot up to kick him in the ear.

'Knobby's, eight o'clock tonight,' he whispered, dabbing his big bleeding ear with a J-Cloth.

'See you there,' she grunted, struggling to her feet and wiping the ear-blood from the instep of a size-five Caucasian foot. As she looked up he was away and flogging his own distinctive feet to the punters.

Knobby's! The exclusive restaurant to the stars, she thought to herself. She'd never been but had read about it in the pages of *Hello!*, *Now* and *TV Quick*. She only really took these magazines to keep her going between *OK!*s.

Ah, *OK!*. It had swept on to the news-stands like a breath of fresh air; yes, it looked exactly the same as *Hello!* but it had replaced the stories of minor royals with more pictures of celebrities at play. Her particular favourites were photos of well-known men out by themselves with a baby. Preferably they are holding the baby, but if it was in a buggy it was fine, just not so good. She had one of Damon Albarn holding baby Missy and then buying an ice-cream, which was really cute, and he was really sweet anyway and his baby looked a lot like him – ah, bless. Then there was the photo, clear as a bell, of Johnny Vaughan and his lovely French wife; she was handing him baby Tabitha as they were getting out of the car and, even better, it looked like it was right outside their house. Jenny strained to see the house number but no, it had probably been fuzzed out. Shame, she knew it was Wandsworth somewhere, but where?

She glanced over at the copy of *OK!* jutting out of her bag. She'd wrapped it in cling film as she always did as soon as she got it home – sometimes outside the shop if she had the time – to keep it fresh and clean and to stop other people from thinking they could read it. She had to steal herself not to just sit down now, put her feet up, pour herself a Red Bull and vodka, unwrap it and chill.

'These feet. Got them in a fourteen?' asked a man. He was sort of rough-looking.

28

'Those are ladies' feet, sir, the men's are over there,' she said.

'No, they're for my wife, but if you're gonna be like that . . .' He walked off in a mood.

Oh dear, she'd lost another sale. She must try not to think about the *OK!*, it was distracting her and she was just not getting any work done. Well . . . just a peek wouldn't hurt. She moved over to the bag, opened her Thermos of Red Bull and vodka premixed at home – if Manny knew he would kill her (he had garrotted his first wife after catching her with a Lucozade-Bacardi concoction in front of *Pebble Mill*) – eased the film wrapper off the *OK!* and flopped it open on her lap.

Head in the clouds now, suddenly she was gone, hooked, lost. A blur of blond hair and teak and onyx that is Rod Stewart at home, Nicholas Cage shopping – no! Surely he doesn't push a basket round like everyone else? But yes, there he is. Okay, it's grainy, taken on a long lens, but it's definitely him. Was that peanut butter in the basket? It was cropped off on the other shot.[2] Wait a minute: where's Lisa Marie? . . . Lorraine Kelly's bathroom . . . she flicked through to the juicy back pages; that was where she would find her prey if there was . . . OH JOY! Johnny, Johnny Depp, and he's alone with baby Lily-Rose Melody; coming out of the house, you can see the number on the door and a toy sit-on train just inside and . . . they've followed him to his car and it's full of sweet wrappers and other junk. Ha, ha! Wait, there's Estrakhan . . . Estrakhan the wise pig at home, beautifully lit and staged with his family photographs. Pre-*Pig Brother* shots of him and the kids nuzzling up . . . oh . . . we're in the bedroom now and the house is just great, lots of teak and gold and pot-pourri, but . . . she flicked frantically through . . . no bathroom. She

2 It was, in fact, a tub of Max Factor all-over tanning cream but placed so close to a loaf of bread it had suggested otherwise – funny how the mind works, isn't it?

was starting to get angry. No bathroom? Why would they not include the bathroom?

The fact was Estrakhan had rather unusual bathroom arrangements.

'Move along now, lady,' said the Earls Court Exhibition Centre janitor. Jenny looked at her watch. Yikes! It was midnight. Another whole day wasted.

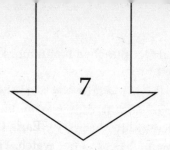

7

The Mums of Navarone

It was a song coming on the radio – 'Jack Your Body' by Steve 'Silk' Hurley – that snapped me out of the coma. I had taken Steve at his word and had indeed 'jacked' my body. As my jacking muscle tensed, it created a tidal wave of blood up into my brain, jolting it out of its complacent state.[1]

I had helped to get an elderly lady out of a coma some years previously. The request came through Zevon, and once they had agreed to the various Postman Pat-alike greeting provisos, I made my way to the hospital. 'You get this kid out of a coma and the corporate work will come flooding in,' Zevon had barked, increasing the pressure on me to heal.

Unfortunately the story had leaked, and as I arrived at the hospital there was a scrum of celebrities at the intensive care unit's door, all vying to have first go at her. Patrick Mower scrapped openly with Cat Deeley, while Ant held Jeremy Vine

---

1 Caution: jacking of the body, whilst wearing tight pants, can result in a tsunami of blood to the brain and can actually burst both your eyes – particularly if in conjunction with a headband.

31

against a wall and Dec punched him remorselessly about the groin.

I inched past them towards the nurse who, apart from wearing a postman's outfit, didn't really look anything like Postman Pat. Thankfully she recognised me (two ego-puff points) and let me in. I made my way over to the old lady's bed. Somehow Jonathan Ross and his wife Jane had managed to slip past the charge nurse, dressed as papal guards. Jane was now reading from her seminal work on *The X Files*, and Jonathan was whistling, nudging the old lady and saying, 'Come on, hup! Come on now! Hello! Oi, you, wake up!'

I went straight to the desk and explained that this was my booking, and four burly security guards appeared from nowhere and bundled them out.

At this hospital they had initially made every effort to keep patients in long-term comas abreast of the fashions. The old lady had gone into a coma in 1967 dressed as a hippy, and they'd kept her in fashion through glam rock in the early seventies, but then in 1977 came the cutbacks and the process was halted. Thus she remained dressed in tartan trousers, a leather jacket done up with safety pins, and her hair shaved into a mohican – the garb of the King's Road punk.

I started out on the wrong foot straightaway.

'By singing a lullaby you might be putting her more deeply into the coma,' said a pretty staff nurse. Yes, quite, I thought. So I just started telling the old girl all about myself.

I was born somewhere over Germany, in October 1944. My mother was one of the elite 'Pregnant Paratrooper Squad' sent over with the express instructions that they discover where the German secret weapons – the V2s – were made, and then ride one back home. Bomber Harris figured that by using pregnant women the German High Command would never suspect them of foul play.

It worked, sort of; no one did suspect a thing. However, the risks to mother and child were enormous, and rather than attracting ladies who were tough, motivated fighting machines, it tended to attract ladies who had developed a pregnancy-related craving for sauerkraut – impossible to get your hands on in war-torn Britain. Also could they get some sausages while they were there, please?

As Mum pulled the ripcord over Eindhoven, her waters broke, and as she landed the jolt caused me to be born. I watched as she rolled up her parachute and hid it in some shrubs. I followed suit, rolling up my placenta and umbilical cord and hiding them behind some other shrubs near to her shrubs but not the same ones.[2]

Problem now was, as she was no longer pregnant and now a postnatal paratrooper, her cover was blown. She needed to get pregnant – and fast. She made her way with me following on foot – you learn quickly when you have to – over the fields to a phone box and gave my dad a call.

'It's a boy!' she said.

'Oh no!' he said, putting down his trowel. He had wanted a girl because he wanted to start collecting Barbies but didn't want people to think he was gay.

'Listen, darling, I need to get pregnant again.'

'Sorry, can't help you,' he said. 'I'm in the middle of something.'

'Then would you mind on this occasion, in view of the special circumstances, if I got pregnant by someone else?'

'Well, just this once.'

'Thank you, darling,' she gushed. 'Wish me luck.'

Dad hung up and returned to his plan. He was attempting to escape from Colditz. Not easy as he was living in Croydon at the time. He pored over his maps and worked out that the tunnel would have to follow the M2 to Dover, go under the

2 Hers a privet, mine a dwarf conifer.

Channel, across France to Germany, then once he'd got into Colditz he could use the same tunnel to escape. He'd got to within twenty miles of the coast and the Kent Police hadn't suspected a thing.

Unfortunately it was taking him so long to walk down to the end of the tunnel every morning that by the time he got there it was time to come back for his dinner. He kept this up for a month, but with the war looking like it was going to come to an end any minute he decided to escape from Maidstone instead. Having fashioned a German soldier's uniform from old blankets, he met with little resistance from the Maidstone townsfolk. The disguise wasn't entirely convincing: they were tartan blankets. He looked like an SS officer who was heavily into the Bay City Rollers. It made the local paper – Croydon Man Escapes From Maidstone But He Looks Kind Of Weird – and he was hailed as a hero.[3]

After the war Dad had tried all kinds of jobs. His big idea had been cold-calling piano lessons.[4] He would knock on people's doors at random and ask them whether they wanted to learn to play the piano. If they said, 'Yes,' he would then follow up with, 'Have you got a piano?' to which the answer was invariably, 'No.' 'Well, do you know someone who has got a piano?' he would enquire. If they did, the two of them would go round to the person with the piano's house and, assuming they were in, Dad would try to teach the first person the piano with the second person's piano. It could be frustrating and although no one could condone it, no one really blamed Dad when having elicited the answer 'no' to 'have you got a piano?' and then 'yes' to knowing someone

3 You take your heroes where you can in Maidstone. The previous person to be hailed as a hero was an elderly man who won three coconuts at the shy at the Maidstone annual carnival. Admittedly over the course of four years.
4 And remember this is long before the TV show *The Apprentice*.

with a piano, he had gone round to the person with a piano's house and, finding them out, had broken in and taught the first person the piano on the second person's piano completely illegally.

Having done it once it was all too easy to call on someone, establish a desire to learn the piano, then take the person to the house of someone they didn't even necessarily know, break into it and teach them the piano on that. It was just a small step from this to knocking on doors, dragging the occupants over to somebody else's house, and regardless of whether they wanted to learn to play the piano or not, teaching the first person the piano on the second person's piano against their will and then demanding a tuition fee.[5]

Well, after a while he even gave up on knocking on the doors; he would just drag people kicking and screaming off the street. It couldn't go on, and an ex-pupil who had been perfectly happy as a housewife and was now a reluctant concert pianist went to the police. Dad was arrested and given a three-year suspended sentence and three months Mark Morrison (the prison community's slang for community service).

'Nurse! I think she's coming out of the coma!' I cried across the ward.

The old lady sat up, pulled the tube from her mouth and spoke. 'Why am I dressed like this?' she said. 'Where's my caftan?'

Somewhere in a dank hospital corridor, Jeremy Vine sank to his knees, his groins swollen out of all recognition.

5 Forced piano lessons were the forerunner to other scams like timeshare flats, solar heating panels and *Ant and Dec's Saturday Night Takeaway*.

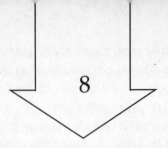

8

Going to Work on a Sheep

'Yo! How ya doin'? Estrakhan the pig jus' chillin' and hangin' loose with my bro' in the Hollywood Hills . . .'

This was how I had started my Estrakhan's Postcard From Hollywood column in the *Daily Express* to a tidal wave of complaints from *Guardian* readers who didn't buy the *Express* but had a friend who did. The *Express*, as a matter of fact, were jolly pleased with the piece detailing, as it did, Estrakhan's search for wider fame in Tinseltown after winning *Pig Brother*.

His road to Hollywood had started when Channel 4 had flown him out to record a special at the Winnipeg Comedy Festival. Estrakhan's bit wasn't part of the festival as such; and festival director Bruvose Haintree had flown into a rage when the idea had been mooted.

'I will not have a pig in my festival! It degrades the stature of what is widely accepted as the hardest job in the world. No!' he bellowed, his usually tight black curls straightening to perhaps a metre and a half and then zinging back into position on his fleshy pink head, momentarily dislocating some bridgework.

'It's a great press angle,' said his sidekick Levfrril.

'No! No pigsshh shand no udder clooffen hoves . . .!' shouted Bruvose.

'What was that?' said Levfrril.

Bruvose put his hand to his mouth and clicked the bridge back into place.[1] 'No pigs and no other cloven hooves in the shows either!' he said, and security immediately started doing spot checks.

How much Bruvose's objections were to do with the festival's reputation and how much with his deep-seated antipathy towards farmyard animals was anybody's guess. The fact was everybody knew his wife, Meerox, had recently taken to riding to work on a sheep.

'I'm gonna ride the sheep to work,' she said one morning and, sure enough, Bruvose watched from the condo window as Meerox Haintree climbed on to the sheep and eased back into the makeshift saddle she'd made from a Tupperware bowl and a snakeskin belt. The sheep grunted as it took her weight. Meerox was far too tall for the animal and to prevent her feet from dragging along the ground had to bend her knees and hold on to her ankles with both hands. This forced her face forward, nuzzling it into the shaggy wool round the sheep's neck. The oily, dirty smell was only slightly masked by the two Magic Tree air fresheners she had attached to each of the ram's rudimentary horns.

Bruvose had been against the whole idea of bringing the ram into his home from the start. Partly from a practical point of view: toileting of the beast, exercise, feeding and so on, not to mention the smell of a farmyard animal in a tenth-floor

1 This particular bridge joined his upper right molar to his lower left incisor thus allowing the free passage of plaque from back to front of the mouth, thus making it easier for him to clean his teeth.

apartment; all their furniture was Ikea too, and just didn't fit with an ovine theme.[2] Also, although he had difficulty admitting it, he felt his position as the dominant male in the set-up was being threatened. The ram would often try to knock him over while he was eating; it seemed to deliberately soil at inopportune moments (their daughter Sarah's third birthday party was a case in point: just as it came to 'Happy Birthday to . . .' a huge rasp was heard, and they looked round to see a big pile of dung over by the Pratok shelving unit). The sheep also made frequent attempts to mount his wife Meerox, and on one occasion had boxed her into a corner behind the settee, stamping and pawing the Leldt mock-beech flooring. So far the great beast had left little Sarah alone, but surely it was only a matter of time. Yes, Bruvose had been dead against buying the sheep, but you know what it's like when you get a really persuasive sheep salesman.

They had gone along to the Ideal Sheep Exhibition out of mild curiosity and for the promise of a free glass of wine and unlimited soft drinks and nibbles.

'We don't have to buy anything,' said Meerox.

They were both immediately disappointed. It became clear from the off that 'unlimited soft drinks' was something of an exaggeration; the organisers had got in four two-litre bottles of Coke and some cans of Seven-Up. Bruvose's request for Diet Coke was met with a disinterested shrug.

'What you see here is all there is,' said the salesman. 'I'm not responsible for ordering the drinks, that's head office.'

'If this is the standard of the catering, what is the follow-up like on the sheep?' wondered Bruvose.

What they'd hoped would be a nice 'cheap night out and then a pizza' was turning into a bit of an ordeal, but having each taken a big handful of dry-roasted nuts, they felt obliged

2 Except the Nank – a moulded plywood coffee table fashioned to look a bit like a sheep.

to stay for the talk. So, to be clear, at the start of the talk neither Meerox nor Bruvose had any intention of buying a sheep. Then the salesman started working his magic.

'Okay, what do we know about sheep? You.' He jabbed his finger out and picked on an unsuspecting member of the audience.

'Um . . .' The middle-aged man was momentarily floored. 'Four legs!' he said, half joking.

'Way to go! Yeah, four legs! How many legs you got, sir?'

'Well, let me check . . .' (Laughter from the room.) 'Two!'

'Right, so sheep are better. You, what do you know about sheep?' It was a red-haired woman's turn now.

'Oh! Um, they have a woolly coat!'

'Right! You have a woolly coat?'

'Not of my own. I have a wool coat . . .'

'Okay, so on two points sheep are coming out ahead.' In this way, and with the help of pie charts, slides and video clips, the salesman gradually chipped away at the Haintrees' confidence and self-belief. They started to wonder how they had ever managed without a sheep. When it came to the final question, 'Who wants to buy a sheep?' they found themselves jumping to their feet with the rest of the class, waving their credit cards in the air, desperate to be included.

It later turned out that despite having bought the sheep, it wasn't actually theirs; they merely had it on a timeshare basis. They would have it three months of the year in two-week chunks and another three families dotted around Canada would have it for the rest. So they couldn't even eat it. All the moving around was rather unsettling for the sheep and had led, in part, to the behavioural problems that Bruvose and Meerox were experiencing.

Bruvose had wanted to give up his directorship of the Winnipeg Comedy Festival and retire, but now found himself having to stay on to pay off the instalments on the sheep. A demonstration of how little they liked the creature was that when they got it home they didn't even bother giving it a name.

Meerox had decided to ride it to work for two reasons: partly so she would feel that they were actually getting something out of it – in other words a service – and partly she hoped that the increased wear and tear would bring about the sheep's early demise, which they were covered for on their insurance (a further hidden expense had been the compulsory insurance policy every timeshare owner had to take out on their animal).

So Bruvose had had enough of farmyard animals at home and he was damned if he was going to have one in his comedy festival.

In the end Estrakhan paid for his own fare and hotels, and booked out a room to do his show under his own steam. I say 'show', it was more a series of slides with Estrakhan in different poses and designer outfits set to music. Then for an encore Estrakhan would come on and go 'unplanned' and answer questions from the audience with the help of his interpreter. The whole thing was more about being near the pig and soaking up the aura that travelled with him than straight entertainment.

Bruvose snuck in at the back on the third night and had to admit the pig had great charisma; to his credit he went backstage to congratulate him. He got to the dressing room and Estrakhan's agent, Nosegay, was towelling him down and whispering flattering word nuggets into his ears: 'You were great!' 'The crowd really enjoyed it; don't be so hard on yourself, they may not have been that vocal but they were all really enjoying it.'

Bruvose entered and proffered his hand. 'Great show,' he said, approaching Estrakhan. But Essie knew all about Bruvose Haintree, how he'd tried to bar his entry into the festival and how he'd badmouthed him behind his back. He ran at Bruvose butting him out into the corridor. He didn't stop there. 'Woah, Estrakhan . . .' said Bruvose, winded and trying to get up on to his feet. Bup! Estrakhan hit him again; Bruvose went flat into a fire door. He was up quicker this time and running, with Estrakhan in hot pursuit. Bruvose burst out of the stage door and cast around for an escape route but Estrakhan didn't give up so easy. Spurred on by psychological pig pain and porcine pride, he snuffled his nose under the Winnipeg Comedy Festival's director and tossed him in a high arc over his head. Bruvose landed on Estrakhan who now paraded around with the hapless character on his back as photographers gaily snapped away.

Just then, on her way back from work, Meerox trotted by on the sheep. The photo of the pair of them made the front cover of the *Winnipeg Gazette*. Bruvose's directorship did not survive the humiliation. Three years later the rotting corpse of the sheep was found buried under their uptown Winnipeg patio.[3]

3 The Haintrees claimed that this was merely a barbecue that went wrong.

9

Pygmy Deposits

No matter how hard I rubbed I just couldn't seem to shift the cream-coloured stain that smelt vaguely of egg – even with a little Jif on my 'J'.[1] What had lodger 19 been up to?

I'd started putting up foreign students as a way of boosting my income when the work dried up in the early eighties. I'd had French, German and Dutch students but could only comfortably fit four into my small one-bedroom flat. That's when I had the idea of getting pygmy students. I got some shelving units from B&Q and could get twenty pygmies in. Just because they're small doesn't mean you don't charge them full price. After all, they're not children. Oh no, the rates are *per human* not per square foot or whatever you measure humans in. I still had the sofa bed free for a full-sized student, so that was one 'lifesize' on the sofa bed and twenty pygmies

---

1 Now of course known as Cif, which makes no sense whatsoever – who says 'I'll be with you in a Cif' or 'Just a Ciffy'. Oddly the word Cif, translated out of the Belgian, actually means 'Snickers'.

on the shelves. I also ran a service cashing their grant cheques or Giros, taking my rent at source, and I charged a hefty commission that Eddie Titchmarsh would have been proud of.

The flat had become self-sufficient overnight. I need never work again, I'd thought, and started turning down all kinds of jobs – even lucrative corporate entertainments.

Of course there were tensions, I don't deny it. Twenty-two personalities operating full time; there were bound to be clashes, and often I had to sedate the pygmies with the maximum dose of Night Nurse. I told them it was medicine to protect them from a disease I had made up called Chinese Takeaway Disease. I'd been trying to think of a name when I saw a Chinese takeaway leaflet, so that's what I called it.

'What's it called, this disease?' they had asked, sceptically.

'Oh . . . er . . . Chinese Takeaway Disease,'[2] I said.

'Oh, okay,' they said, opening their mouths to receive the mild hypnotic.

There were other problems; you only had to get home unexpectedly from work to find one of them using your flannel as a towel, or worse, rolling around in one of your socks with your dad's Barbie – and you get what I'm talking about.

They each had a foam washing-up sponge as a mattress, a panty-liner pillow and a man-sized Kleenex as a sheet. If they were cold I got them to snuggle up, or I would go to the thermostat and pretend to put the heating up, as a placebo (the shelves over the radiators went for slightly higher rents).

Like I say, initially it was fun. The pygmies would spend most of their time out and about, down the job centre, or

2 Chinese Takeaway Disease, it seems, does exist in parts of their native Amazon basin. A number of pygmies who'd ventured into the towns and got wads of menus from Chinese takeaways to use as bedding material then developed a rash – an allergy to the printers' ink. It was only the advent of home laminating machines that circumvented this problem.

amusement arcades, or riding around on the backs of dogs in the park, then in the evening they would regale me and the life-sized student with stories of the Amazonian rainforests.

For instance, one of the stories was about a misunderstanding involving some pygmies and some chips. It seems that amongst pygmies, chips are thought of as having strong powers of leg activation. Whoever eats them will want to dance. Well, a white man visited the Amazon Basin and came upon a pygmy encampment. In order to appear friendly he set up a big fire and started cooking some chips. When the chips were ready he offered them around to the pygmies. They each took a chip, ate it and then immediately started dancing. The white man cautioned against this so soon after eating, 'As it may cause wind or a stitch,' but every time the pygmies took a chip the dancing took off again. In the end the white man threatened them with his guns, yelling, 'Stop dancing!' and the head pygmy replied, 'Well, stop giving us the leg-activation sticks then!'[3]

A nice story but after a while I realised that some of the tales were coming round again and again, often told by different pygmies as if it had happened to them. I would probe around for new stories, asking them directly specific details about what had happened (for instance, where in the jungle had they got the chips from?) but they would change the subject, always bringing it back to one of these same ten or twelve stories.

The life-sized student noticed it as well. So when they'd all gone out I went nosing. Sure enough, under one of their mattresses I found a book, *Twelve Great Stories That Will Make People Think You're A Pygmy*. There they were, the stories in black and white, virtually word for word as they'd told them to me. I could see there was more to this so-called pygmy cabal than met the eye. On closer investigation I discovered paperwork referring to

3 Traditionally chips are not cooked in the pygmy's home but ordered from the 'Tako-dak-to-mari' or 'Chinese takeaway'.

44

sunbed sessions and an order form for Holiday Snaps You Want, a company that falsified your holiday snaps for a country and holiday of your choice (I'd used the service several times myself; even if the holiday had been disappointing, there was no reason why the photos of it should not be sweet).

I had no option but to confront them. I cooked them their usual supper of deep-fried potatoes followed by mango sorbet, and as one of them was about to launch into My Time In The Jungle Clearing When A Marmoset Fell On My Head, I challenged them.

'You're not pygmies, are you?'

'I don't know what you mean,' said Trevor, the spokesman for the group.

'Here,' I said, tossing him the book of stories. 'How do you explain this?'

'Ah.'

'Yes, *ah*,' I said. I gave them forty minutes to clear their shelves and skedaddle, and to their credit they did so without any fuss. Needless to say they lost their deposits. I know what you're thinking – they were still small and paid their rent so what if they weren't genuine pygmies – well, that's because I haven't mentioned to you about the public tours I was holding after dark with night-vision goggles.

So now it was just me and the life-sized student. I'd had the faux pygmies there for so long I'd let all my showbiz contacts go, plus I'd fallen out with the pygmy-supply agent when I'd persuaded the pygmies to quit the agency, thus saving me his 10 per cent commission. The pygmies' deposit money lasted me about a month and I've been stony broke ever since. I still wiped the shelves though, out of habit.

I took a bite out of an old *Daily Telegraph* that I'd been saving – a missing person story. Hmmm, rather cloying, I thought, and reached for a lemon, hoping that the acid of the citrus fruit would balance up the dish.

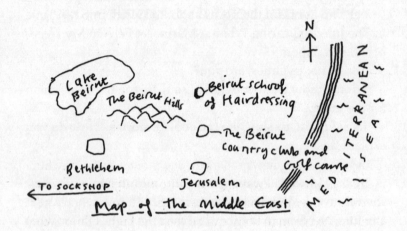

Lake Beirut

The Beirut Hills

Beirut school of Hairdressing

The Beirut country club and golf course

Bethlehem

TO SOCKSHOP

Jerusalem

N

MEDITERRANEAN SEA

Map of the Middle East

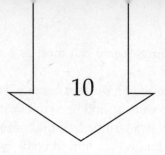

The Beirut School of Hairdressing

I had been eating newspapers to save money. Every day hundreds of unsold newspapers are thrown out by newsagents; I would collect them and eat them. Yes, I know what you're thinking, the human body can't digest the high cellulose content of newspaper. Well, I got round that by pre-digesting them with cellulase, an enzyme that breaks down the cellulose in paper and turns it into sugar. I could then drink the vaguely sweet, bluey-black soup that was left. I developed a taste for certain news stories over others. For instance, murders are good as a main course but you need to have something like an escaped animal or giant cat on the loose story as a side dish to take away the heaviness. Page three made me burp. I'd always regret the media pages of the *Guardian* the next day.

If you eat just newspapers you can live pretty cheaply. I know you're wondering, so why don't tramps eat newspapers, then? Unfortunately under the system that tramps operate, newspapers are classified as bedding, and you wouldn't eat your bed, would you? Where would you sleep?

'Mmmm, yummy,' I said out loud as I munched on the Terry Waite case.

When I'd first read of his disappearance, I'd thought, Who? But as the months went by and he didn't show up, this person who we had never heard of became more and more well known until we longed for him to come back so we could forget about him again.

Imagine how shocked we were some five years later when we found out that he'd merely been on a hairdressing course. I'll never forget seeing the news bulletins as he arrived off the plane, thinner now, older certainly. I can remember thinking, Has he done something to his hair?

He was immediately taken away by Special Branch and debriefed. It seems he'd secretly harboured a desire to cut and style hair for years, and had gone on a five-year course advertised in the local paper in Beirut as Learn Everything There Is To Know About Hairdressing: Five-Year Course. He'd phoned his wife to tell her, and, although surprised, she knew of his desires and thought that the only way for him to work them through was to have a go at it. Also it would give her a five-year break and she immediately went out and bought a copy of *Floodlight*, the guide to part-time study in London, and signed up for a wicker-basket-weaving course. She planned to weave five good-sized laundry baskets for four friends, keeping the best one for herself.[1]

When she'd seen the news and the furore about Terry being missing she was worried that if she said anything at this late stage about his true whereabouts it might jeopardise the number of hours she'd be able to put in on the weaving. Having rashly made promises of a basket to each of the four friends, she shuddered at the thought of only being able to get

[1] Yes, this was extremely ambitious for a beginner weaver; some might even say fool-hardy and the tutor tried to steer her towards a waste-paper basket but to no avail.

four done, or, worse still, three (there were two more worse-case scenarios that she chose not to contemplate).

The Beirut School of Hairdressing was the best-kept secret of the hairdressing world. Located at a hilltop camp, the trainees lived under canvas and were required to lose touch completely with their family, and also their loved ones, so they could concentrate solely on hair care.

The induction week had been very tough on Terry. Designed to weed out those who were unlikely to stay the course, they'd been on a rigorous seven days of haircutting, washing, drying and perming. Basic cuts at first, but when you're tired even something as routine as a bob seemed like putting in a full head of highlights on a curly-haired fidget-bottom. It was tough but Terry loved every minute of it and when at the end of the three weeks he was accepted on to the course full time, his heart leapt with joy. Immediately his mind tripped off into the possibilities of a chain of salons: Waite's Hair Lodges (motto, *Waite* Your Turn), one-stop fast-styling outlets for today's hurly-burly-curly world. A portfolio of celebrity clients: Mel B, Mel C, the Atomic Kitten girls, Princess Stephanie of Monaco, Celine Dion ('. . . and I'll trim your husband's beard for free! Sit down, Monsieur Dion . . .') and even surviving members of the Carry On team ('Leave it with me, Babs! When can you pick it up? Thursday okay?').

The first two years would be basic science – the biochemistry and physiology of hair, right down to the basic DNA structure – then, if he passed his yearly exams, the next three years were purely practical; doing what he loved best: cutting and styling hair. In the final year he would be attached to a high-profile stylist as a 'shadow', learning at first hand how to deal with the most difficult cases, plus specialist techniques like hair extensions.

The course went well, his reports couldn't have been better

if he had written them himself: 'Terry is a lively student much liked by his classmates and has learnt well the importance of the parting in male hairdressing. Well done'; 'Terry continues to work well and contributes much to the discussion sessions. His weakness in the combing area has improved greatly this term. Good work, Terry'; 'Terry's work has been outstanding this term; his thesis on the beehive was a revelation. Still needs a little work on his combing but I have high hopes for his final year exam'. Basically he'd been tipped for a first-class degree with honours, and his classmates, far from resenting him, could see how much work he'd put in and how much he got out of it and felt he deserved to do well.

So, then came the final exam. Set over three days it consisted of two three-hour written tests, one multiple-choice, one paper of questions requiring longer answers and three essay questions. The whole thing finished with a practical exam on the third day.

Terry didn't want to appear too cocky but felt quietly confident about the first day's papers. There had been no real surprises; they'd stuck pretty closely to the curriculum. He'd hit a bit of luck with the essay paper when two of the questions just happened to be subjects that he'd done some extra work on (by studying the past papers from previous years he'd worked out that Problems of Double Crowns and Context and the Fringe hadn't come round for a while).

Then came the practical. He sat in his cubicle, his roll of tools on the dressing table; he checked the hairdryer again, yes it was working fine, the shampoo dispenser, yes, then a swish from the curtain and his subject entered. He took one look at him and his heart stopped. Peter Stringfellow.

'Come in, sit down, have you got the day off or do you work nights?' said a weak, stringy voice that Terry barely recognised as his own.

That night at the end-of-term disco, he sat in a corner drinking himself into oblivion, his dreams in tatters.

Meanwhile, back in their home in Blackheath, Mrs Waite had just finished the third basket, and having run out of wicker and thus lacking the basic building blocks of basket weaving, she'd sat herself down in front of the nightly news. The familiar face of Anna Ford filled her screen and announced that in retaliation for British manufacturers flooding the world craft market with cheap crêpe paper, the rest of the world was enforcing a wicker embargo on the UK.[2]

The next day Terry arrived home, the chance of that fourth basket ever being completed disappearing at a stroke.

2 Remember the Great Wicker shortage? People forced to unpick baskets to supply the wicker furniture that the holiday let business seems to rely on so.

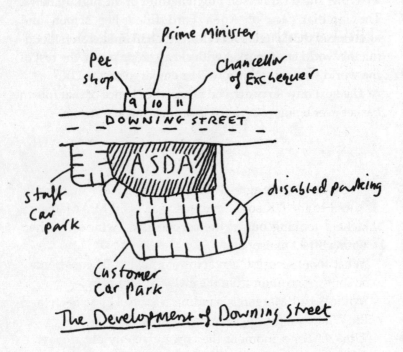

Pet shop

Prime Minister

Chancellor of Exchequer

9 10 11

DOWNING STREET

ASDA

staff car park

disabled parking

Customer car park

The Development of Downing Street

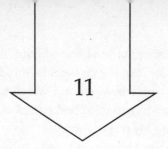

11

The Love that Dare not Beak its Name

'Right then, we're agreed. Deng Xiaoping will make a state visit to the UK sometime this year,' said Mrs Margaret Thatcher,[1] looking out of the second-floor window of her Downing Street maisonette.

'What about security?' said Norman Tebbit. 'There's bound to be some opposition from the artificial-foot people.'

'Willie?' said Margaret, handing over to Home Secretary Willie Whitelaw, putting him on the spot.

'Um . . .' For a moment the curmudgeonly old man was lost for words; he'd zeroed out of the discussion about ten minutes ago and had been thinking about whether there were any laws against marrying a parrot.

Initially there had been opposition to Downing Pets when the new owner had applied for a licence to sell animals from number 9 Downing Street. The Cabinet feared that the smell would distract them from the affairs of state, but they soon

1 Margaret Thatcher is one of our best known women. Indeed many people are able to recognise her over photographs of their own feet.

53

got used to it. In fact some of them quite liked the smell; it reminded John Major of the circus. His mind would go back to when, as a boy, he would sit and watch his father pulling himself into a near-transparent body stocking, then later getting changed to do his trapeze act.[2]

Most of the Cabinet had bought pets during the year it had been open. Michael Heseltine often came out with a gerbil, Norman Tebbit always bought his chew sticks there, plus, of course, there was the passing trade: visiting dignitaries were often treated to a puppy. Margaret would shake their hand and whisper, 'Pop next door and choose anything you like – on us.' Ronald Reagan had gone home with an African lovebird (with the standard warning that 'Any detergent left on the feathers may cause harm if ingested whilst preening').

Willie had seen Helen, an African Grey, in the window a month ago. He hadn't gone in to buy anything, he had just been browsing, killing time before the next Cabinet meeting, but he spotted little Helen almost immediately. She'd put on quite a show for him, winking coyly over one wing, puffing her chest up to impressive proportions then rolling playfully on her back on the open page three of the *Sun* lining the bottom of her cage. Willie could feel his face colouring.

'All right, Mr Whitelaw?' said Ted.

'Um, yes, yes . . .' he said, loosening his tie.

'Pretty, ain't she?'

'Yes, yes, very pretty.'

'Seventy-five pounds to you, sir.'

'No, no, I'm . . . oh good Lord, is that the time? I must be going,' he said, and hurried out.

All that week he just couldn't stop thinking about her. He'd left it a couple of days then he went back. As soon as Helen

2 John's father – John Major Senior – was a trapeze artiste and to this day, if you pass too close to him, he will try and grab your legs.

saw him she seemed to perk up and started rubbing herself against the bars of her cage. Willie gently squeezed his finger between the bars. 'Hello little one,' he said.

'Pru pru pru pru,' Helen purred back, licking the sweat globules from the fleshy pulp of his digit.

He rubbed the soft, downy skin under her beak; it clearly gave her pleasure.[3]

'Give her a nut, Mr Whitelaw,' said Ted, proffering an open bag of monkey nuts.

'Well, I . . . yes, very well.' His plump sausage fingers dipped into the paper bag and selected one of the double pods. He watched as Helen took it in her left claw, and like some sort of bird striptease artiste, slowly stripped the pink kernel of its shell. Willie could feel the hairs on the back of his neck standing up on end, pushing on the inside of his collar, making the top button of his shirt bite into his Adam's apple.

'Another, sir?' chipped in Ted.

'No, no, that's quite enough for one day,' said Willie, flustered. He drew out his fob watch. 'Is that the time?' he mumbled, not really looking and dropping the watch. As he bent over to pick it up, Helen let out a squawk. Did he misinterpret it or had she said, 'Cor! I wouldn't mind some of that'? His hand felt for the doorknob and he stumbled out into the fresh air. Oh God, what was happening to him? Dammit he was seventy-four years old!

Over the next few weeks Ted watched the relationship blossom. He saw how the old man would come in with nuts and head straight for the parrot's cage, how he had started to smarten himself up – hair freshly combed, a clean shirt, the new, strongly aphrodisiac smell of his Hi Karate aftershave.

3 This little piece got a 'Best Homoavian Writing' Award.

Ted chose not to push the sale; the old man was shy and he didn't want to upset him. No, it would come, by and by.

'How about David Yip?' Willie heard himself saying.

'David Yip?' said Mrs Thatcher. 'The Chinese Detective?'

'That's right. He's so good, and I bet we could get him at a good price.'

She hesitated for a moment and then said, 'Yes, I've no objections to that. So it's settled: state visit by Deng Xiaoping, David Yip to do security. Willie? Can I leave you to talk to his agent?'

'I'll see to it right away,' said Willie, getting up to leave. No, I won't, he thought, quietly letting himself out of the side door. He had one little job to do first. He could feel the jeweller's gift box in his pocket pressing against his heart; a heart flabby from years of beating but which now danced to the rhythm of flapping wings. Inside the box a 4-carat diamond engagement ring. He'd decided to do it. Well, you only get one life, he thought, as he'd walked the few yards from Number Ten to the pet shop.

The ring in his pocket and a large bouquet of millet in his hand, he pondered his and Helen's future together. Okay, so he was already married but there was no need for anyone to know about the parrot. No, it would be their secret. Why should anyone suspect anything other than friendship? Except Ted. He thought Ted suspected something – from little things: looks, innuendo – but he also thought he could trust him. If he did leak it to the press, he would just deny it. That wasn't insulting to Helen, was it? Maybe it was; why deny their love? Yes, okay, that's how he would play it: if someone asked him directly then yes, he would say he was in love with Helen and that they were to be married.

He would talk to Helen about it. Not now, no; there wasn't time and with the excitement of it all . . . no, later, over dinner.

He'd got some of her favourite sunflower seeds baked into a cake by melting them up with lard – delicious.

He put his hand into his inside pocket and felt two tickets to the Budgerigar Hotel, Amplemews, in Holland, a small town where by law man and bird were legally able to marry. He'd already spoken to Jim Prior and he'd agreed to be a witness. They'd stay two nights at the Budgerigar, and then he planned to honeymoon in the Maldives. Could he tell Margaret? Would she understand?[4]

He paused for just a second, straightening his tie. He studied his reflection in the shop window. He may be in his seventies but he wasn't a bad catch and, above all, he would look after Helen and care for her. A deep breath, he reached for the door handle – only to have it pulled away from him.

He staggered back slightly and looked up. What? Who? Doctor David Owen striding out of the shop, and under his arm – *no!* What? Some mistake, surely? Helen's cage!

'Hello, Willie. Yes, lovely, isn't she? I've had my eye on her for months!' Owen brushed past, climbed into his mini van and took away Helen in a blink of time. Gone out of his life.

Willie could feel his lower lip tremble, his eyes filling with tears. 'How could you do this to me?' he screamed, dashing the bouquet to the floor and sinking to his knees. His argument not with Helen, not with David Owen even, but with God.

Ted helped the old man into the shop and down on to one of the dog beds. He'd tried to warn Mr Whitelaw about the she-parrot but he hadn't taken the hint. And, after all, a sale was a sale.

'Want a cup of tea, old timer?' he said.

'Yes . . . no, thank you, I'd better be going, I've made such a fool of myself . . . You won't tell . . .?' faltered Willie.

4 We'll never know, but probably not is my gut feeling.

'What goes on under the roof of this pet shop is strictly between you and me, sir,' said Ted.

'Wait a minute.' Willie looked up, his eyes brightening. 'That macaque – for sale, is she?' He wiped his nose on his sleeve.

Ted gently lifted the young bird off her perch and brought her close to the face of the Home Secretary. She nuzzled up immediately, feeling Willie's bristles against her beak and ears, sniffing the powerful oriental scent.

'Her name's Stephanie; I was holding her back for the state visit of the President of the Czech Republic, Vaclav Havel, but you can have her if you like.'

Willie shifted in the dog bed, caressed the tiny parrot's head and felt in his pocket for the seventy pounds. Well, he thought, shame to let those hotel reservations go to waste.

'Er, that's eighty pounds, the macaque,' said Ted, cruelly extorting a further ten from a man in trouble.

'Have you got change of a fifty, Ted?' said Willie, forcing a smile. Better he had found out about Helen now than after they were married.

'Come on, Stephanie,' he said, rising. He turned to Ted and smiled.

Ted smiled back and let Mr Willie Whitelaw out of the shop. He turned the open sign to closed. 'Boing!' he muttered. 'He's on the rebound.' He ran his fingers through the ninety-eight pounds, ninety for Helen from the good doctor and ... 'Oh dear,' he chuckled, 'I must have given Mr Whitelaw the wrong change out of that fifty.'[5] Yes, it hadn't been a bad morning.

---

5 Whitelaw handed over two fifty-pound notes and Ted gave him only two pounds change rather than the correct tenner. Similarly David Owen had given five twenties only to receive one pound fifty in change. Remember, these were vulnerable men.

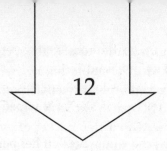

12

I'll be your Privet Dancer

David Yip let himself into the caravan that he had parked in the garden of 10 Downing Street, went to the fridge and pulled out an ice-cold bud. He put the bud in some water and hoped it would open and bloom tomorrow. By keeping the rose-buds in the fridge he was able to control their opening and closing, to get better value for money out of a bunch or bouquet.

He'd picked up the tip at the Chelsea Flower Show. It had been his first visit, and he was impressed by the fancy gardens, fantastic in their scale, all laid out into different themes. He had been most impressed by a garden that was just a pile of rubble with the tail fins of a V2 rocket sticking out of it, but which captured with uncanny accuracy the gardens of the East End of London in the 1940s. He'd wandered on.

There was a huge crowd of middle-aged ladies around Alan Titchmarsh, tearing at his clothes to get a piece of him while his agent, Eddie,[1] directed proceedings from a leather

---

1 Still withered but looking tanned and rested after a holiday with Princess Margaret's withered twin in Mustique.

pouch around Alan's waist. It was Eddie's idea for Alan to go out into the crowd to promote his new Alan Titchmarsh Hormone Replacement Therapy (HRT) patch. It was pretty much a standard HRT patch but with a picture of Alan's face on it, plus it came with a free packet of evening primrose seeds.[2] Well, they were supposed to be evening primrose but they'd been difficult to get hold of and many of the packs just contained weed seeds that Eddie had hastily gathered from a weed-infested lay-by on the way to the exhibition. He reasoned that the old birds wouldn't cotton on, and if they did he'd just blame it on the menopause.

He knew Alan's walk-about would be great publicity for the new product but he hadn't predicted this sort of response. He signalled to the helicopter circling overhead, and the chopper descended. Alan took hold of the rope ladder and the helicopter started back up into the sky. A couple of determined 'Titchies' grabbed Alan's trousers and pants, and as he rose they came off with a twang leaving his private parts covered by only a thin square of muslin, which he routinely placed there on such occasions as a precaution. Diarmuid Gavin, his co-host for the BBC's TV coverage of the Flower Show, quickly placed his hand over the camera lens and cut early to a promo on growing your own gherkins, but you could hear his laughter ringing out across the gardens like an Irish jockey on heat.

Yip strolled past the Alan Titchmarsh incident and stumbled on to a very strange area indeed: a large meadow-style garden inhabited by scantily clad ladies. He looked closer and could see couples writhing in the beautifully trimmed rhododendron bushes.

2 Many experts think that the oil of the evening primrose helps alleviate the symptoms of premenstrual tension but it's still wise to hide the knives during what my mum called 'the naughty week'.

'Hello, mister! Fancy some fun?' a woman in a too-tight top and fishnet stockings hollered from a doorway.

'No, no, just browsing. Tell me, what is this shrub here?'

'Oh, that's *Heptacodium miconioides*,' she said and turned her attention to another gentleman behind him.

David suddenly felt lost; where was he? He took out his Royal Horticultural Society map. Ah, yes, the Red Light District Garden.[3] He put his head down and scuttled off towards the exit.

Back in the caravan Yip sniffed the bud – nothing – and made a pot of tea. It had been a long day, he thought. He still had to pinch himself every now and again to make sure he really was doing this thing. Here he was, a humble actor, organising the security for the state visit to the Yookay of the President of China. He still really couldn't work out how he'd got the job. When Dervil, his agent, had phoned and told him he would be 'acting head' of security, he'd assumed it was an acting job – that is acting the part of head of security – not taking the post *temporarily* of the head of security.

'They've asked for you specifically, David,' Dervil said. 'They want someone Chinese to make the Chairman feel at home.'

It had been Willie's big idea to help put people at their ease. Using this same logic he had booked Duncan Goodhew[4] to cover the state visit of President Gorbachev of Russia: 'Two bald blokes – bound to get on . . .' reasoned Willie.

It was all part of his new 'caring approach' to being Home Secretary. Maybe he was getting old and soft but recently

3 This garden was banned from future flower shows after a spate of unwanted pregnancies.

4 Duncan Goodhew went bald after he fell out of a tree as a boy; the upside being huge savings on swimming caps. Over the years he invested the money he would have spent on swimming caps in buy-to-let flats and now is busy all day Friday collecting the rents.

he'd decided to make people a bit more comfortable. He'd just finished sending out a circular to all the police chiefs requesting that from now on dawn raids should be undertaken dressed as Disney characters – Pooh, Piglet and friends – just in case there were children in the house. He'd already had a very positive response from prison inmates to optional bedtime lullabies.

Yip was kicking himself about that artificial foot. How on earth had the agitator managed to slip through his tight cordon of actors? He would certainly be on the phone to their various agents in the morning. He pressed a button on his intercom. 'Danny? Everyone did get their scripts this morning, didn't they? They all went out?'

He knew the answer was 'yes' as this was part of the script too – and the breach in security – because the whole thing was being filmed as a special edition of *The Chinese Detective*. Dervil had floated the idea to the networks who'd snapped it up. 'It's a kind of reality TV *Chinese Detective* thing. Much of it is scripted, but a small percentage is unplanned and that's what gives it its edge.' There was a subplot involving an affair between David and his secretary, and a Chinese man got murdered by triads. It was going to come out on a video for Christmas.

So now David was confused. Was he acting? Or was he really Head of Security? When was the Duncan Goodhew special coming out? Why was the Home Secretary spending so much time at the pet shop? Why was he dressed as Eeyore?

He yawned. He was tired. His eyes closed, his mind twanged off into sleep. And as he slept, he dreamt . . .

He dreamt that he was the permanent Head of Security for state visits and was on holiday, and they'd got someone else in to cover his absence: Dennis Waterman. He was worried that Dennis would do too good a job and that people would start to notice the holes in his own performance. He replayed the morning's events in slow motion: he saw Deng Xiaoping getting out of the vehicle, and Manny Durban step forward, his hand up over his head holding an artificial foot. He saw Dennis Waterman turn, catch sight of the foot, and dive on the agitator, wrestling the foot from him. He saw the front pages of the newspapers with a photograph of Deng embracing Dennis Waterman,[5] praising him as a hero. He saw Waterman step forward to receive his knighthood. He saw his own name in a roll of dishonour.

'Agh!' He woke with a jolt.

'David! You're needed in make-up!' said his secretary, barging in with a tray of muffins and wearing only a see-through shortie nightie.

'Crikey! Are we on to that bit already?' said Yip, his face colouring.

---

5 Oddly the closest translation of the word Deng in Chinese is Dennis Waterman.

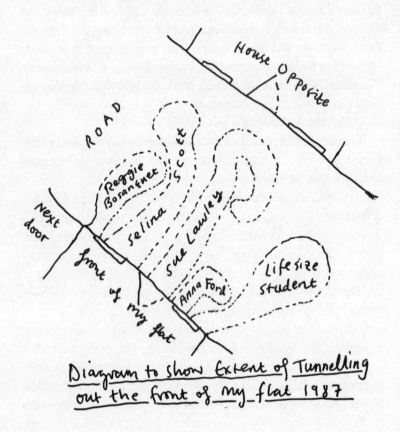

HOUSE OPPOSITE

ROAD

Next door

Reggie Bosanquet

Scott

Selina

Sue Lawley

Front of my flat

Anna Ford

Life size student

Diagram to show Extent of Tunnelling out the front of my flat 1987

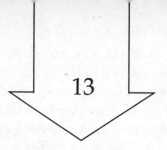

Open up Selina, Shut down Sue

I took out my Sainsbury's reward card, angled it at forty-five degrees and with one deft move got it under the stain and took off the top layer, then wiped it clean with an antiseptic swab.

'There, the last shelf done,' I muttered, and set off down Anna Ford[1] to wake up the life-sized student.

I suppose it was 1983 when I first started to expand my basement flat by digging tunnels under the pavement then naming them after newsreaders. I had no alternative with property prices in London heading up into the high nineties. So far I had four tunnels. It should have been five but a month earlier, with Sue Lawley[2] so nearly finished, I noticed a horri-

---

1 The popular newsreader who was later to fall foul of so called 'Age-ism' at the BBC despite still looking nice – she refused to 'Treble the amount of foundation you use and get a full face of Botox'. At one point she was rumoured to be dating a spaceman – so who had the last laugh?

2 One-time presenter of *Desert Island Discs* who resigned after the turkey king Bernard Matthews chose the same song ten times ('Turkey Trot' by Little Eva) and when asked what luxury he would like to take he named the song again. There were accusations of product placement, so Sue went. No spaceman to soften the blow.

ble smell wafting up from her far end. When I got down there with the lamp I realised I'd fractured a main sewer with my trowel. The last thing I wanted was a visit from the sewage police.[3] Thinking quickly I got a washing-up bowl and started ferrying the sewage out of Sue Lawley and up the stairs to the bathroom, where I deposited it in the loo and flushed it away. Of course, by the time I'd made it back down to the basement the flushings had made their way back into the tunnel. No matter how fast I ran up those steps with the sewage, the tunnel was still full by the time I got back down. The more I flushed, the more sewage came through. In the end I had no alternative but to seal up Sue Lawley and re-open Selina Scott.[4]

I'd only really sealed the Selina Scott tunnel after Selina failed to reply to my invitation to the opening ceremony. All the other newsreaders had sent letters with their quite understandable reasons why they couldn't attend, even after I had offered to change the dates of the launch nights to accommodate them – it's amazing just how much in demand they all are! To be honest, after the knock-backs from the other readers I'd not expected Selina to be able to come and had merely sent her the invite as a courtesy. Unfortunately she was not able to extend to me the courtesy of a simple reply. So I closed the tunnel down there and then, and fired off a letter to her cancelling the launch. I felt that the whole thing had been spoilt and I started work on my next tunnel: Anna Ford.

I know what you're thinking: why not just rename Selina Scott Tunnel, Anna Ford Tunnel? Well, it's not as simple as

3 A crack team of largely French experts armed with smelling cats – cats that had been trained to smell sewage in the tiniest quantities in exchange for vouchers that could be exchanged in any pet shop for catnip.
4 Ash-blonde news anchorwoman and Princess Diana lookalike, known for her outspoken views on the use of the stylophone in early English music.

that because all the tunnels are different and I have the news-reader in mind as I'm digging them, and so their personalities are kind of expressed in the way the tunnel turns out. Oh, I don't know! It's hard to explain unless you've tried it. It's like dogs, I guess: you don't rename a dog just because you've fallen out with the person you've named it after, do you?

So that was that. I closed down Selina and thought nothing more of it.

Imagine my embarrassment when on the supposed launch night, I was sitting watching some old videos of the *News At Ten* and drinking my first dose of Night Nurse when the doorbell went. It was Selina Scott with her 'friend'. She'd never got that letter cancelling it.

Well, what could I do? I told her flatly to her face that the tunnel had been sealed up and told her the reason why. She begged me to let her see it but I refused; I didn't even let her over the threshold. She claimed that the invitation did not state that she was required to respond to it. I kindly bid her farewell and closed the door. She then hung around on the doorstep for about half an hour hurling abuse through the letterbox, leaving only when I threatened to call the police.

I did feel slightly uneasy about the whole episode, as I wasn't completely sure that I had put RSVP on the bottom of her invite, and for some reason I couldn't find the carbon paper from that particular one. Maybe I should have given her the benefit of the doubt, but I didn't.

Of course, not long after that she left the BBC and went to satellite, and has dawdled around on the fringes of TV ever since.

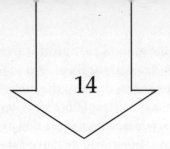

14

My Life with Prince Edward

'You should have let Selina see that tunnel,' said the life-sized student, stirring from his pharmaceutical-induced dream sleep.

'That was two years ago; don't keep going on about it,' I said. 'And get dressed. I've got a corporate engagement at noon and I want my breakfast.'

We operated the 'alternating chores' system of flat share. I do a chore, he does a chore, I do a chore, he does a chore, etc. I wake him up, he cooks my breakfast, I clear the table, he does the washing-up; that way it's completely fair – except when we once got into a loop where, as luck would have it, I was cooking breakfast, lunch and dinner every night, and doing all the washing-up. I then realised he was working out who was going to get what in advance and adding chores accordingly – rigging the system. He was banished un-attended to his tunnel for three days for that, and since then, I'd grab him every ten minutes and spin him round and round so he was permanently dizzy and unable to hatch any of his schemes.

'What are you doing today?' said the life-sized student, crushing those little milk pots you get at service stations for tea and coffee on to some cornflakes (it takes about thirty per bowl but if you take, say, five every time you have a hot beverage, six trips gets you a cheap breakfast); it was a far cry from the butlered service he had been used to while growing up. I poured the milk into the bowl and he ate it. We were stuck, quite accidentally, in an 'I get out a bowl, he pours in the cornflakes, I pour on the milk, he eats it' loop, and laughed to each other about it, he graciously ducking out and allowing me to eat the third bowl of cereal; well, we had to be flexible about the whole thing, we had to remember why we brought in the system in the first place: to make things fairer.

'Did I get any calls?' asked life-sized student.

'Yes, there was one,' I replied. 'The Queen phoned: says have you got a girlfriend yet?'

'Oh God,' said Lifesize, rolling his eyes up to the heavens.

I wasn't planning to reveal his identity but I suppose it was a long time ago – life-sized student was in fact HRH The Prince Edward. When I first met him he had just pulled out of the Marine-training corp, and a Gurkha who knew a pygmy suggested my gaff. I didn't cotton on that I knew who he was until the Queen kept phoning up, by which time I'd got his deposit. To me he was always just 'Life-sized student' or plain 'Lifesize'.

He'd been through a lot of traumatic events on that training course, and after a couple of deep breaths of dry-cleaning solvent he would readily spill the beans. I know that you want me to spill his beans on to you, but I have a mind that they would form a nice couple of chapters for my next book. Maybe a whole book, if I pad out the stories with background information and photographs of the stuff I've stolen off him.

That's right, I steal stuff off my tenants. So what? We all do it, right? Besides, Prince Edward had got so much, there was no way he would ever notice half the things I'd nicked. So far I've stolen: a wooden plaque with a white metal relief portrait of Queen Elizabeth, The Queen Mother, a silver salver, inscribed HRH The Duchess of Clarence, Christmas 1826, a white metal pepper grinder, a book entitled *Royal Institute of Painters in Gouache*, a framed photograph and nine photo frames, five plates in a green box, a framed pencil drawing of Prince Edward, a box containing nightwear, a Windsor family album, a box of crockery and three miniatures, a book entitled *British Music Hall*, a box of Stuart crystal, a jewellery box, two more boxes of crockery, a plate with Prince Edward's crest on it, a rug in a Versace carrier bag, three hats, two oval pictures in a box, a writing case, a butterfly handbag, some colour photographs signed 'Edward's 1986', 226 colour photographs, 71 black-and-white photographs, a tartan sash, a pair of black gloves, a scarf in a plastic bag with a yellow note 'scarf worn in Leeds' attached, an empty photograph wallet marked 'Balmoral '86', a pink laminated label, a number of CDs signed by the Prince: 'La Traviata', Tchaikovsky's 'Romeo and Juliet', *The Classic Experience*, 'Turandot', Tina Turner's *Foreign Affair*, Chris de Burgh's *Flying Colours*, Michael Jackson's *Bad*, The LA Philharmonic Orchestra doing 'Les Miserables', Abba *The Singles*, a Clinique black beaded ladies' bag containing two cotton-wool balls, a Boots receipt, a yellow metal chain, chewing gum and a 2p piece, a beige cloth bag containing six white metal wine corks, a Ratners' clock in orange-and-black marble with mother-of-pearl face and yellow metal trim wrapped in a towel, a red leather Tesco's pouch containing a pair of small white metal-and-gilt spoons, two pink roll-neck jumpers, an Asda cream polyester blouse, some audio cassettes: Supertramp's *Breakfast in America*, Leo Sayer's *Endless Flight*, Jeff Wayne's *War of the Worlds* (signed Prince Edward), Rachmaninov Piano Concerto No. 2 in C Minor (signed 'Prince E.'), Elton John's *Blue Moves* signed Prince Edward,

Phantom of the Opera with Michael Crawford, Phil Collins's 'Groovy Kind of Love', Cliff Richard's 'All I Ask of You', Michael Ball's 'Love Changes Everything', Elkie Brooks's *Backtrack*, an a-ha album signed Prince Edward and a Corby trouser press.

Yeah, I normally managed to shift most of my Prince Edward stuff down the boot sales.[1]

Okay, basically he was unhappy being on the top bunk. That was the main reason Prince Edward couldn't handle the Marines. It seems that the soldier beneath him kept lying on his back and pushing his feet up into Prince Edward's mattress, which kept waking him up. The rest of it – the training, the mucking in with the rest of the guys – that was all fine, it was just this top bunk thing. Like I say it would make a great book.

I explained to ole Lifesize about the Gonk gig, then went to have a shower. I took my pyjamas off down to my pants and stepped into the cubicle. Old Lifesize had insisted that I always keep my pants on around the house. He added it as a separate clause on the conditions of his lease, and like a fool I hadn't bothered to read it when I countersigned. I don't know what it was all about but I always had to leave them on and when I changed them I had to do it in bed and under the covers. The odd thing was that whenever I was under the covers changing them, he would invariably barge into my bedroom on some weak pretence like, 'Have you seen my binoculars?' or 'Have you seen my Clinique black beaded ladies' bag containing two cotton-wool balls, a Boots receipt, a yellow metal chain, chewing gum and a 2p piece?' I couldn't work the whole thing out. How could he know?

Then one morning I took him his morning coffee and

1 Sadly I have a very bad profile on eBay after trying to pass on a slightly soiled Cosmo Jenks hat I'd won in a raffle. My description said 'as new' but there was some wear to the chin strap.

caught him watching a giant screen with a plan of the flat on it. There was a light flashing on what was clearly his room. Then it dawned on me: tracker pants. The pair he'd bought me for Christmas. From then on I changed them round at Zevon's office.

The water dribbled out of the showerhead and wetted my body. I soaped up the flannel and brought it up to my face then recoiled. 'Yuk! Pygmy sweat!' I exclaimed.

Not a great start to the day.

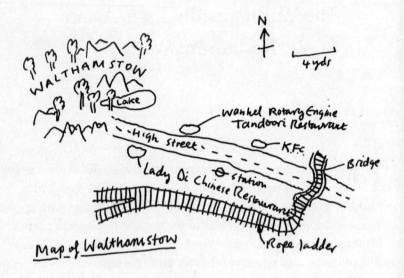

N

4 yds

WALTHAMSTOW

Lake

Wankel Rotary Engine
Tandoori Restaurant

High street

K.F.C.

Bridge

station

Lady Oi Chinese Restaurant

Rope ladder

Map of Walthamstow

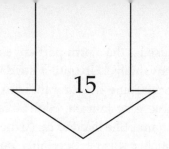

The Walthamstow Inter-Asian
Restaurant Wars

Deng was late getting down to breakfast; Tokwan was already halfway through his Golden Nuggets and Mrs Lamb was busy with the wok. He nodded a greeting to Tokwan and sat down. As he did so Mrs Lamb placed a plate under each of their noses. What is this slop? he wondered. Bits of bacon and egg and what looked like tomato.

'Stir-fried full English breakfast,' announced Mrs Lamb. It was her own recipe. Oh yes, she wasn't too old or set in her ways to adapt. She knew that these Chinese men liked stir-fried food and had reacted to the situation accordingly. Chinese food wasn't that much different from our own food, she quickly realised as she flicked through a manual, they just liked to stir it more. Stir-fried English breakfast, then in the evening, if they were booked for an evening meal (having filled out the necessary forms), stir-fried toad-in-the-hole.

Mrs Lamb had hardly used the wok since she'd bought it at the Ideal Home Exhibition in 1969, but now it was certainly earning its money. She'd also bought a vegetable cutter that doubled up as a rape alarm that same year, which she'd certainly never used – the alarm part anyway, the vegetable cutter had been invaluable. Up until yesterday she'd had a job supplying the local Chinese restaurant with carved radishes. The Lady Di Chinese Restaurant, High Street, Walthamstow, to give it its full name. She liked to carve the faces of political leaders. Mrs Thatcher was her speciality, but she didn't do a bad Michael Foot.

People would come from miles around to see the carvings at the Lady Di Chinese Restaurant, High Street, Walthamstow; word had spread and she got a lot of Chinese gentlemen who had come to see the radishes staying at the B. & B., so everybody benefited. What had been a quiet Chinese restaurant had now played host to Reginald Bosanquet's fortieth birthday bash and the *News At Ten* Xmas party. Robin Day had celebrated his knighthood there, and David Frost had mentioned it in his entry in *Who's Who?* (Hobbies: enjoying the beautifully carved radishes at the Lady Di Chinese Restaurant, High Street, Walthamstow).

It was all going wonderfully well until an Indian restaurant opened up across the road specialising in turnips carved into the shape of that week's top ten in the hit parade. A constantly varied display of whittled root vegetables governed by the peccadilloes of the record-buying public. Even Mrs Lamb had to admire their chef who had to come up with a predominantly new display every week – although inevitably it was often a case of merely changing the order of the existing turnips. The chef had worn a particularly smug look on his face for the thirty-seven-week reign of Wet Wet Wet with 'Love Is All Around'.

Mrs Lamb had her own doubts about the display; his John Denver turnip looked suspiciously like his Elton John turnip, only with a gap carved in between the front teeth, and you'd be hard pushed to tell the difference between his George Michael and his Glen Medeiros. Still, it didn't stop a crowd of kids gathering outside the Wankel Rotary Engine Tandoori Restaurant[1] every Sunday night as the turnip charts broke. A cheer went up as each painstakingly carved head was placed in the window, the name written on it in marker pen so you knew exactly who it was.

The restaurant manager of the Lady Di Chinese Restaurant, High Street, Walthamstow, had responded to the competition by asking Mrs Lamb to vary her radish selection more. 'Maybe do some of the less well-known back bench MPs.'

Mrs Lamb tried to explain that they were appealing to a different crowd to the Wankel Rotary Engine Tandoori. 'They're attracting a young crowd, Mr Lee Con Twix, it won't affect us,' she said, and refused point-blank to start doing members of the House of Lords. 'I believe in an elected second chamber, and if you insist on proceeding down this avenue of carving I will have no option but to hand in my notice.'

Being practical Twix knew that with the salad season almost upon them he would never get as accomplished a radish carver at such short notice. A compromise was struck and Mrs Lamb dropped the Norman Tebbit radish and turned in an MP for the Vale of York Anne McIntosh[2] radish, and a little known balding hopeful, William Hague, in place of Leon Brittan.

Instead of reversing their fortunes, this modernisation had the opposite effect. The regulars, being by nature conservative (with a small 'c' – and all the other letters small, obviously), were dismayed by all the changes; people started leaving in droves, even regulars like the Dimbleby Brothers, Jeremy

---

1 So-called because it had a turbo-charged rotisserie that could revolve a chicken at 1200 rpm, cooking it ultra-evenly but admittedly making it difficult to baste.
2 Whatever happened to Anne McIntosh?

Paxman and the *Panorama* team were seen drifting over the road to the Wankel, who were now having to deploy security guards to keep the crowds at bay. In a stroke of genius they'd opened out the display to include the country-and-western and easy-listening charts, and a smaller section of 'what was number one this time ten and twenty years ago', which broadened the appeal and sucked in traditionally Lady Di customers.

Mrs Lamb knew she needed something big to win them back, and after closing time one Monday night she stayed on in the kitchen.

'No, I'll let myself out, Mr Twix,' she said, delving into her shopping bag and producing a radish the size of a cantaloupe melon. She spread out her knives and started work. She carved all through the night; fingers a blur, radish slivers spraying up into her face, a big pile of shavings gathering at her feet. She stopped only for the five-course 'meal A' for minimum of three persons. At five o'clock in the morning she had finished. She placed her creation in the shop window, put a letter addressed to Mr Lee Con Twix on the counter and left the Lady Di Chinese Restaurant, High Street, Walthamstow, for good, her hands sore from radish juice.

For some reason Mr Lee Con Twix was late that morning, but he knew with the recent fall in trade he probably wouldn't need to get the fat fryers on until just after 12.30. Besides, what was he working so hard for? You only got one life.

As he rounded the corner into the High Street he could hardly believe his eyes; a huge throng of people outside the Lady Di! He started running and as he got level, he pushed to the front of the queue. He tripped and fell forward into the window and looked up. What met his eyes made his heart leap with amazement. A single giant radish carved into all the British Prime Ministers from Atlee to Thatcher, the Mount Rushmore of the vegetable-carving world. She'd done it!

He turned the key in the lock and let the first few customers in. As he did so he looked across at the Wankel: it was completely empty. In the doorway the chef gave him a grudging nod of respect.

Mrs Lamb finished her bacon sandwich and rinsed the plate under the hot tap. She smiled to herself. About now Mr Twix would be reading her letter of resignation. The large, intricately carved radish would buy him some time, then it was someone else's problem; from now on she would devote all her time to the B. & B. and only carve veg for herself. She'd always wanted to go out on top and she'd certainly done that. She watched as the bacon and bread fragments swirled down the plughole like so many chicken nuggets past their sell-by date being put into a vortex.[3]

'Why you give us all this twaddle?' bellowed Deng Xiaoping, startling Mrs Lamb from her reminiscence. He'd been working that phrase out now for three days, using a phrase book and Chinese–English dictionary.

'I'm sorry?'

'Why you give us all this twaddle?'

'Twaddle?' Mrs Lamb was genuinely confused.

'Yeah, twaddle!' Twaddle, he thought, meant 'an inappropriate melding of foodstuffs', as in a 'twaddle of a meal', 'why have you cooked this twaddle and served it up on a plate?' and 'that chef is no good, all he cooks is twaddle'.

Deng immediately regretted his outburst. He was losing his rag more and more with the people around him these days. Maybe I'm not cut out for this leadership thing, he thought.

That's why he had answered an advert for a leadership

3 Um, yes, I'm not happy about this description either, but you get the idea – things being thrown away but rotating at the same time.

training course. I *Will* Succeed, Plus Some Bits About What Happened Between Me And Lady Di, run by ex-England rugby captain Will Carling, was in its second successful year, it had said on the blurb. Deng had signed up for one day of lectures. Also they were due to fly back tomorrow and he still hadn't got down to Tower Records. He hastily filled out the three forms that Mrs Lamb required for him to qualify for an evening meal. A busy day panned out in front of him. He'd do the leadership course, skip the last lecture to get back in time for dinner, pack his things for the next day, then take a trip up to Tower. His ancient heart quickened with anticipation.

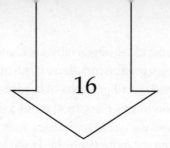

16

Nemesis of the Turtles

'I need a coma patient now!' bellowed Jonathan Ross, slamming his flat, open hand down on the stark stainless-steel finish of his agent's desk, creating a guff of wind that was gently cooling but disappointingly brief.

'Everyone's got a coma patient to bring back to life 'cept me!' he whined, reinforcing the above point but maybe he should have said them the other way round. 'You want me to look caring or not? Well?'

Padua Craw sat motionless in his Charles Kray chair. The elder Kray brother had dabbled briefly with designing office furniture in the late seventies, and the few pieces that remained fetched high prices amongst collectors. Padua had kitted out the whole office with Charles Kray stuff. It was all largely made from rickety bits and pieces that Charlie had found – orange boxes, old shoes, petrified meat – but there was no denying it had a distinctive look. Charlie had got the idea when a piece of meat had got stuck on an orange box[1] –

---

1 Not strictly true: it was a lamb chop on a tea chest but this information reached me too late for publication.

sometimes the best ideas happen by accident. Padua had just got the chair back from the menders. His Kray furniture probably spent on average 80 per cent of the time at the menders because meat and orange boxes are not great materials for building furniture.

Anyway, Padua sat motionless, his eyes closed, hoping that Jonathan would not see him, but Jonny was quicker than that and quickly saw through this limp charade.

'Oh, I get it!' he said, half spitting. 'You . . . you're just enjoying the draught I'm creating with my hands, aren't you?'

'No, no, Jonathan, calm down,' he said, snapping into pro mode now. If the other clients (or 'horsies' as he called them) got wind of some discontent from old dobbin here, there'd be a stampede off to his arch rivals Zevon and Nosegay at Death Management, he thought.

'Listen, Jonathan, the ambulance service assure me that you are top of the list. As soon as anyone comes in with a coma, they'll phone me and we can get you straight over there. The fact is there is a shortage of coma victims worldwide since they introduced the new speed cameras and Drive Safely Through Our Village signs.'

'Well, I'm not happy about it.'

'Have you thought about what I said the other day?'

'I don't think it's a good idea to fly someone in a coma in from the third world, Padua. I just think it would look too desperate and what if the papers found out?'

'No one needs to know.'

'No, it's got to be one of my own people.'

'Leave it with me.'

They went on to discuss the various corporate feed-foods that had come in for JR, which I really don't need to detail here; suffice it to say, awards ceremony, slide presentation, charity bash, awards ceremony, glossy shoot with family, charity football match. All cash.

What I can describe for you is the loving way in which Padua massaged his clients' chins (for a girl) and tummies (for a boy) while discussing contracts. That was all part of his high level of service. As Jonathan left, Pad' popped a boiled sweet into his client's mouth, patted him gently on the cheek, and tickled his chin as he swallowed it down in one. He knew the sugar content would see him through his busy mid-morning corporate taping.

'Goodbye, Jonathan,' said Padua, waving to him from his window.

'Bye, Padua,' shouted Jonathan back. 'Sorry if I . . .'

'Don't worry about it!' shouted Padua. He closed the window, double-locked it and settled gently back into his CK desk chair.

He looked over at the signed photographs of his enemies on the wall; all the top agents in London, and, in the centre, that scumbag Zevon. The rivalry between Padua and Zevon went back a long way. Padua had tried to sign Zellwacker. When Zellwacker declined, Padua had sent out an edict signing up all black men under twenty-three to his agency. His roster had climbed from just fourteen to three million and now he had to do most of his work by standard printed circulars.

Padua turned off his computer and freed up the wax around his mobile phone earplug – it had been fourteen days, a conventional fortnight, since he'd taken it out. Cool air blew over the drum. Suddenly his ear felt naked, and he felt himself taken back to that time. The dirty time. He was twelve and he and his cousin were swimming up at his uncle's pool.

'You dive in, Paddy!'

'Yeah, okay.'

He dived in. The elastic in his swimming trunks, perished from frequent boil washes, failed him, and the trunks were whisked off. The turtle in the Roman end of the pool, which had been basking, was immediately mobilised; it dived down swiftly, grabbed the trunks in its highly evolved beak and was back in the Roman end munching on them[2] before young Padua had even resurfaced.

'You okay, Paddy?' shouted cousin Mike.

'Um . . . yes . . . mm . . . not sure.' He felt the freedom in his lower pieces and the horrible truth dawned. He glanced over at the turtle and watched as the last tassel disappeared. The turtle let out a burp, which was predominantly fishy but with just a hint of the Dreft his mummy used to wash his trunks.

'Ugh! Paddy you haven't got any clothes on!' shouted Mike; he'd worked it out from the burp smell. The clear water didn't leave much to the imagination either.

Wading as fast as he could Padua made his way to the Roman end.

'Paddy's in the nude!'

The twenty-four-girl lacrosse team practising in the adjacent garden all ran to the low picket fence that separated the houses as Paddy, his head spinning, cupping his spice trombone and bells in his hands, stumbled up to the house.

The back door was locked. The girls waved their lacrosse rackets and chanted, 'Nudey! Nudey!' and laughed and jeered as Paddy made his way round the house, and bumped into his headmistress who was visiting friends.

He rang the doorbell and who answered it but Zevon, with his sister – the one Padua had the crush on. There was a flash of bright white light, he felt his retinas fizzing and a burning sensation down there where the light had never flashed before.

2 For this reason the turtle is often referred to as 'The Moth of the Sea'.

The photos of his naked form still turn up on the Internet anonymously and he's pretty sure it's Zevon that's behind it.[3]

From that day on he would hate Zevon and kill turtles.

Padua hummed gently as he daubed the registration plate of his car with fox faeces to obscure the numbers, and hauled his bulky frame into the driver's seat. He looked at the gear stick. Now, he thought, don't tell me . . . He lifted and pulled the stick up and the car jerked back. He leant over and retrieved the roughly drawn diagram from the glove box. Forward for first gear; back for second; forward, forward lift up and back for reverse. He was off, up, out of the subterranean car park.

He glanced at the *A to Z*. The nursing home was only some two miles away; he knew it was wrong but he had every confidence in his clients and was sure that Jonathan would be able to pull the victim out of the coma, so what was the harm in putting them into it? He pulled up a hundred yards from his target; that should be a long enough run-up. How fast did you have to be going just to knock them out and not kill them? He thought back to Jonathan's specification: Caucasian female, then looked again at the gate to the Nemesis Rest Home. It was just a question of waiting . . .

3 I can't give you the web adress for legal reasons but just google 'turtle tassle headmistress lacrosse Padua Zevon' and you'll probably find it.

17

Estrakhan the Wise

Yo! I am Estrakhan the Wise Pig. I dunno if I is so wise as such. They call me wise 'cos on the *Pig Brother* show I seem to offer good advice to my brother pigs, well, they fair seem to look up to me. Truth to tell I'm just bein' me. I don't set out to be clever or nothin'. Fact is, on that dumb show you don't got to be that clever. Remember, none of us had a choice to be on it, we was just chosen. None of us 'cept maybe Deirdre wanted to do it. Man, was Deirdre ever wantin' to be on TV! With her saucy display and cussin'. I warned Deirdre, 'You is makin' a spectacle of you sel'.' Well, she done ignore me, and as you well know she was first off to the slaughter.

Okay, call me wise if you want. Some of the jobs they give us to do in the house was pretty dumb, like 'make a horse from yoghurt pots', 'see who can ruck a hole in the floor', and someone tell them the trotter doesn't lend itself to shadow puppets – they all come out looking like my man Hezza.[1] But I knew I could win; I really knew that.

---

1 A common nickname for then Trade and Industry Secretary, Michael Heseltine.

When they voted my wife out of the house I was sad, but also part of me had had enough of her. Three years is about enough; after that the little things start to bug you, like, 'Don't come over into my area and start rooting for grubs because that's where I get my food, man. You may be my wife but still, show me a lil' respect. That smell you got as well; we may root around in dirt but you don't have to smell so bad, honey. You don't get me or the kids smellin' like that so have a bit of respect, huh?' Recently we'd been arguing a lot more, in front of the kids, too. I guess bein' in this house together kind of showed up the weaknesses in our relationship. Don't get me wrong, I never wanted her slaughtered or nothin', although maybe that's for the best 'cos it draws a line under things and I know she won't come back. I wouldn't a killed her myself though. No, you don't do that; she's my wife for Chrissakes.

Then when they voted the kids off, that did kind of get to me. I mean, they my kids, man! Yeah, they diss me sometime but, you know, you do your best for them, you look out for them, but, you know, on *Pig Brother*, when you in the house it's them or you, man, and I gotta say, yeah, dey my kids but I don't want to die, Lord. My time ain't come now. Anyways I want to meet Davina again. My lady McCall. You know she not at all like she appears on the TV, all showy and so. No, when you get to know Davina, she all concerned about how you all was coping, and very human and that. Nice lady. Remember, it wasn't her idea, she just works there. She jus obeyin' orders. I know a lot of us was hoping for Ulrika because she seems more touchy-feely but I heard through the grape that Ulrika's kinda cold.

Now I won this thing I'm gonna try and crack America and maybe manage other pigs. I figure I can pass on a lot of my experiences, you know, and do some good in the world.

I'm still smarting from the criticism I got for that column, which I ghostwrote with Estrakhan from the grunts and oinks that I observed while watching the *Pig Brother* show, and from interviews I did with him and his interpreter. The liberals said I was giving Estrakhan a kind of black voice and this offended a lot of people, but it wasn't a black thing; I just wanted to make him sound like he's off the street, plus that was how he talked. After all, I'm the one who spent all that time with him and bothered working out a way of decoding what he was saying. I don't care what Tom Paulin, Germaine Greer, Dominic Lawson and the other one have got to say about it, I worked with that pig, I know how he speaks. Fact is, as usual it's just the whites that minded; a lot of black guys and gals came up to me and said they liked it. I got a nice letter of support from Trevor McDonald. The column was very popular and, as every one knows by now, Estrakhan went on to conquer the States and become a big star.

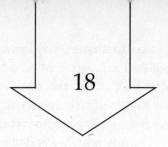

18

Sewer Cats

It was after the Estrakhan column came out that Zevon got a call from Andrew Lloyd Webber asking whether I'd be interested in writing a musical with him – not the tunes, no, he would prefer to do those, but the words. He'd already written one with Ben Elton about a football-playing Irishman who gets kneecapped and then is only able to pass backwards, called *Begorrah Me Knees: Leave Me In Peace!* (referred to by the crew simply as *Knees*).[1] He'd followed that up with a musical with Tracey Emin doing the words called *Why Are You All So Horrible To Me? Bollocks To You, I Just Don't Need This* (the crew just referred to it as *Need This*),[2] so we'd kind of been waiting for the call.

His last one *Bernie!: The Bernie Clifton Story*, co-written with Melvyn Hayes, had bombed[3] so they needed a hit. Part of the problem with *Bernie!* was that the man they got in to play

1 Folded after two performances.
2 Folded after the interval.
3 Closed after three weeks so in some ways this was actually a bit of a return to form.

young Bernie refused to shave off his beard. They'd auditioned him with it and just assumed he'd be shaving it off. Instead he insisted on playing the twelve-year-old Bernie with the beard, albeit with it covered in silly putty and painted pink. The contract was signed so they couldn't get another actor in, which is how his performance came to be judged as 'less than convincing' (Sheridan Morley, Radio 4).

The show was picketed by a group of short-sighted ornithologists who somehow thought Bernie was genuinely riding around on the back of a real ostrich. They chanted all through the first half, 'Ossie Out.' This was doubly confusing as the part of Bernie's Spanish agent was played by Argentinian midfielder Ossie Ardilles, who looked anxious throughout the show and tended to hang around the wings. This annoyed Bernie as the wings were an important part of the ostrich and he needed space to be able to flap them.

In the second half, one of the short-sighted bird lovers rushed the stage, dragged Bernie to the floor and tried to liberate the ostrich, only to find that it was really mostly Bernie. Finally getting the joke, the protestor collapsed into a laughter-induced seizure and was thrown out. The rest of the ornithologists rebooked for the following night and, observing it now from a different perspective, loved the show.

Nuff said. Lloyd Webber needed a hit. Could I help? He sent a car for me, an S-series Mercedes with metallic finish (two ego-puff points), which I made wait a full ten minutes (one puff point) before getting in. The driver held the door open for me (a further ego-puff point), and this act was witnessed by a neighbour (doubling it up to two). Those were the days.

'You're going the wrong way, driver,' I said as we swung into Penge High Street. 'This is nowhere near Bayswater.'

'Leave the driving to me, sir,' he said, his voice vaguely

familiar, his pudgy eyes studying me from the rear-view mirror.

He slammed his foot down hard on the accelerator and swung a U-turn, heading back towards Elmers End. I quickly worked out why. Alexei Sayle was tailing us, trying to get in on it. Rik Mayall and Ade Edmondson were in another car, and the whole thing was being controlled by the secretive shadowy figure behind the *Comic Strip*, Peter Richardson, working from a room above the Curry Cottage, Beckenham High Street. None of the *Comic Strip* had had much in the way of feed cash since their glory days of the early eighties, and seeing how Ben had made a wad of dough out of *Knees*, they saw Andrew Lloyd Webber as their meal ticket to a third home each. Oh, they all had second homes now but there were various other properties they had their eye on. You know what it's like when you get on the mailing list, they just keep sending you all this stuff about beautiful homes with pools in Florida, the Caribbean and so on. That kind of money doesn't come from voiceovers alone. They needed some Lloyd Webber cashmeat.

Realising we were being tailed, my driver suddenly pulled on the brakes and the car went skidding sideways down a back alley. Rik and Ade collided with Alexei's car and a puff-ball of flame engulfed the stricken vehicles.

'It's okay, they're not hurt,' the driver said, and he indicated a small video screen set into the dash. The three great alternative comics had rolled to safety and were supping down a double skinny latte each in the Café Rouge on the main Penge thoroughfare. They threw back their heads in laughter. Diners in the Curry Cottage heard the faint sound of a fist passing through a partition wall. Peter was angry.

'It's a shame,' said the driver. 'You know that they are next on Andrew's list.'

'How do you know?' I asked.

The driver turned and pulled down a latex rubber mask to reveal Lord Lloyd Webber himself.

'You cheeky monkey,' I said, immediately wishing I hadn't. I'd meant to say something like 'You wily fox' because it can be taken as a compliment, whereas 'cheeky monkey' just sounded silly and made me seem a bit silly too.

The car was rapidly approaching a large bush too fast.

'Brake, Andy!' I screamed, covering my face. I waited for the impact but the bush folded neatly down flat and we drove over it and through a door that opened in the rock face.

'You saucy ape!' I exclaimed; there, I'd done it again.

'Come with me. The girls will get you changed out of those ugly clothes.'

A set of slender fingers that I recognised as belonging to Sarah Brightman fumbled with the toggles on my duffel coat. I smelled the acrid scent of Tizer. The grey-black clouds of unconsciousness welcomed me like Germaine Greer's hair on firework night.[4]

I awoke tanned and refreshed some three minutes later in full kimono and those flip-flop shoes that they wear. Brightman offered me a glass of Pond Breeze – cranberry juice and pond water with a dash of lime.

'Mr Lloyd Webber-san will see you now,' she purred, feigning a Japanese accent. 'Follow.' She led me out of the narrow doorway to sunlight. As we walked along Wardour Street in London's Soho, I suddenly felt very silly. People pointed and laughed. My feet were cold and a cigarette butt had lodged itself between my toes. This was crazy!

'Sarah. Um, where are we going?'

'No questions,' she snapped. 'Follow! He is testing you.'

---

4 This phrase doesn't seem to make any particular sense but actually accurately describes the feelings I had at the time and is not just a needless pop at the well-known feminist's googly mane.

She led me through a hole in the ground opposite Lee Chapman and Leslie Ash's show restaurant Teatro, and down into the sewer. There he was, seated at a huge bureau. The sewer was immaculate, spotless, the tiles polished and the sewage stripped back to reveal the original features.

'You like my subterranean office, yes?' said Lord Lloyd Webber, flicking a piece of faeces from his jacket. 'These beautiful old Victorian sewers have long been neglected. I bought them up; I now own two-thirds of all the sewers in London.'

'What happens to the sewage now, Lord?' I said, suddenly caught up in his world.

'I've had it redirected. There are many tunnels in London.'

Don't believe what you read; in person he is really quite handsome, his face covered with a fine downy hair that gives the appearance of Fuzzy Felt. Tufts of coarser black hair protrude from his ears like quotation marks.

Sarah brought us tumblers of Tizer and a tray of water biscuits and Lord Lloyd Webber set about explaining his ideas.

'*Dog Breeder: The Musical*. The simple story, told in song, of the day-to-day running of a dog-breeding kennels. What do you say?'

'You brazen baboon!' I shrieked, barely able to contain my excitement. My mind started racing. It was brilliant! Oh joy! Cascades of words pounded my cerebrum like so many pasta shapes being poured into a colander.[5]

'Stanley knife!' I cried, and started to carve words on to anything I could get my hands on: a piano, table mats, the wooden panelling. As I wrote Lord Lloyd Webber hit the keys of his piano in a set order to make different tunes.

After what seemed like five minutes, but was in fact two days, and fourteen meals later, we collapsed into each other's

---

5 Yes, I know but I wanted a kind of tumbling metaphor and was preparing my dinner at the time.

arms, the work done. Andrew called in his staff. They listened in silence as he played the overture.

'My dogs got diarrhoea!' I sang.

'And my dogs got worms!' sang Lord Lloyd Webber.

Then together: 'One of me dachshunds is ill!'

The staff sprang to their feet in applause. It was really going to happen; it was really going to happen this time!

'Do you think you could get Estrakhan to be in it?' He broke off.

'Pardon?' Surely I hadn't heard him right.

'Estrakhan the pig. You know him, don't you? I've been trying to get him to be in it but his agent won't return my calls. I wondered whether you could pull a few strings . . .'

So that was it; he was using me to get to Estrakhan! I was disgusted and gagged up a tiny sachet of stomach contents.

'You filthy macaque!' I cursed, pulling on my duffel coat.

'What's wrong?'

With a yell I grabbed a Canaletto – *Venice: The Entrance of the Grand Canal* – from the wall and smashed it down on to his head. He fell back against a long Chippendale table and reached up, grabbing Canaletto's *The Molo, Seen from the Basin of San Marco* and rammed me fair and square in the ribs with it. I countered with a *The Bucintoro at the Molo on Ascension Day* in the teeth; he staggered back and as he fell to the floor I jumped on top of him, thwacking his bruised phizog with Capriccio: *Palace with the Clock Tower and Roman Arch*. He rolled on top of me and I saw in his hand the flash of gold and many bright colours – and I realised he had a Klimt.

'Yes! All right! I'll see what I can do . . . about Estrakhan . . . I'll have a word!' I shouted, frightened now.

'You sure?' he said, bringing the German expressionist painting up to my neck.

'Yes, yes, I'll see what I can do but I can't promise anything; he's his own pig.'

'Very well,' he said and loosened his grip.

As I stood up I grabbed any painting I could and brought it with a kerump! Down on his skull, knocking him out. The painter? Why Egon Schiele, of course!

I had to hand it to A. L. W. though; he certainly knew his art weapons.

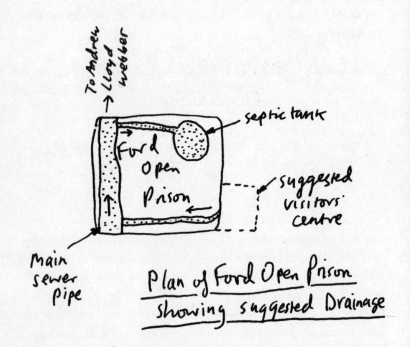

To Andrew Lloyd Webber

septic tank

Ford Open Prison

suggested visitors' centre

Main sewer pipe

Plan of Ford Open Prison
showing suggested Drainage

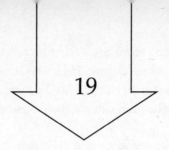

19

Lady Aitken Bakes Exceedingly Good Cakes

Manny Durban took a sip of tea, pulled the soft feather double duvet back on top of him and rolled over on to his side. His face bore the creases of a good night's sleep. He rubbed his good eye, then his glass one so as not to make it feel left out. One eye looked west the other east, which made close relationships difficult, and more often than not his wife would just end up addressing his large bulbous nose. He licked the dandruff from his lips and suddenly remembered where he was.

'Would you like me to bring your breakfast to you this morning, Mr Durban?' asked the guard who was dressed as Peter Rabbit.

'No, just leave it there; I'll be up in a minute,' said Manny. All his life he'd been a Ford man: first the Cortina, then the Escort, then the boxy Granada. He was driving a Scorpio when he was arrested over the now notorious Caucasian size-twelve artificial-foot incident. Oh yes, he'd tried many of their cars but never one of Ford's open prisons.

They'd picked him up from Wandsworth and no sooner

was he through the front door than he felt the prison lurch forward and slowly accelerate. He looked out of the window and saw Wandsworth change to Putney and Putney to Kingston as they headed out on the A3, stopping only once for petrol.

'What's the fuel consumption on a prison this size?' he'd asked his guard.

'Oh, fifteen, twenty miles to the gallon on a run, less in traffic.'

'As much as that?' said Manny. He was surprised; he only used to get twenty-eight out of his Cortina.

'Yes, well it's diesel, remember,' said the guard.

Ah, that explained it.

He swung his legs round and tucked into the scrambled egg and smoked salmon. Things had certainly improved since they'd employed CenterParcs to do the security.[1] Prison was prison though, and Manny had one or two scores to settle on the outside before he was prepared to be caged. There were a number of others who felt the same way.

Manny had got together an escape committee to discuss methods. After a preliminary chat it was agreed that he would be the leader and Jonathan Aitken[2] his second in command. Manny figured he needed someone at his side with an impressive background in lying. So it was Manny, Jonathan, three murderers, a rapist, two of the Guinness clan who had been done for fraud and assorted thieves. They all agreed that the best way to escape and avoid detection would be to build a visitors' centre.

Manny had to admit it was a pretty smart idea; he couldn't see how it could fail. They would secretly build a visitors'

1 With Group 4 you were offered only a continental-style breakfast – juice, bread basket and choice of preserves.
2 Conservative MP for Kensington and Chelsea who was banged up for pretending.

centre from bits of masonry, fixtures and fittings taken from other parts of the prison, plus some brought in from the outside, where the budget allowed. Once the visitors' centre was completed, they would put up a partition wall, gently ease themselves away from the prison and then they were free.

Of course, all this depended on them getting planning permission. It shouldn't really be a problem, providing the centre was in keeping with the existing architecture. Besides Jonathan reckoned he knew someone in the planning department.[3]

Manny immediately started working on the designs. He wanted it to be as open plan as possible, to give it a nice airy feel so the visitors would want to visit again and again. They'd recognised from an early stage that the visitors' centre needed to be financially viable; they didn't want to be sponging off handouts. Manny was hoping that at the end of the day this escape might be the first ever to make a profit, but it was important, too, to get the right balance between education and commerce. He knew that the first year was all-important and, of course, that would include the set-up costs. Things were going to be tight but he felt confident they could do it.

It wasn't until after he consulted the planning regulations that he realised they would probably have to have disabled access and toilets, something he hadn't budgeted for. Straightaway he went to see Jonathan in his cell.

Jonathan Aitken was sitting working on his tattoos with a compass needle and bottle of ink. He quickly dropped the implements and hastily pulled down his trouser leg. 'Ah, Manny! How are the drawings coming along?' he said.

'Got a problem, Jono,' said Manny, unrolling his paperwork on Jonathan's bed. 'See here?'

3 But he may have being pretending.

'Oh, oh dear; any way round it?'

'Not that I can see. We don't have main drainage, do we?'

'Couldn't we move the tills?'

'But surely that would mean moving the exit? Besides I've got a power point down there coming directly off the mains in the governor's office.'

'Hmm, I've got it!' he said, leaping to his feet.

'What?'

'A macerator blade. You know, one of those loos you have with a macerator blade in the outflow that allows you to plumb effluent through regular-bore piping. You don't need main drainage, that's the point.'

'Got a source?'

'No, but I'll find you one.'

And he was off, sourcing the macerator-style loo, popular in bed and breakfasts up and down the country. Ah, what a wonderful lieutenant he was, thought Manny.

Once he had the rough designs he called a meeting of the other members of the escape committee and they honed them up. There were various discussions as to whether to have hand dryers, paper towels or roll towel in the loos, and there was the choice of door handles and other fixtures and fittings; everything had to be covered if the Ford Open Prison Visitors' Centre was going to be a success.

They all agreed that shelf space was important and Tommy the Neck, one of the murderers, suggested smoked glass with chrome supports, as it would look classy. In the end that idea was dismissed as it was felt it would give the centre too much of a 'bathroomy' feel. Tommy was initially annoyed and Manny thought for a moment that he was going to have another one of his murder attacks, but it seemed that the Murdering Instinct Control Classes were paying off and he did little more than pull the legs off a spider (as part of the new progressive regime, they had brought in a behavioural therapist who had initiated the Negative Emotion Insect Transference Programme; basically instead of murdering someone, you take it out on an insect).

'What about stock?' asked a highly respected cat burglar.

'Well,' Manny said, 'you must appreciate that the visitors' centre will take a good six weeks to complete after we've got planning permission, but yes, I have no objection to some of you having a think about some of the merchandise we could sell in the shop.'

'Is it a shop or a visitors' centre?' asked another.

'It's a visitors' centre, in other words a place where you can find out about Britain's best-known mobile prison, but also a place where you can buy souvenirs of your visit.'

Manny was aware that they needed to get this balance right. If it appeared they were just keen to turn a fast buck, the planning department might well reject their application and, more importantly, it would not attract the kind of through put that they needed to make it a viable business.

Between them they carved up the various responsibilities: Manny would set about getting hold of the tools and equipment; Jonathan would handle the paperwork, including applying for a Prince's Trust Award. The others all had a role too: in an attempt to placate Tommy the Neck, Manny gave him the job of choosing the floor coverings.

When the idea of the visitors' centre was first floated, Manny realised that they would need a lot of tools and had contacted his wife, Mrs Jenny Durban, asking her to bake some basic tools into cakes and get them over to the prison. So far all she'd managed to bring in was a handful of rivets pressed into some cherry bakewells.

'No, love, we need Phillips screws, not rivets,' he'd said, but she seemed disinterested, almost as if she didn't want him back.

He was getting pretty fed up about it, and mentioned it to

101

Jonathan who straightaway suggested his mum, Lady Aitken. Manny wasn't sure; he didn't want to seem as if he were imposing on the old girl, but when he mentioned it to her in passing, Lady Aitken said she was up for it and, as a gesture of her commitment, on her first visit turned up with a cake baked and iced to look like a pickaxe.

Manny quickly took her to one side and explained that they didn't want cakes that looked like tools, but normal-looking cakes with the tools hidden inside. She went away and came back a week later with three sanding discs inside a beautifully moist carrot cake (so difficult to keep moist at the best of times). A week later a Black and Decker drill turned up inside a gloriously rich fruitcake covered with sweet franzi-pan – they were off! Another week went by: a vice turned up in a big Madeira (oddly rather dry); a further week saw a hand-operated lathe in a huge Victoria sponge (real fresh cream).

Unfortunately Manny, being a diabetic, couldn't eat the cakes in any quantity. Oh sure, the other inmates were all doing their bit and they could palm some of the stuff off on the guards, but there was a hell of a lot of equipment they needed to get in and therefore a load of cake to eat too. After three months of cake-tool smuggling they'd all put on an enormous amount of weight. The average prisoner was now eighteen stone. Most men had to have their prison uniforms let out with additional panels and vents. Several had fallen down and been unable to get up.

Manny was up to seventeen stone, which made his dia-betes wildly unpredictable. When his blood sugar was high he would go into an odd sort of fugue state and start singing Simon and Garfunkel songs until jabbed with life-saving insulin. The singing was usually a good sign that he was going hyperglycaemic. It was a tricky one though, because sometimes Manny liked to sing Simon and Garfunkel songs regardless of his blood sugar level. To avoid confusion, the prison doctor sent out a memo saying that if Manny sang more than three S&G numbers in a row, he would like to be called. You got to have rules, and if not rules then at least guidelines.

It soon dawned on the porky prisoners that at their new size the visitors' centre was now far too small. For them all to fit into it they would either have to lose the weight prior to the escape, or find some extra space from somewhere. Losing the weight was out of the question in the time they had before the putative launch so they decided to apply for a loft conversion. As well as giving them more space it would also add value to the property.

Jonathan adjusted the drawings to include a spiral staircase (classy!) and two dormer windows in the upstairs area – officially a stockroom. There were immediate objections from the planning department and instead it was agreed they would fit Velux windows – which, in fact, would be easier for them to do.

In the meantime the entire inhabitants of the prison had become so bored of cake that disposal of it was really beginning to limit their progress; there was a huge backlog, and as the cake became stale it was even harder to get the inmates to munch it down. Someone had suggested that Lady Aitken cook the tools into savoury items like pasties or samosas, but no, Manny was quite certain that cake was the only traditionally tried-and-tested method of tool smuggling and he wasn't about to risk the entire operation on going savoury. What if the meat juices corroded the steel of, say, a hacksaw blade? No, they needed to stick with cake but work out a way to shift it big time.

Then some bright spark had the idea of winding down the windows of the prison and just slinging it out as they were going along. So that's just what they did; for a week the lads would spend twenty or thirty minutes a day just flinging handfuls of cake out of the window. Of all types.

Well, you don't have to be a brain scientist or computer to see how that was going to backfire on them; far from just lying there in the gutters to decompose, the cake attracted all kinds of fauna: mainly birds but also some foxes, squirrels and, of course, a huge number of rats. The birds would follow the prison on its route, squawking and swooping down for lumps of cake. Rats and other vermin would line the route fighting each other for the largest scraps. This in turn had an effect on the ecosystem, and cake took over from nuts and berries as the principal food source. The creatures, not used to such a rich diet, developed appalling dentition, and it was a common sight to see an all-but-toothless vole sucking on a dirty piece of Battenberg.[4]

Not that it bothered the members of Manny's escape committee; no, they sat back lobbing huge chunks of Lady Aitken's cake out of their windows. The entire prison became covered in great dollops of bird dung. The governor would stop at a junction and it would take twelve changes of the traffic lights before the gypsy girl with the bucket and squeegee had got the front windows clean. 'And the back, sweetheart,' he'd say, and nine times out of ten would speed off without paying.

Lady Aitken, meanwhile, had tired of her job as principal baker and was starting to get careless. A couple of times, Manny had had to reprimand her when she had turned up with a 'cake', which was little more than a spirit level that had been iced and put in a cake box. Another time she'd got a shovel and just written 'Happy Birthday' on it with a marker pen. Manny hit the roof.

4 Okay, I'm exaggerrating but a lot of the small mammals had a mouthful of fillings.

'She's got to go,' he said. There was no room for complacency in this operation and Jonathan and Manny, in consultation with Lady Aitken, had agreed to downsize her contribution. Jonathan resisted it at first; he loved his mum's cakes, although everybody else thought they tasted a bit 'cabbagy now you come to mention it'.

So, go she did. I think she was secretly relieved. The pressure had begun to show: her normally immaculate hair and make-up had taken a knock, and she was developing something of the 'Wild Man of Borneo' look. A neighbour had recently phoned the police after seeing her walking across Bodmin Moor, claiming to have spotted 'something like a puma: a monster', thus the legend began.[5]

It was agreed that thenceforth she would supply only the simple equipment; for the heavier plant stuff they needed someone who could bake some really accurate cakes.

5 The so-called Beast of Bodmin Moor has had many explanations – big cats, evolutionary throwbacks, Jeff Capes on a picnic – but the truth, as is so often the case, is rather more pedestrian. It's Lady Aitken.

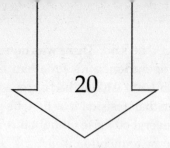

20

Who Framed Gerald Scarfe

Jane Asher was more expensive but they all agreed hard to
beat for accuracy. To look at her cakes you would never
dream that they contained an important piece of construction equipment. Manny for one would never forget the day
she turned up with the JCB cake. A JCB baked into a chocolate
sponge with fudge icing and Smarties on it, so that it looked
like a Clanger from the children's TV show (the Smarties
formed the two eyes, and there was quite a fight over those,
as you can imagine).

She'd delivered it herself and had kept the screws talking,
regaling them with stories of Paul McCartney, London in the
swinging sixties and her collection of pewter tankards
(second-largest collection in the Borough of Kensington and
Chelsea). It had gone through without a hiccough. They'd
needed a reason for Jane to visit though, so some friends of
Tommy the Neck had had her husband Gerald Scarfe framed
for a robbery.

It was a pretty clever crime and one that Tommy had sort
of been saving for himself but, in an uncommon act of

community spirit that his prison psychologist would have been proud of, had sacrificed it for the greater good.

Like all great ideas, it was beautifully simple. Wanna hear it? Okay get a pen and write it down – it's a peach.

Right, you pick someone rich who has a son at boarding school. You sneak into the boy's dorm and while he's sleeping, chloroform him, then while he's unconscious you take a mould of his face. That's it; you're out of the school, that was your only contact with the kid, and he has no knowledge of it except for maybe some bits of mould fibre round his ears and a whanging headache from the chloroform. You take the mould and make a latex rubber mask of the boy's face. Then you dress up a short man or midget (avoid pygmies as you don't know what you're getting) in the boy's uniform. Wearing the latex rubber mask and uniform the small man goes to the rich fellow's house and pretends to be the boy arriving home early from school. With him he has a note that reads 'I have lost my voice and been sent home early from school to recuperate'. Fine, no problem, in he comes. Then, that night, you get the midget to burgle the place and let himself out of the front door. Genius? Yes? Try it; believe me it works.

So, how did they implicate Gerald Scarfe? They planted the rubber mask in the boot of his car and tipped off the police. Oh, it was only circumstantial evidence, but the police needed a conviction, and Gerald had not exactly made many friends in the upper echelons of society with his cruel cartoons. He went down for two years. Perfect.

It was the JCB cake which had finally pushed Manny over the edge and into a diabetic coma. He'd covered both sides of the much acclaimed *Bridge Over Troubled Water* album, and was two-thirds of the way through the title track of *Bookends* when they found him, his hands and face thick with JCB sponge cake stodge.

107

The governor slipped the prison down into third gear, checked his rear-view mirror, indicated, overtook the Nissan Young Offenders Unit and drove the prison straight to the local hospital where Manny was taken immediately to intensive care.

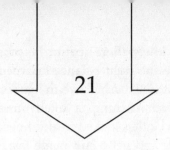

21

The Great Brian Conley/
Des O'Connor/Bradley Walsh/
Shane Ritchie Mix-up

It was only a matter of hours before Jonathan Ross heard about the coma and started going through his wardrobe for something suitable to wear. He had a staff nurse on every ITU in the country on the payroll and one, it seemed, had tipped him off. 'Male Caucasian, inmate of Ford Open Prison' had been the call and he'd scrambled. He'd waited so long for this.

Then doubts. As he got more information he could see how resuscitating a convict could backfire on him. Of course he'd heard of Manny Durban, the Artificial Foot Freedom Fighter and okay, the artificial foot thing gave it a culty angle, but as Padua said, it was a little too 'Channel 4' and that it would 'undo all the great mainstream ego-puff points that have been slung your way. Hold off, Jonathan, and a better coma will come along.' Jonathan faltered; what to do?

It was then that the old lady was brought in, found unconscious outside a nursing home. Hit and run. Jackpot! It seemed too good to be true.

He went along the rail – the snakeskin suit? No, that was

too showy. He knew there would be press there and he needed to strike the right balance between successful and concerned. What else did he have in that wardrobe? A high-buttoned Edwardian thing, a lot of crushed velvet ... Suddenly all his clothes looked freaky. I need to get down to Ozwald Boateng and get a suit made fast, he decided. But Padua said there wasn't time. It was then that Jane had suggested he go in a black bin liner.

'Black bin liner?'

'Yes, it's like you're saying, I am nothing; I am here only to help.'

He liked the idea straightaway and pulled on the garbage bag with armholes cut in the top, got into his Mazda MX5 and headed off to the hospital. He hit a fat band of traffic as he crawled out of Hampstead and on to the A11, traffic that was largely due to an ageing partially sighted flying eye.

'Come on, come on!' he steamed, glancing at his watch. He knew that as soon as word got out all the usual suspects (Eubank, Feltz, Woody from the Bay City Rollers) would converge on the hospital and he'd be at the back of the queue again.

As the car swung round into the car park of the Coca-Cola Hospital, Boomsheerary (a fascinating partnership of private and public finance), he could see only his photographer. He breathed a sigh of relief; it looked like he was going to get away with it. He parked up, posed for a couple of shots in front of the hospital, then some more in front of the accident-and-emergency department, then made his way up to the third floor to the intensive care unit.

His soundman had already arrived and set up, and as Jonathan pushed open the swing doors to the unit, his play-on music started. A big brassy raunchy sound that immediately commanded the attention of the ward. In fact, so attention grabbing was it that the old lady in the coma coughed, pulled the tube from her mouth and sat up.

'What's he doing here?' she exclaimed, pointing at Jono.

Jonathan suddenly went cold. It dawned on him that he was not within the curtainable area round the bed, which was necessary if he were to claim the coma wake-up as his. Without a pause for breath, he made a dash for the zone. The charge nurse blocked, Jono tried to dodge round him but he knew it was too late; it was no good, all the staff and other patients had seen what had happened and the medical registrar was busy filing his report to Matthew Wright at the *Daily Mirror*.

'Put this one down to experience, shall we?' said the charge nurse.

'Damn! Damn and blast!' shouted Wossy; he'd been so close this time. 'Won't anything go wight for me?'

The coma wake-up was claimed by the session musicians who had recorded the play-on track and who immediately sent their claims for expenses to Wossy who was obliged to pick them up. On top of that Jonathan had no other clothes with him and he ended up at the Groucho Club with pasta sauce all down his garbage-bag outfit singing 'Honky Tonk Women' round a piano with Danny Baker and Victor Lewis Smith.

When he finally got home he discovered that Jane had come home with the wrong kids.

She'd taken them to a fête where they'd had their faces painted – one as Brian Conley and the other as Bradley Walsh – and it was only when they got home that she realised that the two kids she'd taken home had their faces painted to look like Des O'Connor and Shane Richie. She rushed back but too late. Jonathan was furious and the next day pulled the kids out of their private schools and booked them into the local comp; he was damned if he was going to pay all that money on private educations when they weren't even his flesh and blood.

Two days later, whilst shopping, Jane thought she'd spotted her own children and bundled them into the back of the car; they put up quite a struggle and it was only when she got them home and started to undress them for their bath that she realised they were the real Brian Conley and Bradley Walsh out on a spree. Naturally embarrassed, she zipped them back up into their jumpsuits and let them out the back way with an apple each.

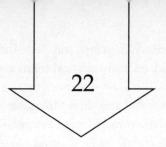

22

Return of the Supercad

In a large breakfast-cum-dining room, a hand pulled playfully on a joystick, flitting between various monitors each labelled with a different capital city: Birmingham, capital of the Midlands; York, capital of Yorkshire; Hastings, capital of coastal East Sussex. Two clear blue eyes, fringed with fat black lashes, surveyed a huge map marked with various coloured diodes; as the cities lit up the picture on the monitor changed too. We follow the hand up, past the navy-blue sleeve of an old rugby-club blazer, past the soft button-down collar and rugby-club tie to the dimple-chinned face of Will Carling. His feed-food face garnered the information, his brain mentated it like some kind of friastonic hardware into photodaptated pre-rolls.[1] He nodded, pleased.

Since he'd set up his I *Will* Succeed, Plus Some Bits About What Happened Between Me And Lady Di course, things had really taken off. Strange to think his first conference had been held in his car, using drawings that he'd done on the

1 Many of these words are made up because words don't exist for this kind of thing.

steamed-up windscreen, some puppets and the use of forward and reverse on the tape cassette to create different moods.[2]

But the fact was that the three delegates that day – Clive Sinclair, Freddie Laker and Gerald Ratner – had been really positive about the event. As he'd let off the child-safety locks and released them into the early evening, Clive had given Will his home phone number and said that he'd 'really enjoyed it, particularly the bit about what he got up to with Lady Di'. Will had put in the bit about Lady Di as a carrot to get them to hang on in there for the less racy material about 'what shoes to wear when clinching a deal' and 'why shouting doesn't work'. All this and he'd never taken a formal psychology degree; no, he reckoned as so much of psychology is unproven, why shouldn't he just make up his own rules?

Here he was, eighteen months later, running forty separate 'I *Will* . . .' conferences without having to leave home. With the new technology of CB radio and long cables, he was able to oversee things from his control centre which was in fact his Mum and Dad's kitchen. Mum and Dad were really pleased with him, especially as he was now in a position to pay for the odd pub lunch. He'd based himself at Mum's house initially to keep the overheads down, but it was nice being back in his old room, nice to wake up to Mum's smell.

He had twenty 'Will Carlings' working for him now. Graduates of the course could apply for a Will Carling franchise and go out as Will. They got a Will Carling kit, with blazer, tie, button-down shirt, black wig and detachable chin dimple (supplied by the Embalming Centre), three mood cassettes, a set of slides and leather-look wash bag as a free gift. After that they were pretty much on their own unless they got into really serious trouble, in which case Will stepped in.

2 A hire car, the cost recharged to the business.

Suddenly a light flashed on the map. Oops! A distress call from the Beaconsfield Travelpost Inn.

The freckled, sun-burnt face under the Will Carling disguise struggled with the remote control on the slide projector, but the same slide just kept coming up over and over again.

'Um ... leadership is important as we found out in part one ... er ...'

What? He glanced at the manual: press play on cassette player to create motivational mood.

He pressed play but accidentally pressed fast forward at the same time; far from creating calm the speeded-up mood music that ensued turned the class into a nervous rabble.

President Deng Xiaoping of China tried to follow what was going on in his translated version of the seminar. What was happening? Surely there should be an illustration of poor leadership at this point, a slide leading on from Part One: Where Hitler Went Wrong? He flicked back and forth through the text. This Will Carling woman! She didn't look anything like the chick on the front cover of the pamphlet. He raised his hand to ask a question.

Oh God, no! Someone has got their hand up! thought the faux Carling, the adhesive on his dimple beginning to work loose under the hot light of the slide projector. He decided to ignore it in the hope that the Chinese man would give up.

'Ahem!' coughed Deng. Why was this girl ignoring him? She had seen him; he saw her look straight at his face. 'Ahem.'

'Breaker one-nine! Request assistance,' whispered the man into his CB, simultaneously pressing a button under the podium.

Carling sat forward and jostled the joystick; Beaconsfield came up on the screen and he saw the worried, sweaty face of his trainee, his dimple hanging by a single strand of spirit gum.

He leant forward. 'Okay, take a deep breath; it's Will, I'm going to talk you down. Place your left hand on your dimple and bring it up to meet your chin . . . okay, that's good.' He watched as the creature on the CCTV link-up followed his instructions. 'Okay; now accept the question from the man with his hand up—'

'What? But I can't!'

'Accept the question!'

'I can't—'

'Look, just accept the f***ing question, you f***ing moron!' bellowed Carling, his eyes bulging, his dimple all but gone under the sudden increase in skin pressure.

The faux Carling, frightened, bolted from the podium, the dimple finally breaking free from its mooring and rolling under a chair in the front row.

Damn! thought Will. Damn him for making me shout like that; I didn't mean to blow my stack!

Heart pounding! Must get out, get out of here! Throat tight, eyes exploding, lights! Bright lights glare, unfriendly faces, argh! Cooler air, leaves brush face! Ouch – what? Penned in! Glass wall – no!

The man pulled off his clip-on tie and threw it to the floor. Without the dimple we recognise him as none other than Supercad James Hewitt.[3] He sank on to his rear end and sobbed uncontrollably. 'I not cad! I leader,' he said. A cleaner proffered a helping hand and led him shaking out of the conservatory and function room area of the Beaconsfield Travelpost Inn. His wonky wig, now set back on his head, revealed a shock of red hair.

'Pub lunch!' bellowed Mrs Will Carling Senior barging into the breakfast-cum-dining room. Will, forgetting the waiting delegates in Beaconsfield in an instant, joyfully put the monitor on standby and strolled off to his mother who was waiting in the lobby.

3 An odd course for Hewitt to sign up to since he had been running his own Princess Di related course 'Lovin' The Lady – How To Get Off With Someone Who's Anti Landmines But Not Heather Mills'.

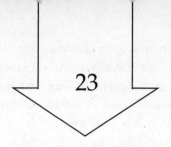

23

Touch Me, Pierre Trudeau, I Wanna Feel Your Body

The delegates waited for forty minutes. When Will Carling failed to return they gradually drifted off, some passed into the lobby to look at the 'I *Will*' merchandise – 'I *Willed*' T-shirts and badges and so forth[1] – others returned to their rooms and had a bath.

'Does this mean there will be no disco?' said Jeremy Thorpe, a late, but ever-hopeful, signatory to the leadership course.

George Bush Senior and Junior went off to the table football and Senior heaped a big pile of 20p pieces on the side. He needed no lessons in leadership but he was keen to get his boy through. In the event of a close presidential election result at a later date, this leadership course and certificate might well tip the balance in the boy's favour.

President George Bush Senior was the first to admit that

---

1 Top seller was a plastic effigy of Will naked except for a barrel around his waist. When you inserted two AA batteries (not supplied) and pressed the top of his head the barrel dropped and he urinated into a hat.

with the pressures he'd been under in office he had neglected his relationship with the boy, and he looked on this three-day course at Beaconsfield as a chance for them to get closer. George Junior didn't know it yet but George Senior had a little surprise laid on for him later.

They were pretty evenly matched at table football, and out of the twenty-seven games, George Senior won fourteen to Junior's thirteen.

'One more game, Dad!' said Junior.

'No, no, son, it's late; remember we got the rest of the course tomorrow, we'd best get us some shut-eye.'

'Okay, Dad.'

They walked down the corridor to their room. Senior looked after the key and adjusted himself deftly with one hand in order to retrieve the bulging fob from his tight George jeans. He made it a rule to always try to get along to Asda any time he was in the Yookay ever since they'd launched the George label. Well, he reasoned with Barbara, as she tried on a large, floral roll-neck smock, why pay more? Hey, they got my name in too!

He let the two of them into the room and turned on the light. The TV flickered its welcome: Beaconsfield Travelpost Inn welcomes George Bush Senior and Junior. He helped himself to a complementary banana and started to make up the camp bed.

'Let's go through your worksheets quickly before bed,' he said.

Junior's face turned sour.

'Listen, I know you don't want to do this but I got a surprise for you. You go through the worksheets with me and . . .' He opened his bum bag and retrieved a fresh, unopened pouch of tobacco. 'I'll roll you one of those tobacco cigarettes that you so crave!'

Junior looked amazed. 'But . . . what if . . .'

'Who's to know? Let this be our little secret,' he said, repeatedly hammering the smoke alarm with the heel of his boot. They both chuckled and Junior threw himself into the work, knowing he would garner his nicotine fix at the end of it.

The young future president looked over at his sleeping father, then at the digital alarm. Nought nought nought o'clock: that couldn't be right. He looked at his own watch: half-past ten. He crept quietly from the bed, released his chinos from the Corby trouser press, pulled on his cagoule and made his way downstairs to the disco.

George W. Bush was momentarily disorientated by the throb of the music and bright disco lights, but knew straightaway that this was where he wanted to be. He glanced over at the DJ who shot a wide gapped-tooth smile. The Hits From September 1987 Disco just played hits from September 1987; it was niche music marketing of a highly specialist nature.

As he stood taking in the heady atmosphere, he felt a tap on his shoulder. It was Jeremy Thorpe.

'Excuse me, could I have this dance?'

George needed to think only briefly about the offer and returned, 'No thanks, old timer,' turned his back to the old man and headed for the bar, jostled as he went by the other dancing delegates.

'Here's a hit from September 1987, "Star Trekkin'" by The Firm . . .'

'Star trekkin' across the universe . . . It's life, Jim, but not as we know it . . .'

Immediately everyone was back on their feet and dancing. There were only three girls at the conference, and only one, Judith Hann,[2] had come down for the disco. Sleepy and with

2 Judith Hann was a presenter on *Tomorrow's World*, the TV programme which showcased futuristic ideas that couldn't possibly ever happen, such as spray-on eyes for the blind, magnetic shoes for walking up a fridge and dental floss for Esther Rantzen.

a drawn face from the day's studies, she was beginning to tire of the endless whirl of male suitors, so it was kind of agreed that the fellahs would dance with each other – not a gay thing, just for fun, otherwise no one would be dancing.

'Snowball, please, barman,' said George W.

'I'll get that.' It was the Prime Minister of Canada, Pierre Trudeau.

'Hey! Hi, Pierre! Enjoying the conference?'

'You bet! Well, up until when our lecturer ran off.' They both laughed. 'I hear we're getting a new Will Carling tomorrow, though.'

'Great,' said George, sipping the sweet, eggy, advocaat and lemonade drink.[3]

'Um, fancy a dance?' said Pierre.

'Why not?' said George, and led Pierre to the dance floor. They danced three songs together, and as they finished George heard a familiar voice.

'George! To your room now,' boomed George Bush Senior, standing in the doorway in his dressing gown, hair mussed up and face unshaven.

'Goodnight, Pierre,' muttered George, slipping shamefaced towards his father.

Pierre returned George Senior's steely gaze. Why did the Yanks always seem to get the better of the Canadians? he wondered bitterly. He turned towards a yelping sound as Jeremy Thorpe strangled a dog in the fireplace.[4]

Deng Xiaoping had returned to the Tower Records Bed and Breakfast, Walthamstow, to find no meal waiting for him. It

3 Maybe you could try sipping a snowball as you are reading this bit to really get into the atmosphere. It's about two-thirds lemonade to one-third advocaat.
4 It wasn't actually a dog; it was a dog glove puppet that JT would bring with him to such functions to get attention.

seemed that he had not pressed hard enough on the top sheet of paper and the tiny ticks had failed to turn up on the lower copies rendering the order form invalid.

He'd snatched a couple of hours' sleep and now turned to see Tokwan, eyes rolled up, tongue lolling out, snoring his head off. Deng ran a wet finger through his eyebrow, broke open the padlock on his window with the wire cutters, eased it open and climbed out on to the flat roof. He could just see the glimmering lights of the city ahead in the distance. He took a deep breath of the cold night air and jumped into the tree.

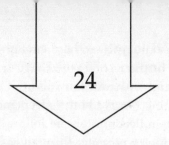

24

Please Don't Stare At My Wing Buds

I remember when I first started inhaling dry-cleaning solvents; Mum had got hold of some from a friend in the trade, and we had opened up the big cans in the kitchen in an attempt to do a little home dry cleaning. That was a pretty crazy session and it was while under the influence of that fluid that Mum had decided to go ahead with her over-the-counter non-prescription-medicine religion. All I can remember is trying to hoist her coat into the sink filled with fluid, but as I got close my face would go numb and my arms get heavy and I would fall back down and spend twenty minutes just staring out of the bay window. The thing is we didn't have a bay window in the kitchen. Then Mum would try to get the coat into the sink but the same thing would happen and she'd fall on top of me. We were both in a heap just laughing.

We did this every day for three months. Mum lost her job as headmistress at the local primary school, I missed my O levels and the coat was no cleaner at the end of it. We only stopped because we ran out of the solvent. I can honestly say though, they were the happiest days of my life.

Nowadays we only really get the solvent out if we're celebrating: a royal birthday or christening, or if it's just a bit drizzly outside and we need cheering up. Certainly no need for the dry-cleaning fluids today, not with Zevon's exciting call about the gig in Leeds.

The car was due to pick me up at twelvish. I packed an overnight bag and a few things to do on the flight. I had been reading the same book, *Little and Large: Our Story* by Bonnie Langford's legs, for fifteen years. It was taking me so long because I couldn't read and rather than take lessons I thought I'd just jump straight in there and teach myself. Don't get me wrong, I can write okay, but I can't read what I've written. I think it's a legacy from all that dry-cleaning fluid because I used to be able to read. Oh, hang on, I just read that, so maybe I can read after all. Whatever, I'll find out when I die, I guess, and God, or whoever it is, goes through all the stuff that happened in my life.[1]

I've often wondered: when you become an angel (okay, I'm making a few assumptions here), do you get fully formed wings straightaway or do they sort of grow on your back over a period of time? I prefer the former idea, fully formed wings straightaway, because I think I might feel a bit self-conscious about my wing buds when I'm getting undressed in front of all the other mature angels. Or if they do grow gradually, I hope that the young angels like me are all in one area together so there's no wing-bud envy or leg-pulling. As I thought this I found myself unconsciously drawing my arms protectively round my chest, as if the suggestion had sparked off some latent movement pathway in my brain. This suggested to me that the wings probably grow gradually – just my luck.

---

1 Yes, I believe that as various events happen in our lives some celestial being is taking down the minutes which will then be collated at the end and handed to us in some sort of folder, but maybe there is a condensed version of highlights too.

I put the book, my medication, wash bag and a change of clothes into the suitcase and filled the rest of the space with scrunched-up paper so they didn't rattle about so much.

I was ready to go and it was still only half-past ten, but I had some work to be getting on with. I took the cassette out of its padded envelope and put it in the tape player (I don't know where Prince Edward was at this point; maybe he'd gone out or maybe he was tidying up his tunnel) and started to transcribe the series of grunts and squeaks that were on it. I got these tapes from a mole I had on Estrakhan's staff. He secretly taped the starpig's phone calls and general gruntings and I deciphered them for my column.

Normally it was just Estrakhan going on about what he'd had for dinner and what he was planning to have for lunch, or complaining that he couldn't swim and going on about how his rabbi was refusing to see him, pretty mundane stuff. But this tape, this tape was different – he was going so fast I could hardly keep up. He was saying something about how he was unhappy being paraded around, and felt like a big piece of pie that got rolled out and everyone took a big bite. I thought, this is dynamite!

He continued by saying he was fed up with his management pushing him into mainstream movies and game shows, that he wanted to write other things, maybe a novel. Wow! This was powerful stuff!

Suddenly my conscience was pricked as I scrabbled to transcribe it all. I realised that what I was listening to was a pig in trouble. I'd got his most private gruntings here; should I really make them public? I went quietly over to the tape machine and pressed eject. I took the tape out, kissed it in a rather dramatic way and threw it into the incinerator in the middle of the room. I watched the gruntings carbonise. Then it dawned on me that by burning the tape the thoughts were going directly up to heaven. In a way wasn't that worse than publishing them in a newspaper? I hadn't listened to the rest of the tape. Maybe there was stuff on it that Estrakhan didn't want God to hear, maybe blasphemous stuff that he didn't necessarily mean but just said in the heat of the moment. Too late, the tape was gone, the grunts were with God now – and his angels. Make of them what you will, sweet Lord and master, and hey! don't stare at my wing buds![2]

2 I know, this whole chapter does make certain assumptions that many of you will not be comfortable with. For the record I'm not sure whether there is a God or not but I do know that it's more fun if there is, or maybe God put that idea in my brain too. If, when I die, I can get a message to you to let you know either way, I will as I think I might just be the person to do this and settle it once and for all for humanity. I might use Derek Acorah to get the message to you so make sure you keep up your subscription to Sky TV.

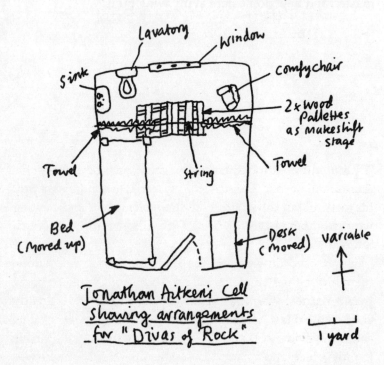

To staff Car Park →

Lavatory

Window

Sink

comfy chair

2 x wood
Pallettes
as makeshift
stage

Towel

string

Towel

Bed
(Moved up)

Desk
(Moved)

Variable

↑

Jonathan Aitken's Cell
showing arrangements
for "Divas of Rock"

⊢——⊣
1 yard

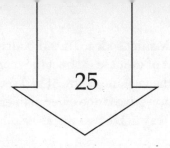

25

Talkin' 'Bout Nut Bush

Eton-educated Jonathan Aitken sat munching through his mound of cake, the rich icing smeared around his mouth, his teeth all but rotten from the sticky mix. He'd come a long way from being the top Tory with a house in Lord North Street to this.

He glanced down at his fresh prison tattoos. He'd done them himself with a compass and a bottle of Quink. His new friend Barney, who had killed a man with an oven-ready chicken (he'd just held it over his face for seven minutes then eaten the evidence), had shown him how. On one knuckle Jonathan had tattooed 'vodka' on the other 'tonic'. There was a reason for these words but he couldn't remember what it was. He'd put two altogether more impressive tattoos on his shins – Tina Turner on the right and Sam Fox on the left – and would rub his knees together in front of a mirror as part of a tableau he'd created called 'Divas of Rock'.[1]

'Jonathan Aitken's Divas of Rock Show', to give it its full

---

1 Why not ask Jonathan Aitken to show you his prison tattoos next time you see him?

name, had been Manny's idea. They'd both agreed that they needed some sort of event to distract the screws on the night of the launch of the visitors' centre; it had seemed obvious to use Jonathan's impressive tattoo entertainment system, which had come a long way in the two weeks he'd been working on it.

He could still remember how nervous he had been that first night. He was using a corner of his room as a stage and had constructed some rough wings from blankets tacked to the ceiling. He peered round the two towels that served as his curtains to watch as the audience gradually filed in. There were seven of them: two rapists, a pickpocket, three Guinness fraudsters and, of course, Manny. Tough crowd, he thought. He ran quickly through his lines; he would start with 'Nutbush City Limits', move on to 'River Deep Mountain High' and finish on 'Private Dancer', and then introduce Sam Fox who would come on and do her hit. By 'come on' he meant that at this point he would roll up his trouser leg to reveal the Sam Fox tattoo, but to him these pictures were real people; he had to think of them that way – if he didn't believe in the divas, how could he expect his audience to? He knew that if he could communicate to the crowd just one fraction of the talent of these ladies, then it would be a great show.

'Are you ready?' he shouted, the lights dim now as he played a torch around the makeshift set. 'Jonathan Aitken can't hear you! I said, are you ready?'

'Yes!' shouted the felons.

'Okay, ladies and gentlemen, please welcome, from The U.S. of A . . . Miss Tina Turner!'

His fingers fumbled with his tracksuit trouser legs. Damn this stretch fabric! he thought, making a mental note to get Lady Aitken to smuggle in some flares in a sausage roll.

As he launched into 'Nutbush! Talkin' 'bout Nutbush!' the

response from the crowd was electric; they were up on their feet dancing and clapping. Buoyed up by this and in a voice strong, yet slightly posher than Tina's, he bellowed out hit after hit. Suddenly he felt alive for the first time in his life; he was ad-libbing, doing stuff that wasn't in the script but which felt perfectly natural. It was at this point that he realised that what he was experiencing was an adrenalin high.

The encore took him completely by surprise – what could he do? So he just started the whole show again. Two hours later he collapsed into the sack, exhausted; his back sweaty, his shins red raw from trouser friction. This was it! This was what he was going to do with his life. Fuck the priesthood! I'm in show business!

The next morning he was mobbed by prisoners:

'When's the next show?'

'Where can I get tickets?'

At elevenses a screw knocked on his door and said the governor wanted to see him.

'This show of yours,' said the governor, slipping the open prison into fifth. 'The boys tell me it's pretty good.'

'Oh well, I try my best, sir.'

'Tina Turner and . . . er . . .'

'Sam, sir, Sam Fox.'

'Yes, Sam Fox, that's right. You know no women are allowed in the prison except Jane Asher?'

'Oh no, sir. I use my legs and knees. By flexing the different muscles in my legs I can make my knees appear to sing.'

'Hmm. Indeed.' He paused, intrigued. 'Do it.'

'What here?'

'Yes, do your show for me here,' said the governor, tossing a chicken leg out of the window.

'Oh no, I . . .'

'DO IT!' bellowed the governor, taking his foot off the gas, indicating left and slipping into the inside lane.

With that Jonathan started up. 'Good evening, ladies and gentlemen, please welcome, from the U.S. of A . . .'

The governor had to pull over on to the hard shoulder. The show had 'hit' written all over it.

Jonathan brought his mind back to the present. He finished his cake allocation for the day, wiped his mouth and pondered the big show for the opening of the visitors' centre. He had a surprise for the punters quite literally up his sleeve, for on his forearm, working from a photo in the *Radio Times*, he was adding a tattoo of Bonnie Tyler. He wouldn't be caught without an encore again.

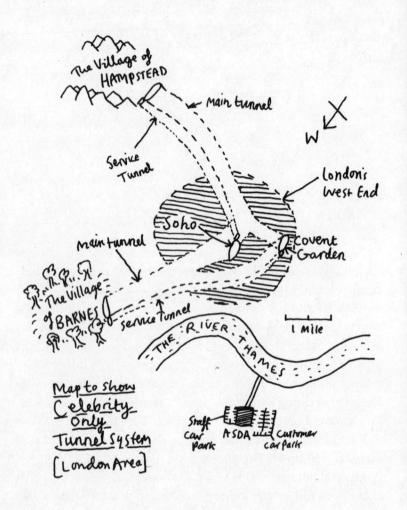

The Village of HAMPSTEAD

Main tunnel

Service Tunnel

W

London's West End

Soho

main tunnel

Covent Garden

The Village of BARNES

service tunnel

THE RIVER THAMES

1 Mile

Map to show
Celebrity
Only
Tunnel System
[London Area]

Staff car park   ASDA   Customer car park

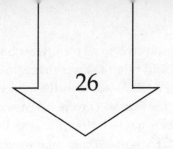

Catch 22-and-a-half

The car picked me up at noon. I recognised the driver straightaway as Paddy Zellwacker, the twelve-year-old comic wunderkind and latest of Zevon's signings.

'Hello, Paddy,' I said, shaking him by the hand and gorging myself on ego-puff points like a wildebeest supping at a watering hole. I didn't want to embarrass the boy by asking why he was in the driving seat but he came right out with it, eager to unburden his brain load. It seems he had amassed huge debts doing a dummy London residency.

'Dummy London residency?' I said. 'Run that past me.'

It had been Zevon's idea to raise Paddy's profile after the ITV show flopped. The youngster's twenty minutes of material could not reasonably be padded out into a full-length TV show but a full-length show in a West End theatre was exactly the sort of thing to create enough heat around young Paddy to tempt in the TV fat cats once again. It was a catch-22, well, sort of (Paddy had written to Joseph Heller to check this out but was still waiting to hear back).

The scam was this: Zevon, using Paddy's money, would

take out full-page adverts in all the arts sections of the broadsheets, *Time Out* and other listings magazines, advertising a London Residency, 'Zellwacker in Residence', at a fictitious West End venue, the Burton Theatre (the name suggested that it could have been named after Richard Burton maybe; I dunno, it was just the sort of thing they would do. Anyway, it had an air of authenticity about it).

Okay, so you're thinking, wait a minute, if the show's advertised what's going to happen to the people who turn up to see it? That's just it, Paddy's so out now, no one's going to want to go to see it. The TV fat shots certainly won't; all they see is a residency by that Zellwacker guy handled by Death Management, and straightaway they're falling over themselves to rebook him.

That was the theory. Problem is it's expensive. As Paddy found out. If no one's going, no one's buying tickets; there's no money coming in, just overheads going out – those adverts don't come cheap. He had lost seventy-two thousand pounds in twelve weeks and was still waiting to hear back from Alan Yentob at the BBC. That's why Zevon had him driving executive cars around town. The fees, including tips, went straight into Death's coffers and Paddy was paid a small allowance just to maintain his body weight.

Ironically, a week into the run he heard back from Joseph Heller explaining that it wasn't technically a catch-22 situation, as instead of doing the run, Paddy could have waited until he had amassed enough material to do a full show.

'I find out next week about the BBC show, but Zevon says it's pretty much a certainty and the money I get from the series will pay off the debt,' said Paddy brightly. It was then that I noticed his hair wasn't hair at all, but iron filings stuck to his head. I was about to point this out but then I thought, no, that's probably another story, and what's in it for me? So I deliberately tried to think of some pretty images but all I could muster was a puppy in a poncho playing with a pork scratching.[1] I gave up and reached for the *Daily Mirror* that was tucked into the leather pouch-pocket on the back of the seat in front of me; I was feeling peckish.

Paddy steered us down into what looked like a subterranean lock-up garage. The Celebrity Only Tunnel System, or COTS, had been the brainchild of Neil Morrissey after he'd got stuck in traffic one morning and been late for a voiceover. The job had gone to his arch rival Yoko Ono (he'd pipped her at the post for the Bob the Biulder gig) and left him over a thousand pounds out of pocket. He took the twelve hundred pounds from his next job and used it to send letters out to all the major celebrities asking them to donate money to build a network of celebrity priority tunnels under the capital. It had taken eighteen months to complete the main routes: Notting Hill to Soho, Hampstead to Covent Garden. They were two-lane and could take a standard executive car. Once you'd made your initial payment you then paid a yearly subscription; if you were new you paid a joining fee and subscription from then on. The only condition for entry was that you had to have been photographed on holiday by a tabloid newspaper.

It was a brilliant system and much better than the old purple-flashing-light one started up by Noel Edmonds in the early eighties (basically if you were caught in traffic on the way to an engagement, you stuck a purple flashing light on your roof, which was meant to mean 'Give way, celebrity in transit', but it never really caught on, and when Anthea Turner was caught with her purple light on just nipping round to Grant's place for a light supper, people were understandably up in arms about it. These days 'sticking a purple'

1 I was hoping for Denise van Outen walking in a cornfield whilst Lee Meade created crop circles around her by rolling on his back but I couldn't imagine his nose.

was more likely to end up with your path being blocked by other drivers, and you being dragged from your car and beaten up by rage-invected mothers on the school run).

We approached the opening funnel of the tunnel and pulled up at the barrier; then I realised that my subscription had lapsed.

'Look, it's me,' I said, showing the toll operator my face then matching it with a photograph of me sunbathing in Ibiza, clipped from Matthew Wright's column in the *Mirror*.

'Sorry, sir, you know the rules.'

Damn and blast! There was a flash and I realised we've been snapped by one of the many paparazzi who hung around the tunnels. Snapped doing a U-turn from the Celebrity Only Tunnel System. The next day there was a very embarrassing spread in Rick Sky's column of me being turned away. Not a great morale booster for the staff of the Leeds Gonk factory. They immediately phoned Zevon and tried to reduce my fee.

I knew what Zevon would say, though: 'It's when they don't snap you that you've got to start worrying.' He saw the whole thing in those simple terms. Get your face in the papers, get your face on TV and everything else follows.

'But what of love, Zevon?' I asked him (admittedly I had spent that morning with Mum doing some 'dry cleaning').

He looked at me completely confused, and then his face cracked into a smile. 'Ah! You nearly had me there!' he said, his head rocking back on its hinges, the chicken-food-faggot teeth exposed for all the world to see. Zevon had no time for such ethereal thoughts as love.

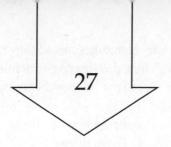

27

The Genesis of Death

He'd come from pretty much nothing had Zevon. He'd grown up in a coastal town which had taken a direct hit from a nuclear bomb. The Ministry of Defence had hushed it up and everyone had received a cash pay-off well into four figures, but the bandstand was still all bent and a lot of the kids still turned out strange – strange in the head and strange looking. I mean, the yearly knobbly-knee competition was really something.

Zevon had got away pretty lightly; his left leg kind of turned outwards a bit, the only knock-on being that if he ever went swimming he kept going round and round in circles.

After the nuclear bomb dropped he changed his outlook, became disillusioned with life and the values he'd grown up to believe in, and got involved in the punk rock movement. This was 1986 though, long after the last punk band had had its day. He formed a punk band called Poinsettia with his friends, and they started doing odd spots in pubs. The other members of Poinsettia were mostly in their late forties with high-powered jobs in commerce, and it was difficult for them to juggle their family commitments, so they rarely played and rarely recorded. They did manage to release one single, 'Bollocks To You', set to the 'Happy Birthday' theme:

> Bollocks to you,
> Bollocks to you,
> Bollocks to you-hoo,
> Fuck off

It hung around the lower end of the charts for weeks without really taking off, until Estée Lauder picked it up and used it in their blusher advert. It hit number one, stayed there for six weeks, then stayed in the top ten for a record thirty weeks, beaten only by Wet Wet Wet's 'Love Is All Around'.

Zevon had used the considerable sum he'd made from the record to invest in a big office, computer and phone network, and, for a while, used to go into 'work', as he called it, but which was basically sitting down all day trying to think of things that he could do. Then he met Nosegay.

Nosegay had been a science boffin and member of MENSA; he'd been studying quantum physics at Oxford University, had a string of letters after his name, and was widely tipped to become one of the top thinkers – maybe even to rival Clive Sinclair.[1]

Then one summer afternoon, having just spent the morning in the lab, he'd inexplicably felt drawn to the West End of London. Without really thinking, he'd skipped lunch, bought himself a Poundstretcher and got on a train to theatreland. Almost robotically he walked up from Charing Cross through Covent Garden and into the matinee performance of *Mamma Mia* the Abba musical, the first live entertainment he had ever

1 Inventor of the first electric three-wheeler and also of the dog food ball gun which fired balls of dog food at your dog to save on the washing-up.

seen in any form. Straightaway he mentally threw away his life-script and knew exactly what he wanted to do: he wanted to sell ice-creams.

He'd marvelled at the way the girls held them out in the tray, a huge range of tubs and ices. He'd sidled up to one in the interval and asked her a few questions about what exams you needed to get into it and she had rebuffed him thinking he was trying it on. 'Please let me carry your tray for you,' he'd said. He'd missed the second half of the show and followed her outside to where she was changing. A move that cost him a slap in the face, but he was smitten.

He never went back to Oxford. For all he knew his pencil case was still lying open on his abandoned desk. No, he'd walked back to Charing Cross and as he'd passed the arches, he'd seen the men lying rough and joined them. The following day he presented himself to Lord Rix at the Whitehall Theatre and asked for a job as ice-cream salesperson. He started that night and he had a real flair for it; he shifted ice-creams like no one's business. Within a couple of months of signing him, sales were up three-fold; they were making more on the ices than on the tickets.

Nosegay took an interest in the merchandise as well, going on tasting weekends around the world, paid for out of his own pocket. He'd been the first in London to introduce the Lord Toffingham ice-lolly,[2] which he'd first seen in Papua New Guinea. He imported other ice-creams from places like the Amazon Basin and the South Americas.

Then, during one matinee of the new farce *Are These Your Wife's Pants?*, who should enquire about the cost of a Strawberry Mivvi but Zevon. He'd observed Nosegay's sales skills with the crowd as he'd stood in the queue, and recognised straightaway his huge potential. Although he'd only

2 Toffee flavoured ice cream enrobing a tongue of real toffee.

stepped up for a Strawberry Mivvi he'd found himself returning to his seat with two tubs and a Calibre Con Citronie (a kind of Cuban Calipo).

Zevon hung around afterwards and approached Nosegay as he was about to get his bus home. He chatted to him loosely about forming a business partnership, explaining his ideas on promotion and talent management, and gave him his empty tub with his phone number written on the bottom. Well, needless to say, Nosegay didn't sound very interested in the project and Zevon didn't hear back from him for three years. It was only during the particularly cold summer of '84, when ice-cream sales had slumped so badly, that Nosegay, chancing upon the hastily scribbled tubnote, decided to contact him. The famous partnership of Death Management was born.

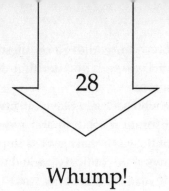

28

Whump!

Their first act was a fellah called Brian Gould – just a bloke they'd seen playing the piano in a wine bar. The pair of them had followed him home and offered to sign him up there and then. Brian didn't want it though; he was Labour MP for Hartlepool. So to impress him they started promoting him anyway.

It worked. Despite never having heard him play, people were clamouring to find out where he was performing next. The fact was he wasn't playing anywhere; he never played the piano in public and had done it just the once on a whim. So when he saw the posters advertising *The Solid Gould Music Show Showcasing Brian Gould*, boasting a thirty-date national tour, finishing up with twelve nights at the London Palladium, he nearly threw up. They couldn't hold him to it, surely?

'Legally, no, we can't hold you to it, Brian,' said Zevon. 'But with it looking like a sell-out, this could make you a very rich man indeed.' Brian looked at the figures, at his eight children all needing new shoes and school uniforms, at the wonderful holidays you could go on these days with the advent of air travel[1] (especially after that dreary summer), and reluctantly agreed.

Well, for a man who had only played in public once before, Gould was an absolute revelation and wowed the crowds wherever he went. It was a master class in piano singalong. The front three rows were routinely packed with celebs: Russ Conway, Bobby Crush, Ted Hughes, and taking notes on opening night Jools Holland and Liberace. All the piano-playing top brass sat mouths agape at the skill of this balding fifty-something wunderkind, dressed simply in grey slacks and corduroy cardigan. He sang and played and did back flips; he skipped the light fandango and turned musical cart-wheels in the air.

He only broke even though and never did it again (but with 15 per cent of the gross, Death did very nicely indeed). The main reason for the lack of revenue to Brian was the over-heads. When asked for his food and drink requirements or 'rider', instead of the four cans of quality lager, cheesy biscuits and 'Frube' yoghurt that he'd decided he wanted to be in his dressing room on his arrival, Brian had mistakenly given Zevon his list for that week's shopping. Any other time the weekly shop would have been an affordable sixty pounds-odd, however that week Mrs Gould had a big fiftieth-birthday party planned, so the shopping list came in at some four hundred and fifty quid. Every night Brian would arrive at the venue to find his dressing room packed full of enough party food and wine to feed forty middle-aged adults. Mrs Gould's old adage of 'Better to have too much than too little' had taken on a rather haunting quality.

The rider was accepted as a part of the contract and legally binding, and many of the venues had already got in

1 For instance, France.

the non-perishables in advance. Theoretically Brian could have taken the food away with him and tried to resell it, but practically that was impossible – the van was already loaded up with his keyboard. So rather than see the food go to waste, he was regularly joined after the show by the forty or so people who had been invited to Mrs Gould's party. They were only too keen to cash in on the itinerant bean feasts. Brian would watch every night as his profits disappeared down the gullets of his nearest and dearest.

Naturally he started to resent them. He finally cracked on the last night of the Palladium run when his brother-in-law, Michael, sidled up and asked him, 'Is there an end-of-tour party?' Brian punched him in the face. Mrs Gould was pretty upset by that and the ensuing argument, stretching as it did over the next three weeks, inevitably led to the breakdown of their marriage.

By then, of course, Zevon and Nosegay had moved on to their next project, Whump!. They had been on a bonding conference for the workforce in Scarborough. The workforce at that stage was just Zevon and Nosegay, so it basically involved them booking a double room (twin beds, no funny stuff) in a plush bed and breakfast and going out for trips (Rabbit World, Monkey Domain, Jorvik – the Viking settlement reconstruction in Leeds, I mean York).

They had been woken up one morning by the banging and crashing of the bin men outside their window. Zevon looked at Nosegay, Nosegay at Zevon; they had realised the sound was a bit like music. They immediately went downstairs and signed up three bunches of bin men and Whump! was born. It consisted of the men – wonderfully earthy, working-class characters – coming on stage and clearing away a whole bunch of bins. The banging and crashing noises set a sort of rhythm.

Zevon and Nosegay knew this wasn't quite enough to be a

show so they booked Jonathan Pryce and Elaine Paige who dressed up as pieces of garbage (he as a discarded flannel and she as an empty tin of tuna). They did some old show tunes that sort of fitted in to the bin-men motif, and there was a vague plot about the garbage trying to avoid discovery and being allowed to live in peace.

Everyone agreed that it was an incredibly bad idea but somehow it worked. The buses would trundle in from the Home Counties night after night, filled with menopausal mums and the Barbour-clad recently retired, to partake in this curiosity. Wave after wave of fetid garbage stench would waft from the stage out into the stalls, and at one point it wasn't clear whether the audience were clapping or trying to waft the smell away. Zevon, the bright spark, had replaced the opera glasses with air fresheners – available at 20p a time – and to stop people walking off with them he stationed sniffer dogs at the exits.[2]

It ran for three years and saw thirty-six changes of cast (although Prycey and Paige stayed on throughout), and it should have set up Death Management for life. One day, however, after a power lunch with Cameron Mackintosh, Nosegay and Zevon compared notes and realised that neither of them had been paid since the company started. They were aware that Jakob, their accountant, hadn't been in for a while, and had had two and a half of the last three years off for various illnesses. Some days he'd turn up with his arm in a sling saying he'd fallen, the next week he'd have his leg in plaster; other times he'd arrive with a big tub of E45 and ask one of them to massage his calves. Whenever either of them had asked for a cheque, Jakob had told them that he was 'waiting for certain invoices and receipts to come in', which had seemed plausible.

2 And the incoming crowd were frisked for Magic Tree.

Zevon and Nosegay left the restaurant and unable to get hold of Jakob broke down the door of his office. The room was completely empty apart from an incinerator in one corner, and a desk and chair in the other. On the desk was a thick layer of dust, a packet of Wet Wipes and a single well-thumbed book – *Hutchinson's Signs and Symptoms of Illness*. Not a single invoice or piece of paper charting any of the company's transactions from the last three years had survived. As soon as customs and excise found out they were beaten black and blue, with fines for non-payment of VAT.

'Why didn't you sack him earlier when he started bunking off work?' I asked Zevon.

'It's not that easy to sack someone,' said Zevon. 'And his symptoms were just so convincing.'[3]

There was nothing for it but to persuade Brian Gould to go back on the road.

Naturally he wasn't keen but it was Mrs Gould (they had by now remarried) who was vehemently against the idea. Zevon and Nosegay sent flowers, chocolates and all kinds of presents[4] but she wouldn't budge. In the end it was a smoked ham from Harrods, gift-wrapped, which finally changed her mind. The fact was that Brian had quite enjoyed the performing part of the tour, and as long as they got the problem of the massive rider sorted out, it should be okay.

So it was that Brian Gould found himself on his second national tour. But the intervening years had left him rusty and although once or twice you could see the old flair and sparkle, the show wasn't really a patch on the previous one and ticket sales were down.

3 For instance he'd achieved a textbook case of *necrotising fasciitis* by painting a section of his abdomen with those little tubs of enamel paint you get in Airfix model kits.
4 A copy of the Rolling Stones album *Sticky Fingers* signed, but only by Bill Wyman, and a copy of Bill's single 'Je suis un rockstar' signed, but only by Mandy Smith.

After Death Management had taken their cut, the Goulds merely broke even again. On top of that forty family and friends would routinely turn up and expect to be wined and dined in the manner to which they had grown accustomed on the last tour. Fights would break out over the four cans of lager, cheesy biscuits and Frube yoghurt, and the whole thing soured relations with Brian's friends, and old family feuds (particularly that with brother-in-law Michael) which had previously lain hidden were once again brought to the surface.

Death was much more cautious after that, making it a rule not to take on anyone with real flair but to stick with plodders: people who just chipped away gradually, doing what they did best, not taking any real risks but bringing in a steady income. Presenters, hosts and DJs was pretty much an accurate description of their current stable and Zevon had gone out on a limb with young Paddy Z.

Of course their main moneyspinner had been the pig.

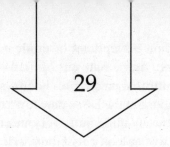

29

Eye in Sky Needs Monocle

We'd hit a great big snake of traffic. Stuck fast, Paddy Zellwacker turned up the radio.

'Now we go to Joey in the flying eye.' It's Chris Tarrant (I love Tarrant but it was only when I met him recently that I realised he is made almost entirely from metal[1]).

'Er . . . yes, Chris,' Joey faltered. 'Er . . . there is . . . er, lots of traffic about heading out of London.'

'The Westway pretty chocka, I imagine?' suggested Chris, a little testily.

'Er . . . yes, that's it! The Westway backed up to Euston Tower.'

'Thank you, Joey, and here's the new one from Amazulu,' said Chris in his usual upbeat way, but behind that he was furious. As 'Too Good To Be Forgotten' started up, he turned to the sound desk, ripped off his headphones and bellowed at his producer, 'He's got to go, Kenny!' He was sick of covering for that bloody man!

Joey Fedora had been City Radio's Eye in the Sky for thirty

1 Actually, only his teeth are predominantly metal but it gives the impression that more of him is because of his height.

years and relied on his updates of traffic congestion for his bread and butter. Traffic had put his kids through private school; it was traffic that paid for his holidays and bought him a big detached house in the Essex new town of Boomsheerary, but his eyesight was failing and every morning when Chris came to him, he would look out of the window of the helicopter and just see a kind of blurred mass with some moving objects in it, which he assumed were cars, and he would be forced to make things up. He had once famously mistaken the River Thames for the Westway and described it as flooded, and inevitably motorists who'd then got stuck in traffic looking for alternative routes had phoned in to complain.

Barry, the pilot, had been feeding him some of the answers but Barry couldn't always fly and look at the same time. The people in the office liked Joey, he was like a part of the furniture, but what was the point of a flying eye if you weren't getting any useful information out of it? Chris was starting to get short with him.[2]

The problem for Joey was, if you're a flying eye you don't really have any skills that can be applied to any other job. Joey was caught; he knew that if he was spotted visiting an optician the press would have a field day and he would be finished. He put his feelers out and through a friend in the underworld made an appointment to see a bent optician. You know, the sort of optician you'd go to if you were in an armed robbery and lost your glasses.

Doctor (he wasn't a real doctor) Hubert Headfrey operated from a safe house in Clerkenwell. The premises were set up as a twenty-four-hour photo developing shop, the Snap Shop, but it was just a front as countless holidaymakers found out to their cost (one man had been waiting seven years for his prints of a lovely two weeks spent in the Maldives).

2 On the 8.15 bulletin Chris had once called him a Twazzock, live on air.

Hubert had pointed out that if Joey were to suddenly start wearing glasses it would immediately alert the media to his myopia. Then anyone who was interested could look back at Joey's past year's traffic advice, put two and two together and pretty soon the City fat cats would be queuing up to sue him for the man hours they'd lost sitting in traffic. That's when Joey had decided to order a new windscreen for the helicopter – a huge lens that Dr Headfrey was making up to his prescription.

'It seems to be clearing,' said Paddy, driving off the pavement that we'd been weaving along for the last three miles and back on to the road.

Pretty soon we were pulling off the M4 and waving at the tiny passengers in the miniature Concorde that sits on the approach roundabout to Heathrow Airport (if you look hard you can just about see them).

I thought back to the last time I flew. I'd been going Premium Economy Class to Amplemews, Holland, to attend a homoavian wedding. I was seated next to an old man; we got chatting, and he turned to me and said, 'Would you like to see a picture of my granddaughter?'

Humouring the old boy, I said, 'Of course.' He then completely surprised me by producing that month's *Penthouse* magazine and, turning to the gory centrefold, crying, 'She sure grew up pretty, don't she?'

I pressed the call button and asked to be moved.

I got chatting to the air hostess and asked her what the other classes of air travel were like. She took me silently by the hand and led me down the aisle to Club Class where she showed me how the seats were slightly larger and reclined to 75 degrees, and you got your own telly and choice of menus.

She dragged me on to First Class. 'Here the seats recline to horizontal, you have your own telly, plus a wider choice of menu,' she said.

'What's through there?' I said, pointing ahead to a further curtain.

'Come,' she said, and pulled me towards it. There before me was a sight I will never forget.

'Here the seats recline all the way back,' she said, as I watched a man who was tipped right back on his head whilst two air hostesses silently milked the blood down from his feet into his head to the tune from the British Airways advert. His head was bright purple now and two hat sizes bigger than normal, his tongue was swollen and lolling out of his mouth as a third hostess poured champagne on to it. Two stewards then approached with a 26-inch TV whose screen had been moulded into a cup. The head of the passenger was then greased with royal jelly and passed into the televisual alcove. The passenger let out a narrow grunt as his expectations were finally realised.

The menu? An alphabeticised listing of all the near-extinct species in the world, all served with chips. The steward began to announce them through a megaphone: 'Osprey-egg omelette . . . braised snow leopard shanks . . .'

'What comes with the snow leopard?' grunted the fat passenger.

'Chips,' says the steward.

'Just chips?' says the passenger.

'Sorry, yes; we don't have the facilities to cook more than one type of potato . . . I can show you the Club Class menu if you'd prefer . . .'

The passenger begins to wail, the tears gather in the base of the cup and moisten his hair.

'What class of air travel is this?' I asked the hostess.

'Fools' Class,' she said.

I dunno, maybe that's what happened. I'd had a couple of Bacardi Breezers, you know, I was pretty breezed up.

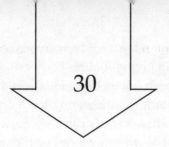

30

A Sudden Sense of Guimpt

As we pulled up outside the terminal I immediately saw the familiar figure of Zevon. He was standing on one leg, resting against his driver. He was wearing his patchwork-quilt coat with fur trim, and duckbill toggles. His skin was a livid red that reflected the colours around him. His shoulder-length hair was plaited into a topknot held in place by a silver skull-and-crossbones bunchie holder. His partially stove-in head bore the scars from a minor operation to remove terrapin claws. His tum was swollen with CO_2 from that morning's Rennies and strained for the freedom offered beyond his terracotta satin shirt with floppy collar. Standard-issue leather trousers held up by swastika braces completed the look that he described as 'Gangsta Arts 'n' Crafts'.

I noted that his vehicle had a champagne metallic finish while mine had a standard black paint job, and I saw one ego-puff point evaporate. I approached to take a look at the upholstery but he slammed the door before I was able to get a good look. I noticed his look of guilt mixed with triumph, which I mentally refer to as 'guimpt' (pronounced gwimpt).

My nostrils expanded and drew in precious air, the smell centre of my brain noting that his body-odour level was running low but breath odour high. He clicked out two pound coins from his black, plastic spring-loaded pound-coin dispenser and gave them to the driver.

The driver took them and wasted no time in clocking them into his own pound-coin dispenser. He thought back to the night before on the slot machines. Pound coin out of the dispenser and into slot, three plays, then another coin, nudge, nudge, hold, win, ten coins spew out. Reload dispenser then on again, three plays, nudge, nudge, hold, play, dispenser, slot, nudge, nudge, hold, play, dispenser . . . until they were all gone.

The dispenser had not known a night like it, exciting but at the same time exhausting; but it knew it needed to refill its four empty punnets if it was to stay the driver's friend, and gratefully received the coins, squeezing its black plastic buttocks, which still ached from last night's activities at the amusements, to retain them.

My manager made a dash for a lone trolley that had broken away from the main group; it was wounded with one wheel manky. As he grabbed the handle of his suitcase to yank it on, a smart-suited lady – probably a city dweller or maybe worked on a computer – pushed him back. He fell into the polished glass of the airport exterior and banged his head with a loud 'bump', then he went to wrestle the trolley back from the woman. She reared up and stretched the fabric of her jacket taut across her back in a display of strength. Zevon thought twice and backed down. He shot a look of guimpt across at me and saw that I had witnessed the entire trolley-woman-wrestle-back-arching incident. I saw that he saw me; I shot a look back and gained one ego-puff point.

We tugged our suitcases through the giant revolving door and I noted beads of sweat on his brow and nasal sub-zone, and predicted increased body odour readings to follow but did not check these at this moment. I pretended not to see as Zevon wrote out a cheque for two thousand pounds to some hobo travellers in exchange for their trolleys.

'Found some!' he said cheerily, pushing the trolleys towards me.

We walked up the concourse and checked in on Air Canada flight 845 to Leeds. The lady asked me if I had left my bag unattended at any time and I explained that I had left my suitcase unattended for three years, which was the last time I went away, but that there were other bags with it at all times, and if I went out I always left the radio on so it was never really alone. Then I realised she only wanted to know if I'd left it unattended since I packed them for this flight.

Just then Alanis Morissette approached me in a distraught state; she was crying and her hair was stuck to her face with a high-sodium mixture of tears and saliva, which she called her 'self-made Pritt Stick'. She said she was anxious because she had set her VCR to record *Heartbeat* (the tale of police folk set in sixties rural Britain) and she was worried because she could not remember whether the red light on the VCR was on or off when she left.

'Think back,' I said.

'Okay,' she replied.

'Are you there now? In the lounge?'

'Yes,' she said, her eyes closed in concentration.

'Right,' said I. 'Look at the VCR, got that?'

'Yes.'

'Now, is the red light on?'

'Yes, yes it is.'

'Okay, you can relax now; your programme presets are fine.'

'Oh man, thank you,' she said, her eyes brightening, and she started to crack the hair off her face with nail clippers to expose pretty rosebud cheeks and broken veins.

153

'Those can be mended with lasers,' I told her.

'What?' she said.

'Those broken veins on your face can be lasered dry.'

'Oh fine, no, wait; do I need to leave the TV on for it to video something?'

'Yes,' I said. 'Yes, you do. The TV needs to be on if you are to video stuff off of it.' With that I scurried off.

Zevon by now had weighed in the suitcases; they appear on a list that is published once a month of weights of suitcases. My best suitcase was only at number forty on the imperial chart, while Zevon's was at eighteen, beaten by Idi Amin's, which apparently still resides on a Ugandan carousel unclaimed.

'Let's go get some marinated chicken breast, nine pound ninety-nine, approximately fifteen minutes,' said Zevon.

He has memorised the menus at Heathrow and is able to conjure up specific items including prices and approximate waiting times. That's kind of what I pay him for.

We stepped up to Garfunkel's, the restaurant and ground-meat outlet opened by Paul Simon in the seventies.[1] I heard a bawling noise and looked out of the upper galleried area. Down on the main trudgeway I saw Alanis; she was screaming at a tradesperson from the Heathrow branch of Dixons. He kept her at arm's length with a stun gun. I imagined wresting the stun gun from the assistant's grip and poking Zevon with it; better still, getting a jelly fish and dropping it in his drink.

'I think I'll have the chicken,' said Zevon to the waiter.

Suddenly I was back in Heathrow again; this daydream of harm befalling your agent is extremely common, apparently. Oh, how I longed for a cheque! It was probably caused by a slight imbalance between the Night and Day Nurse that I use

1 Art Garfunkel countered by opening the Paul Simon Carpets chain.

to maintain my biorhythms. It's all part of the over-the-counter non-prescription-medicine religion that Mum's got me on, and to which I alluded earlier.

'I too the chicken,' I said. 'Does it come with chips?'

'No, but it can do,' said the waiter.

I stared at Zevon and noted that the B.O. levels were rising in accordance with the graphs we had prepared back at Mum's house.

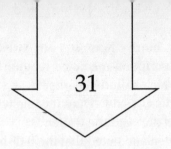

31

Long Day Nurse Journey into Night Nurse

Mother is a biochemistry PhD (Open University) and uses her knowledge to prepare tables of predictions.

She started taking Night Nurse for a cold back in the late seventies and quickly realised that if she could control her nights, then why not her days? By keeping our lives perfectly rigid using over-the-counter prescription medicines and dry-cleaning fluids, the only variables then become other people. Remove the constants and you can, Mum maintained (admittedly in the face of current scientific opinion), predict certain outcomes. Zevon's B.O. levels were our first pilot study – but if we were right on this, well, you can imagine the knock-on effect.

'This is the big one!' shouted Mum. She was standing on the coffee table in her small warden-controlled flat, my sister and I looking up at her. It was a rallying cry to keep morale up on the B.O. study. 'Get out there and measure B.O.!'

She explained how we must always be impartial and maintain our own B.O. levels at a constant rate so that we did not become part of the experiment. She dismounted, wiped off the coffee table, and we rewound the video footage of the rally, deleting frames where she was not happy with the image portrayed.

Ever since some amateur home-movie footage of her wedding surfaced some years ago, Mum has been obsessed with controlling what other people see of her. She wore only a long, plain canvas mailbag with the bottom opened out to release her legs, and holes cut for head and arms. She wrote different slogans on the front and back of the bag, words that summed up her mood for the day and motivate us – my sister and me. Today's words were 'FRIARSTONIC HARDWARE' (front) and 'SESTATIC COGNITIATIVES!'[1] (back).

I watched her as she eased herself into her *Jim'll Fix It*-style chair with drawers in the arms. She pressed a button and the drawer (left arm) opened with her medication: two pieces of paracetamol-fried chicken. This is chicken dipped in a coating of paracetamol and deep-fried; not only delicious but takes the edge off that whanging headache you get when you come down off a Percodan sleep. You get those strange nightmares on Percodan? The ones where you're on *Millionaire* and each time they go up a level it's the same question and no one notices and you can't believe your luck. You win the million then they explain to you that due to a fall in the exchange rates you owe them money.

'Dismissed!' barked Mum, and my sister and I filed out. It was inspiring to see a seventy-four-year-old lady so full of life.

It had not been quite the same scenario the year before when the sherry in one of Mum's trifles, not properly titrated against her medications, caused her to lapse in and out of a coma. Not wishing to involve the authorities we set up a

---

1 The meaning of these words is not easily explained but, boy, it felt good to read them when they were on Mum and she was on the coffee table.

makeshift life-support machine by connecting in parallel the washer dryer, the dishwasher and the fridge, and taking the resultant gaseous mixture to a hose held delicately to her face with double-sided tape. The theory being that the life force from the active youngsters on children's TV would be purified and enhanced by passing through the dishwasher, then warmed and made cosy by passing through the dryer. There was some delay in getting the backing off the double-sided tape, but she seemed to respond quickly to the warmed-up Andy Peters wind that coursed through her lungs like a hare on heat.

I think it was due to an overhang of Tixylix cough mixture interacting with the Percodan but I'm not sure. Since then she had cut back on her Tixylix and increased her Triludan (the antihistamine) and titrated the sedative effect with slurps from her miniatures. Remember, one vodka miniature equals approximately four spoons (20ml) of Tixylix. But she had to be careful not to operate heavy machinery, although there was no reason why she could not operate light machinery, such as conveyor belts, hole punches or certain items of rivet-manufacturing equipment.

I suppose it was in response to these sorts of problems that Beechams came up with the answer in one neat little bottle: Day Nurse.

Okay, maybe it's a pretty weird way to conduct yourself. You say what you like about my mum but she hasn't had a cold in twenty-five years.[2]

2 I know what you're thinking, 'Get on with it!' and 'What about the trip to Leeds!' and you're right really, but it was nice to meet my mother, wasn't it?

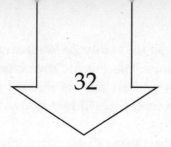

32

Of Mince and Men

'Did I tell you the latest on my Jesus-o-saurus idea?' said Zevon, arranging a small piece of chicken into the gap in his teeth where a tooth should have been. He'd lost the tooth a week earlier in a bare-knuckle fight with Alan Yentob. He'd been negotiating the big Paddy Zellwacker deal.

'Paddy is perfect for BBC1: he's Irish – everyone loves the Irish; he's black – which fits in with the channel's policy on ethnic minorities; he's from Suffolk – so he's in touch with the countryside; and he's related to Liverpool acting dynasty the McGann brothers,'[1] said Zevon, opening the meeting.

Yentob was unwilling to proceed with the signing until he had definite proof of the McGann links, but Paddy was refusing to take a blood test.

The deal had the potential to be fantastic. Twenty million quid over two years, plus a fruit basket in the dressing room.

---

1 Indeed, one of them – Paul – was Dr Who for a while, so you know, that's quite important.

'For that you get the Paddy Zellwacker name and branding, but Paddy doesn't necessarily have to be in the shows or be involved,' said Zevon, leaning forward in his chair and craning to see Yentob perched high above him on a raised podium.[2]

Zevon knew that during Paddy's monthly anxiety attacks, the boy would barricade himself into his home and refuse to come out. They only lasted a couple of days but that sort of behaviour could play havoc with a TV schedule. He could feel the deal beginning to fall away and was starting to get desperate.

'This is a deal breaker, Alan. You get the name but not necessarily him.'

Alan peered down from on high. 'The bottom line is this: we can accept Paddy not turning up to the shows or being involved, and we can accept the loose McGann connection without documentary evidence, because I think you're over-estimating its effect anyway,' said Yentob.

Zevon shrugged, prepared to concede this small point.

'On one condition.' Yentob had taken off his shirt now to reveal massive tattoos of Esther down one arm, Trisha down the other and Crystal Rose across his back. He always did this when he was about to close a deal; it was a primitive effort to intimidate the other party.

Zevon shifted uneasily on the wooden bench that Yentob had placed him on, his neck aching from constantly staring up at the BBC controller whose desk was so high his head was brushing up against the ceiling. This guy was a psycho!

'The condition?' said Zevon. Even he could feel his body-odour levels increasing markedly and made a mental note

2 This gave Alan a psychological advantage; oh yes, he'd read *Manwatching* by Desmond Morris.

to go straight out after this and buy an aerosol of Lynx 'Sport-smell'.

'No fruit basket,' said Yentob, down on all fours on top of the desk, arching his back to make himself look bigger and staring directly into Zevon's eyes.

'No deal,' said Zevon. With that Yentob launched himself at the hapless agent with a high-pitched screech, knocking him back off his bench. Zevon, now pinned to the floor, bit the man firmly on the tummy button. Yentob recoiled and grabbed an ornate floral tray – a present from Bobby Davro[3] – and brought it down with a crunch on Zevon's head, who was sent reeling, then steadied himself on the sideboard and cast around for a weapon. Meanwhile Yentob was up on the plinth again and fumbling in the desk drawer for something. Zevon grabbed a Golden Rose of Montreux, awarded for a particularly strong episode of *Rosie*[4] and flung it at Yentob, who ducked, letting it smash through the window behind him to the street below. Zevon rushed the desk, but Yentob's fumblings had paid off. He lifted the blowpipe to his lips, firing a single sedative dart into the hapless agent's neck. Zevon's momentum kept him moving towards the desk but his eyes didn't see the corner as it came up to meet him.

Oddly, it wasn't the collision with the desk that caused Zevon to lose the tooth. No, once Zevon was sedated, Yentob unrolled his dental tools and gently set to work liberating an upper pre-molar and adding it to the rope of agent's teeth that he wears around his neck.

'I wish he was my agent,' said Yentob ruefully.

Since losing the tooth, Zevon would always order the

3 To be fair, Les Dennis had chipped in to buy it but Davro had 'forgotten' to put his name on the card.
4 BBC1's mousy bobby-on-the-beat played by Paul Greenwood.

chicken, and save a piece back, which he would roughly hew into a tooth shape and wedge in the gap, thus saving money on a costly dental procedure. I think a lot of the time his bad-breath odour was due to forgotten rotten chicken tooth replacement nuggets.

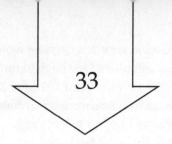

33

The Jesus-o-saurus

Zevon's big idea was this character 'Jesus-o-saurus', a son-of-God dinosaur who appeared in six animated short films set in the Jurassic period. The plots were simple and based on the Bible stories, so you could have T-Rex killing, say, a stegosaurus, but then Jesus-o-saurus brings him back to life. Maybe a diplodocus gets a skin disease and Jesus-o-saurus sorts him out. Get the idea?

In this way kids get three things out of it: violence, dinosaurs and Christianity. Also there would be innuendo stuff that goes over the kids' heads so adults get something out of it too. Plus, of course, there would be the usual tie-ins: action figures, trading cards, a real-life film version of the cartoons, a musical and hopefully an ice show. He already had a letter in to Andrew Lloyd Webber who said he was interested if he could get Ken Dodd to write the words.

Also he'd been praying every night just to get some sort of permission through from God, but so far nothing. He'd lit a candle every time, so it wasn't like the prayers weren't getting there.

'I understand God is very busy arranging earthquakes and that but could you ask him to get back to me as soon as possible, otherwise I'll have to go to Allah,' he'd said as he pitched the idea to the Archbishop of Canterbury in his Lambeth office. He had hoped to get the Archbishop's blessing and, better still, financial backing.

'No, Zevon, he doesn't arrange the earthquakes,' said the Archbishop.

'He doesn't?' said Zevon.

'No, God arranges all the good stuff like butterflies and the first new buds of spring.'

'So who organises the earthquakes, then? There's a lot to organise in an earthquake; you're not telling me they just happen?'

'Um, I don't know, maybe it's the Devil who organises them.'

'I wasn't sure that the Devil existed as a separate entity; I thought we were the Devil, that it was a representation of the bad side of man?'

'Look, God doesn't organise earthquakes, okay?' snapped the Archbishop of Canterbury. He hated it when people said bad stuff like that about God.

'What about the baby turtles?'

'Huh?'

'What about the baby turtles that get picked off by seagulls as they flip-flap clumsily on their first journey from the egg to the sea. Who arranges for them to be killed?'

'Look, I don't wanna talk about that, okay? Just accept it!' This whole Jesus-o-saurus idea was really beginning to get on his nerves. At first he thought it might be something the Church could go along with, as a chance to see some of this new money that seemed to be floating about but at the same time keeping within the spirit of Jesus's teachings. It looked like a great idea on paper, as one line shouted across a church car park, but when he looked a little deeper there were all kinds of holes in it. Like what happened to Jesus-o-saurus at the end?

'Ah yes, I thought of that; there are these small creatures with the faces of children but bodies of voles who have the ability to use tools and so are able to overpower Jesus-o-saurus and nail him to two mighty pine trees that have fallen over into the shape of a cross.'

'Don't be ridiculous! You can't just make stuff up to suit your needs!' yelled the Archbishop.

'Listen, okay, I don't know whether the Man-voles actually existed, but you can't prove they didn't. So what if they're not in the fossil record? Maybe the relevant fossils just haven't been found yet, or maybe their bodies were too fleshy to be able to form fossils. In a million years time will there be a fossil of Bruce Forsyth? Huh? Well, how will we know if he existed?' countered Zevon.

'From the video tapes of shows like *Play Your Cards Right*,' replied His Grace.

'Video will be an outdated format by then,' said Zevon, dismissing his argument out of hand. 'Anyway, how come there isn't a fossil of Jesus? You still believe in him!'

There was no reasoning with Zevon when it came to his Jurassic Bible idea. He really was convinced that this was going to be the big one.

'So, did the Archbishop invest?' I asked as I ate my chicken.

'No, no; he wants more time to think about it.'

'Have you had an appointment from the hospital about your stove-in head?'

'No, no, nothing.'

'I don't really think what you've done to it works,' I said. Using the chicken idea further, he was mushing minced beef on to the stove-in part of his head where he'd

hit Yentob's desk, then painting over it with thick foundation cream. The mince was days old now and was
beginning to throw off its own odour. He was spraying it
with Lynx but the fetid-mince odour was still managing to
seep through.

'It'll do for now,' he said.

'No, listen to me, Zevon,' I said, my voice rising. 'Go and
change your mince.'

He hesitated for a moment, wondering whether he could
take me on. I could see him gulping air into his stomach to
make it look bigger, but I casually opened my duffel coat to
reveal a fully puffed-up stomach and he backed down with a
large burp.

'Buuuuuuuaaaaaarrrrrruuuup!' he said, as he made his
way to the kitchen in search of fresh mince.

I heard a kind of wailing noise, then a crash and I
looked up from my chicken dinner to see some sort of
fracas going on over at the British Airways check-in desk.
A rope barrier had tumbled over; someone had penned off
the Club Class passengers from the First Class with a rope,
but then one of the First Class passengers had somehow
got under it and finding himself amongst Club Class passengers had reared up in panic. This in turn scared the
other highly strung First Class passengers who, breaking
free of their cordon, were now stampeding up through the
concourse.

They headed up towards Coffee Republic and past an elderly lady who was accompanying her husband's body back
from Cyprus. He hadn't died there, she'd just taken the body
with her on holiday; old habits die hard. He'd been dead for
over a year now but still looked pretty good. A lesson to be
learnt that when you get someone embalmed it pays to get a
recommendation from a friend. Get a warranty, if possible.
Two years. Get two quotes.

She still took him on holiday and it was actually more enjoyable; they didn't argue so much, he could travel free as luggage and still appeared in the holiday photos. Dammit, she'd thought, Arty's going to enjoy his retirement!

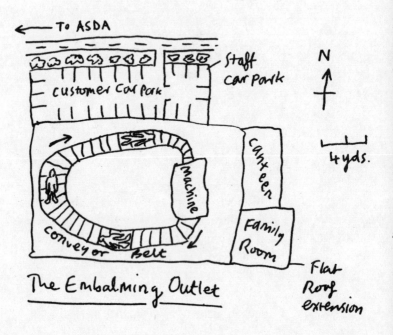

← TO ASDA

Staff Car Park

customer Car Park

N ↑

⊢—⊢—⊢
4 yds.

Canteen

Machine

Family Room

conveyor Belt

The Embalming Outlet

Flat Roof extension

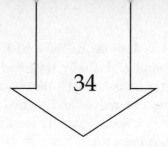

Who Embalms You, Baby?

Arty had been the foreman at the big embalming factory in Weston-super-Mare. They'd been told not to call it a 'factory' as it gave a rather impersonal impression; 'embalming outlet' was the preferred term, although the fact was that with the conveyor belts loaded with bodies, it did give it more of a factory feel.

This was, of course, all hidden away from the public. No, if anyone ever wanted to go 'backstage' after a gig they were taken to a wood-panelled room with sober pictures of wading birds.

'The birds remind us that we are human,' said Lenny, who had meant to order pictures of Christ and his disciples but ticked the wrong box. This reminded him that he was only human.

There was a bowl of pot-pourri that was once replaced every other day, then weekly, then once a month, then instead of being replaced it was 'refreshed' by spraying air freshener on to it. Then they started to hide an Airwick Solid air freshener behind a false panel in the wall, but they found the Airwicks were only lasting a couple of days when really a new Airwick should give out a steady level of smell for two or three weeks. Arty kept taking them back to the cash and carry and complaining.[1] Initially they had replaced them without a fuss as the Embalming Outlet was a good customer but then a new manager arrived and queried it. He refused to exchange the Airwick Solids, so Arty started sending them back to Airwick headquarters.

Arty sometimes thought it a shame that the Airwick people had decided on the name Airwick as it would have been a better name for an airport than Gatwick. Airwick Airport. Come to think of it, they didn't need to have the 'wick' bit if they were making the name up from scratch. 'Wick' doesn't have anything to do with flying. Air . . . hmm . . .? Air service? Air . . . port! Yes, airport, why not call Gatwick Airport, Airport Airport?[2]

The chap from Airwick headquarters came down and worked out that because the pot-pourri had lost its smell it was now absorbing smells direct from the Airwick Solid, therefore the smell was only travelling the short distance from the Airwick Solid to the pot-pourri. His advice was to remove the pot-pourri and just have the Airwick Solid. This was exactly the situation they had been trying to avoid by having the pot-pourri in the first place because it looked quite attractive in the bowl. So, grudgingly, they went back to restocking the pot-pourri once a week. The Airwick Solid chap was pretty good about it, but relations with the cash and carry were permanently soured.[3]

As he'd worked at the factory – sorry, outlet – Arty automatically got a discount, and the fact that he'd been handling

1 That's not the name of the store: 'The Cash and Carry and Complaining'.

2 Okay, it might be confusing but they may well pick up extra trade from people getting into taxis and asking for 'the airport, please', and the driver taking them automatically to Airport Airport (formerly Gatwick).

3 A month later he was turned away because he hadn't taken his cash and carry card with him. Yes, strictly this was the rule but come on! He's a regular! When the manager of the cash and carry's mother died he had his revenge by only embalming the top half, but charging full price. Such is commerce.

formalin for most of his life meant his hands had become partly embalmed already, which gave the embalmers a head start and Arty's widow a further discount.

Arty's speciality had been the face, and putting a suitably peaceful expression on it. So difficult when you didn't know the person. He would work from photos and nine times out of ten people were happy, well not 'happy', obviously, but pleased, no – what's the word? Anyway, you know what I mean. Satisfied, most of the time they were satisfied with the results.

One lady had been most upset though. Arty had got the deceased mixed up with the person standing next to the deceased in the photograph he had received. It was a photograph taken at Harrods of the dead man standing next to Telly Savalas. Arty had thought it odd as he had shaved the head . . . The widow went crazy: 'How dare you! Is this some kind of a joke?' she screamed, yanking on the lollipop protruding from her dead husband's mouth. She was placated with a heavy discount, a talk from the manager and a tour of the canteen.

It had given the Boss an idea though:

Embalmed In Your Eyes
Fancy-dress Embalmings
for an extra fee you can be embalmed as
the celebrity of your choice

said the initial run of twenty thousand promotional leaflets, delivered to all the nursing homes in the region. It created quite a buzz. It worked for a while but they just got too many people requesting Carol Vorderman.[4]

There was also a complaint from the Archbishop of Canterbury who was anxious that where the embalmee was

4 Not easy to do, as it's difficult to get that quantity of chiffon.

embalmed as someone already dead, there might be some confusion when they got up to heaven.

'No, your Holiness, the soul goes to heaven, the mortal remains are left here on earth.'

'Well, they must have some sort of physical presence in heaven.'

'Well, if that's the case, what about cremations?' said Lenny.

'What about them?'

'Well, the body's burnt, isn't it?'

There was a long pause.

'Look, I'm going to have to get back to you on this one, but if I find out . . .'

In the end Carol Vorderman sued saying it was a breach of her copyright and they were forced to stop the scheme. Where there's a hit there's a writ.

Arty was promoted from knees to face, but had much preferred knee embalming; there wasn't quite the same pressure to get it right, as most of the time people wouldn't bother inspecting the knees. That's where you tell a good embalmer from a bad one; always check the knees.

Arty had died of a diabetes-related illness – he went blind and was run over by a bus. He had known that he too would be embalmed. Now he was up in heaven he was dismayed by the number of people up there who looked vaguely like Carol Vorderman. He looked down at Ruby, his widow, as she waited for his embalmed corpse to turn up on the baggage carousel and was proud of the old girl's determination. It wasn't easy getting a corpse on to one of those trolleys single-handed – attagirl. At the same time he wished she would hold the holiday photos still for longer so he could get a proper look at them; things still annoyed him about her, even in death.[5]

*

5 Due to the bright lights in heaven everyone permanently has 'red-eye', like in flash photos.

McDonald's activated the security shutters just in time as the breakaway group of First Class passengers came careering round the corner. A porter transferring two disabled passengers on an electric buggy vehicle was in hot pursuit, yellow light flashing and noise beeping. He managed to corner them in the lift-well by the toilets and nappy-changing area, blocking their passage. The toffs were shrieking in high-pitched nasal voices, and were only calmed when a beautiful air hostess went amongst them with complimentary champagne and hot towels. Their breathing patterns became more regular and they were slowly escorted back.

The Economy Class passengers were dismayed but understood that these high achievers were bound to be highly strung; they were in awe. A call went up: 'Three cheers for the First Class passengers! Hip Hip!'

'Hooray!'

They looked up to the First Class passengers.

The Club Class passengers wanted to join in the reverie, but felt self-conscious, not knowing whose side they ought to be on.

The hostesses breathed a sigh of relief and checked the knots on the security ropes. As they'd suspected: grannies.

Grannies had sabotaged the knots in the night.

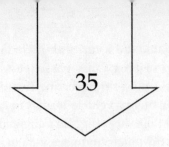

35

Bernie's Son

Chairman Deng Xiaoping emerged from King's Cross Station, perspiring heavily. He glanced at his watch: he'd been dancing for almost forty minutes. Well, you know what it's like when you come across a really good busker.

He'd heard someone singing 'Bridge Over Troubled Water' as he'd disembarked from the tube train. Although, of course, Deng, not speaking any English apart from 'Why do you give me this twaddle', knew the song only phonetically. So 'Bridge Over Troubled Water' was 'Biged Oaffert Rubbled Dorter', and 'Let It Be' by the Beatles was 'Leddybee'.

By the time Deng got to the busker he was playing Quo's 'Waddevro Ont'. Deng slung a Downing Street food voucher into the man's guitar case and started dancing. When the busker finished, Deng shouted 'Sweek Arroline! Sweek Arroline!', and the busker, realising he was on to something, launched into a medley of Quo's hits while Deng danced furiously and moaned the words.

'Cum own sweek Arroline, cum own sweek Arroline . . .'

A crowd gathered and Deng was spurred on by the rhythmic clapping of the commuters, their jobs momentarily forgotten for this fantastic display of footwork. Sensing the crowd's enthusiasm, he began to work them, flicking out his feet and spinning his arms, then spinning round and limbo dancing up to particular commuters and rubbing his face against their coats.

Then the busker launched into his favourite 'India Me Now', the very track he was seeking from Tower Records, but the slow driving beat just seemed to lose the audience. Deng tried doing the funny walk off the Genesis video, but even that couldn't stop the slow exodus from his display. The busker shrugged. 'Well, we had a pretty good run you and me, maybe it's time to go our separate ways.'

But Deng didn't understand a word of it; he insisted they go on.

'Down down, deeperendown . . .'

They carried on for another thirty-five minutes but it never really scaled the same heights.

'Would the dancing Chinese gentleman on platform two please desist,' barked a voice over the tannoy and that was it. The busker, not wishing to jeopardise his future, refused to play on. Deng tried to move the man's hands over the strings, producing a discordant twanging, but he knew it was over.[1] He attempted to give the man his address, scribbled in Chinese on a piece of paper, but he refused to take it and turned his back on Deng. Deng, hurt and close to tears, headed for the escalator; he could feel the other travellers looking at him and hear in his head their mindtalk: 'There he is, look: the busker's friend.'

Outside the station Deng looked around for a rickshaw –

1 A young Thom Yorke was passing at this point, filed the noises away and later *OK Computer* was born.

nothing in sight. So he jumped on a passing woman's back and shouted, 'Tower Records.' And off they set.

Back on the platform, a man approached the busker and placed a calling card in his hand.

'I heard you playing back there. I am a record producer; maybe I could help you? What's your name?'

'Bernie,' said the busker.

'Hmm, I like it. Listen, Bernie; I'm on my way to the recording studio now; why don't you come with me and we could try and lay down some tracks?'

'Okay,' said Bernie, aware that he still had another twenty minutes of his busking patch to go, but it had been a good morning so far.

'Let's go,' said the man, and they headed off.

Bernie the busker sank down into the plush leather seats of the Lexus, suddenly aware of how shabby his clothes were. He glanced over at the record producer in his sleek canvas trousers, hobnail boots and fluorescent green waistcoat with 'Highway Maintenance' written on it.

The car travelled out of the town, the urban landscape giving way to trees and fields. 'Where are we going? I thought you said the recording studio was in Hammersmith; this is Devon,' said Bernie some three hours later, not anxious as such, just curious.

'Listen . . . what did you say your name was again?'

'Bernie.'

'Bernie, right. Listen, Bernie, I'm going to have to 'fess up. I'm not a record producer; I work for the road-sign maintenance part of the Department of the Environment. The job means I have to travel a lot and sometimes it's nice just to have a little company. I hope you understand.'

'You mean we're not going to a recording studio?'

'No, no, Bernie, we're not, but listen, I thought that seeing as I've taken you a little out of your way, I would buy you something.'

They were passing through a village and he pulled up outside a small Post Office and General Store called the School Children One at a Time Only. They got out of the car and the man held open the door of the Post Office for Bernie.

'I'd like you to choose anything you want from the shop, Bernie.'

'Anything?'

'Anything,' said the man from the road-sign maintenance part of the Department of the Environment.

Well, Bernie couldn't believe it; was this really happening to him? He walked slowly towards the counter. The lady at the far end smiled at him and looked at the man, nodding her approval. As Bernie walked down the aisle, A4 pads jostled for his attention with jamboree bags, giant felt-tip sets with all the colours from lemon-yellow to mahogany, boxes of brightly coloured elastic bands, a family-sized bottle of Copydex. Oh, what to buy, what to buy?

Then he saw it. A cardboard box with a hole in one end, through which you could see all kinds of brightly coloured silvery items.

'One of those, please,' he said.

The man nodded to the woman who got a little stepladder and fetched a packet of crisps out of the box with the hole.

'Salt and vinegar do you?' she asked.

'Yes, thank you.'

The man stepped forward, produced 7p and paid for the item.

'So long, Bernie, and thanks,' he said, turning to go.

'Not at all, thank you,' said Bernie, watching as the man got back into his car and drove off.

He was disappointed about the recording session, but also kind of relieved. One thing he'd come to realise about himself was that he didn't really want that kind of pressure.

It was only as the man from the road-sign maintenance part of the Department of the Environment's car disappeared off into the distance that Bernie realised he was completely stranded with no means of getting home.

Bernie settled in the village, sleeping rough initially and making just enough money to get by singing in the local pub. He met and married a local girl, the daughter of a landowner who gave him a job in his construction company. He quickly rose to the top, and four years later when the old man died, took it over completely, divorcing his wife a year later. It was Bernie who was responsible for demolishing the Post Office and General Store, and building executive homes on the site. He never ate that packet of crisps. No, it stood as a potent talisman for his new life.[2]

2 Salt and Vinegar.

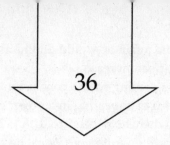

36

Acorns and Water for Suite 42

In his luxury suite at the Four Seasons Hotel, Los Angeles, Estrakhan the wise pig rolled over in his bed, brought his hind legs up flush with his body and, thrusting them back out with a jerk, pushed the female groupie from his bed. She landed with a squawk between the bed and the partition wall and immediately gathered up her clothes and skedaddled.

They knew the score: it was a one-night-only engagement. Oh, not that anything, you know, *funny* happened, no, nine times out of ten they would just sit awkwardly staring at each other until one fell asleep, but no one else needed to know that. As far as Estrakhan's entourage were concerned, he was gettin' it every night of the week with a different sow, and the girl pigs would return to their sty with a broad grin, implying that they'd had a very engaging evening with world-famous Estrakhan.

Just 'cos nuthin' happened it didn't stop Essie from feeling dirty. Before the *Pig Brother* show, he'd had a lovely wife and family. He didn't really go for this showbiz lifestyle and he could see the look of pity in the groupies' eyes as he refused all physical contact. These days, more often than not, he just had this hollow feeling inside that he couldn't really understand,

and every now and again he would find himself just bursting into tears for no apparent reason.

He was slowly coming to the conclusion that he wanted out. At first the idea of appearing in his own sit-com had been appealing, and when he'd been told that *Essie* was being devised by one of the writers of *Cheers*, he thought it could really be a great opportunity to develop his skills, but the script he'd been sent stunk worse than Zevon's mince toupe. The situation was this: Estrakhan was a supply teacher working at a school for mentally handicapped people in the Bronx. Where was the comedy there? Well, in all the 'interesting characters' who populated the staff room: Matty the English teacher who was Puerto Rican and spoke very little English, Teddy the PE teacher who was incredibly fat and out of shape; Jessie the piano teacher with no fingers . . . need I go on?

The pilot show kicked off with one of the students developing a crush on Essie – I mean, I ask you?

'It's like *Welcome Back Kotter* meets *On The Move*,' said Estrakhan.

'Just do it,' said Nosegay bluntly. He'd waited a long time for a whiff of some Yank nosebag and wasn't about to have it gypped away by a pig with artistic pretensions.

Estrakhan had had enough of the constant round of meetings and lunches with these so-called Hollywood head honchos. He was beginning to feel like just a piece of meat. A meal ticket for the food cats. He had that hollow feeling again and could feel his eyes brimming with tears.

This morning he'd woken with a particularly uneasy feeling that something bad was going to happen. He'd had another one of his *All Creatures Great and Small* nightmares where he was taken ill and needed an operation. He would be taken to the vets' surgery and seen by James Herriot – played by Christopher Timothy – but then, during the operation to remove a Mini Clubman starter motor from his digestive tract, he would wake up to see it wasn't the accomplished young vet Christopher Timothy doing the operation, but Siegfried Farnon's younger cack-handed brother, Tristan – played by Peter Davison. Davison looked down at him and smiled, saying, 'Feel that, did you?' Whenever he had this dream it was nearly always a harbinger of doom.

He lay back in the giant, black satin sheets and listed his problems in order of importance. Need acorns, want water, like mud, must finish novel. He rolled out of bed, snuffled the phone of the hook and pressed the large, specially adapted red button on the console. Down in the hotel kitchens a red light flashed.

'Acorns and water for suite forty-two!' Straightaway a large sack of acorns, fresh from the UK, was cracked open and two large shovelfuls scattered into a bone-china bowl.

So the acorns and water were on their way. Essie knew he wasn't going to see any mud until later that morning when Nosegay took him to the mud club. His skin felt dry and itchy and longed for mud. But he decided he could wait.

That left the novel. He'd started writing *Dumb Crowd: The Politics of Dumbing Down in Popular Culture, Volume One* a year ago, and had had one encouraging turndown from Random House: 'It's brilliant writing, wonderfully witty and refreshingly original, but too non-linear for a list like ours.'

How could it be 'brilliant' but not get picked up? wondered Essie. Maybe it was because it was written strictly in his porcine patois. They had been really positive at the meeting and Essie had encouraged them to get down on all fours when reading passages because it made their grunts that bit more convincing, but they plainly didn't really understand what it was about.[1] It was always going to be a problem being a pig in a human's world.

'They created this problem for me,' said Estrakhan – out

1 They hadn't actually got down on all fours, they'd merely said that they were going to. Though one of them read it lying down under an infrared light as they'd remembered seeing a sow doing this once on a farm visit.

loud – and he struck out with his hind leg again, sending the digital alarm clock/radio flying across the room. The clock landed on the TV remote control, firing the TV into life – still on the porno channel from the night before.

He'd always had a problem with human adult material; he found the images pleasing but the language – the grunts emitted by the indulgees – was very off-putting and invariably a weird collection of non sequiturs. Take the scene he was watching now: the lady was saying, 'The acorns are on the top shelf . . . the satsuma has rolled under the picket fence . . . has anyone seen Keith Chegwin recently? I mean, since the *It's a Knockout* thing, which I thought was pretty good . . . my sea monkeys are hatching and I have run out of growth food!'

Oh God! he thought, what kind of life was this? Sometimes he just longed for the abattoir. He was thirty now; pigs just weren't supposed to live that long.

'Room service!'

A knock at the door and the bellboy wheeled in the table covered with a neatly pressed white linen tablecloth. He lifted the big chrome dome to reveal a huge bowl of acorns. To the side there was a glass of water with ice and lemon.

Essie grunted and dismissed the servile box-hatted nerd. He shuffled down the bed, put his front trotters on the table and began to scoff. All mental processes were blotted out as he gorged on the bitter oak seeds.

There would be other publishers.

He finished the acorns and trotted over to his suitcase. Flipping it open with his snout he procured his Dictaphone and started dictating: (translated from the grunts) 'Chapter Fourteen. Reality TV and the Quest for Mediocrity . . .'

Two floors below him Nosegay stirred to a knock at the door. He slipped on a towelling robe and answered it. A farmer stood there with his young sow, a tear in his eye. Nosegay recognised the sow as the groupie from last night.

'Wait there,' he said and went back into the room. Returning with his wallet he peeled off a wad of dollar bills and slapped them into the farmer's open hand.

'Come on, Sonia,' said the farmer, turning towards the bank of lifts.

'Um, the service lift, if you don't mind,' said Nosegay. 'And cover her with this.' He threw a soiled sheet at the farmer, who looked hurt but bit his lip and headed off. Nosegay couldn't run the chance of the sow being seen by the press leaving the hotel, well, not until the time was right anyway.

He shut the door and turned back to the room, stopping to pick up the night's faxes. He sorted through distractedly, tossing them one by one into the bin. A charity request for some money to enable someone with dyslexia to swim with dolphins – bin. Another wanting money for a kid with dyspraxia wanting to swim with turtles – bin. Another from an Essex man trying to raise enough money to swim naked with Susan George – bin. A letter from Richard Curtis asking whether Estrakhan would 'Do Something for Comic Relief', 'Maybe a song with Gail Porter'. Hmm, thought Nosegay, this sounded interesting; might be a good party afterwards, mingle with some other potential clients. He ticked this fax and moved on.

There were requests for various signed 'personal' items for auction (Nosegay always sent towels stolen from hotels smeared in pig's muck) and . . . wait a minute, what was this?

Nosegay sat down on the edge of the bed and stared at the childish scrawl.

TO FAT PIG, YOU WILL FEEL PAIN SOON SNOUT
FACE. TIME CLOCK TICKS AWAY AND SOON YOU
WILL BE BACON. CAN'T WAIT, YUM YUM

A death threat. Yes, quite clearly this was a death threat. 'Dynamite!' he said, and was straight on the phone to the press.

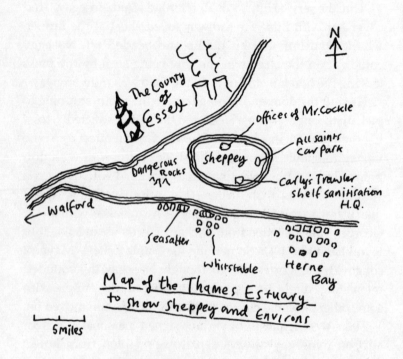

The County of Essex

N ↑

Officers of Mr. Cockle

Sheppey

All Saints Car Park

Dangerous Rocks

Carly's Trawler Shelf sanitisation H.Q.

← Walford

Seasalter

Whitstable

Herne Bay

Map of the Thames Estuary
to show Sheppey and Environs

5 miles

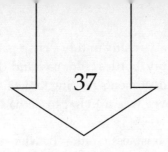

37

Carly's Gonk

'I'm going to River Island to see if Carly still works there,' said Zevon. Well, I barely looked up from my chicken dinner. Carly was Zevon's sister and worked tidying up the shelf by the steering wheel on the fishing boats on the Isle of Sheppey. Because Sheppey is an island in a river, Zevon had become confused. He kept checking the clothes retail outlet River Island to see if she was there. He would go in and call, 'Carly! Carly!' The staff in most of the branches knew him by now and even invited him to their Xmas parties – shambolic three-day events held, bizarrely, at the Schooner Inn on the Isle of Sheppey. On several occasions he had been downing prawn cocktail in a tangy Marie Rose[1] sauce as unbeknownst to him his sister Carly was tidying up a shelf on a trawler literally feet away.

Carly had been a trawler maid now for fourteen years. She'd noticed that the shelf by the steering wheel on a lot of

1 Named after Henry VIII's flagship that sank in the Solent due to its close proximity to prawns.

the boats was always really untidy – crisp packets, half-eaten fruit pieces, empty bottles, old pay-and-display parking tickets, sensitive documents relating to the fishing business – and reckoned there was a living to be had by tidying the shelves up.

She called the business Gonk's Trawler-shelf Sanitisation Service. 'Gonk's' because often when working she'd find a discarded Gonk there. She always carried a Gonk as a mascot and he was known around Sheppey simply as 'Carly's Gonk'. Carly's Gonk was quite a character and was extremely popular with the sailors. People were always saying to Carly's Gonk, 'You should be on the stage,' or, 'You should have an act, you should,' so it was kind of inevitable that one day he would go into the entertainment business. As far as Carly was concerned though, her Gonk had just gone missing.

In the early seventies Sheppey had been a melting pot for new ideas, the place to start a new business. There was something about estuary folk; they just had a very can-do attitude. Despite this, no real successes had come out of the island and the business community on the mainland referred to it jokingly as 'Failure Island'.

Carly remembered the surprised look on the face of her bank manager as she had presented her Gonk's Trawler-shelf Sanitisation Service business plan. She thought the look was probably confusion, though her bank manager had suffered a Bell's palsy some years earlier leaving the right side of his face paralysed, so it wasn't easy to tell. Many people pitching their business plans to him gave up on seeing his reaction – even a favourable one came out like disgust/sneer face (odd that, because 'Disgust Sneerface' had been his nickname at school[2]).

She could see he knew little about tidying trawler shelves

2 And Sheerness the capital of Sheppey.

186

and blinded him with phrases like 'dusting the top of the shelf', 'clearing it of stuff', and 'judicious use of a dust buster'. She also falsely claimed to be able to cure his half-paralysed face. 'How do you propose to dispose of the shelf tidyings?' he asked. He was fascinated by this woman called Carly who bore an uncanny resemblance to Carly Simon. In answer to his question, Carly gave the bank manager an envelope, which contained pieces of chewed garbage.

'I propose to chew the stuff into a pulp and then to compost it down with these love letters I've kept from my second husband.'

She'd then distil down the result into a perfume 'L.O.B. (Love of Business)', which she would hawk round Sheppey's up-and-coming brat-pack business community. So the whole thing was very eco-friendly.

'This is a high-saliva-turnover job,' said the bank manager.

Carly dribbled into his ashtray for a full ten minutes and that clinched it. He agreed to the loan, and as she left he did think that maybe his face looked slightly better.

'Stop staring at it!' said his secretary, barging into the bank manager's office with morning coffee. 'We're all used to it now,' and he hastily tucked the hand mirror away into its leatherette pouch.

The shelf tidying was boring but simple work and she'd been running at a loss since she'd started. The main flaw in the project was it only takes about ten minutes to tidy a shelf so you can't really charge much more than a pound a time. That meant she had to tidy a lot of trawler shelves to make it pay. Really she needed to tidy three hundred trawler shelves a week just to cover her costs.

There were only six working trawlers left on Sheppey and realistically you probably only want a shelf tidied once a month at the most. Three of the trawlers did it themselves. You don't have to be a Casio calculator to work out that's thirty-six pounds a year, and even if the other three trawlers changed their working practice, that was only going to double.

Alan, Carly's second husband, was one of the three trawler men holding out against Gonk's Trawler-shelf Sanitisation Service. He didn't believe in nepotism and felt it was important that Carly make a success of this business by herself without a leg-up from him.

I say second husband, but the first didn't really count; it was one of a spate of Rohypnol marriages. She had met him at a party and after a brief introduction she'd asked if she could set up a drip on him. Curious, he agreed. Carly infused the powerful sedative and within minutes he was in the back of a Transit van where a vicar was waiting. The two witnesses and the best man were also asleep and the vicar was pumped full of steroids which had been crushed up in his dinner so he had an aggressive desire to join two people in holy matrimony.

The vicar was grunting and snorting impatiently, the veins on his neck prominent, beads of sweat on his forehead. The groom and witnesses were snoring, their tongues lolling about. It was a beautiful ceremony and, in the middle of it all, Carly was nervously fiddling with the groom's drip.

Why go to all this trouble? you're thinking. Simply because Carly had heard that second marriages were more likely to succeed than first, and she wanted to get the first one out of the way nice and quickly so she could move on to Alan who she already had lined up. She had planned to divorce her new husband the day after the wedding but he gave her the slip, running off as soon as he woke up. Unable to track him down she couldn't divorce him, and was forced to commit bigamy with Alan, which was far from ideal. On top of that it turned out that she'd got the statistics about second marriages wrong; in fact second marriages are more likely to fail than first ones so she breathed a sigh of relief that the divorce hadn't gone through.

Carly couldn't really understand how she had lost touch with Zevon. The move to Sheppey had been a sudden one, yes. When you get an idea like that you don't hang around. She had contacted him before she left though; she'd left a message on his answering machine. What she didn't know was that the machine had been playing up and had only recorded odd words. Her message was: 'Sorry **I** missed you; I guess you are at **work** anyway. I'm on my way to the Isle of Sheppey, it's **in** the **River** Thames estuary and I'll contact you as soon as **I land**'. It just recorded the words in bold type and that's how Zevon came under the misconception that she worked in River Island.

As she entered the fifteenth year of the shelf sanitisation business, she was starting to face the fact that it really wasn't going to get off the ground. I guess it really hit home when she noticed that she was increasingly relying on bins as her main source of food. The last straw came when two of her best clients dropped out, leaving her just the one shelf to tidy – and he'd cut down her visits to just once every other month.

But it wasn't just her business that was suffering; everyone on Sheppey was feeling the pinch, ever since Mr Cockle had left.

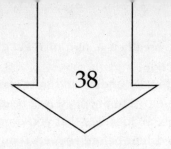

38

Supercockle!

Mr Cockle had been an extremely charismatic cockle salesman and for the locals had come to stand for everything that was good about Sheppey.

Mr Cockle knew everybody on the island and made it his business to welcome new people; as a result when Mr Cockle came to call on a Friday night, most of them would buy a couple of pounds of cockles, a quarter of crabsticks, some prawns, whatever. He was welcomed to the pubs with open arms, a queue would form wherever he set up his stall and people would try to outdo each other on the amount of stuff they could buy.

It wasn't that the food was particularly good; most of it was frozen and imported from the Balearics, and often you'd discover the middle of your cockle portion was still frozen solid. To be honest, at the end of the night most of the seafood would end up in the bin. No, it was more about having a chat with Mr Cockle and, more importantly, being seen in his company.

For eight months he was a regular fixture on the Isle. Then

he disappeared. Just like that. No goodbye; there one minute, gone the next. Sold the business, bought a massive house in Basildon, was a millionaire.

It left the townsfolk disillusioned and devastated; they felt used. The whole Mr Cockle thing had been an act. He wasn't really interested in their little projects, their families, their hopes, their dreams; he'd merely feigned it to shift cockles and make money. And that was the other part of it that hurt. Many of them, despite their own failing businesses, had poured money into Cockle's pockets. They should have taken the whole experience for what it was: a hard lesson in business practice. You need that ruthless streak, Sheppey, to get on. Take a page out of Cockle's book or go under.

It was the Church of England, of course, that suffered the backlash. The Archbishop of Canterbury had the idea to buy Mr Cockle's business; he saw it as a way to make a little money and get a footing once more in the community.

'Let's take Sheppey as a model for the whole British Isles,' he'd told his bishops. 'Get Sheppey right, we get the whole country right, and then who knows – maybe the whole world.'

The bishops nodded in agreement; they knew something had to be done. The Archbishop himself had taken a personal interest in the project, and had studied Mr Cockle's order forms and approved exactly the same quantities of seafood to be imported from the Balearics.

The first week they didn't shift one cockle, the second, much the same and so it went on. The church hall was packed full of stinking, unsold cockles and reclaimed painted crab-meat. Worse still, the smell was actually putting off the few regular churchgoers they had left, lowering the attendance figures even more.[1]

1 Despite a Glade plug-in behind the organ.

The Archbishop, angry with God now, ordered the bull-dozers in to level the ancient Anglo-Saxon church in a move that astonished the synod. If God wasn't going to play ball then he would have to get tough with him.

'Let the church demolition be a warning to you!' he yelled, standing on the concrete slab of what was now the Church of England All Saints Car Park, Sheppey, shaking his fist at the clouds. 'Either you help us, or I'll stick one on that big, smug, bearded face of yours!' he shouted, then confusingly added, 'Amen.' He was taking it to God direct, and had stated in prayer that unless attendances in churches in Britain were up by the end of the month, he would systematically start levelling churches, one a week, until things improved. It was not a step he'd wanted to take, but he couldn't stand by and be made a monkey of again.[2]

2 Did God hear the warning? We'll never know. Fatally, the Archbishop failed to light a candle, so the message may not even have got through.

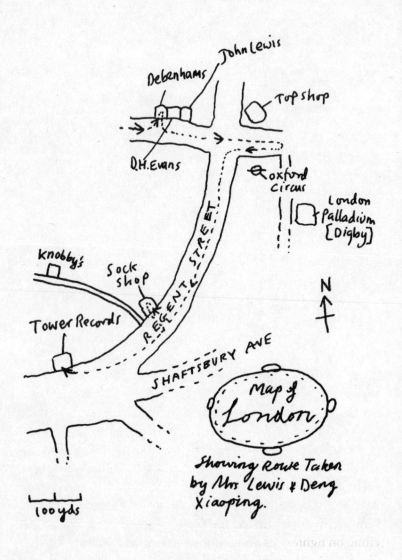

John Lewis

Debenhams

Top shop

D.H. Evans

Oxford Circus

REGENT STREET

London Palladium [Digby]

knobby's

Sock shop

N

Tower Records

SHAFTSBURY AVE

Map of London

Showing Route Taken by Mrs Lewis & Deng Xiaoping.

100 yds

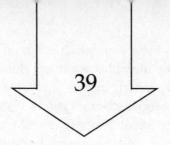

39

Riding the Chairman

'Ouch!' cried Mrs Joan Lewis, as Deng Xiaoping whacked her rump with the flat of his hand. 'I'm going as fast as I can,' she shouted. They'd just made it through Holborn and were rounding the corner and heading down and to the right to get on to the Strand.

At first she'd made good progress along Marylebone Road, past Euston, then left at the lights into Bloomsbury, then she'd started to tire as she entered Tottenham Court Road, and the buckle of Deng's belt[1] was rubbing the small of her back. It was at this point that she begged Deng to let her put him down for a minute. But the elderly Chinese man would have none of it, knowing that once he'd let her put him down it would be very hard to get her to pick him back up again. Joan tried to shake him off, swinging first to the right then to the left, but he just clung on tighter, his arms squeezing her neck. She sunk to her knees but he bent his legs up and backwards so he was still suspended and she was still taking his weight. Then she rolled

1 Engraved with the legend 'I am macho man'.

on to her back so she was now resting on top of him; he brought his legs up round her waist and clutched on.

At this point her elderly mother, up for the day to see if she could get some cheap electronics goods, walked through the barrier of Goodge Street Tube Station. She pushed her way through the throng of rush-hour commuters and looked down to see her daughter wriggling on her back on top of the Chairman of the Chinese Communist Party.

'Joan! When I think of the money your father and I spent on your education, and this is how you repay us!' said Mrs Shirley Lewis, then promptly turned tail and headed off to Sashonic Megastore in search of a 25-watt shielded rectangular tweeter. She'd already tried Tandy but they were out of stock and thought maybe Mr Sashki at Sashonic might be able to help. She had been playing around with some of the options on her hearing aid when she'd had the idea to beef up the sound with a subwoofer and shielded 60-watt bass midrange speaker, but because she was losing a lot off the top range she needed a tweeter to balance it up. A miniature domed tweeter with a ferro-fluid-cooled voice coil and encapsulated magnet assembly with extended frequency response and more balanced drive should do the trick.

That would show Lady Mayoress and President of the Women's Institute, Mrs Paddy Lockyer. She may be married to the mayor, but Mrs Lewis couldn't wait to see Lockyer's face when she walked into the W. I. meeting with this new souped-up hearing aid. Respect in the house, I think. Lockyer had a simple two-way speaker set-up, state-of-the-art at the time, but she hadn't bothered to upgrade; fine for low volumes, but it had been completely overstretched at the AGM and she was left, on occasion, looking confused and amateurish.

Yes, not long now, thought Mrs Lewis, a smug smile breaking out over her face like some sort of tooth convict. Not long and I will be in charge. When Kenneth steps down as mayor in a year's time, she'll just be another ordinary woman like the rest of us. That's when Mrs Lewis planned to make her move.

'I will sell you this tweeter, Mrs Lewis,' said Mr Tommy Sashki. They all knew her by name along the T.C.R.; in fact Mr Sashki had shared a villa with Mrs Lewis in Spain only last year. 'But I have to warn you that the extra weight on your ear may well interfere with your bifocals.'

'I understand what you're saying, Tommy, but I'll take it anyway.'

'Then I must ask you to sign this disclaimer.' Tommy placed a piece of paper in front of Mrs Lewis and offered her a pen attached to a chain attached to a desk, which was in turn chained to the floor, which was concreted in through deep foundations, thus hopefully reducing pen theft.

Tommy didn't agree with the way these old girls souped-up their hearing aids but figured that if he didn't sell her the gear someone else two doors down would. That's why he'd brought in the disclaimer. Though not technically a legal document – it just said, I KNOW I AM BEING NAUGHTY, MR SASHKI TOLD ME ALL ABOUT IT, BUT I AM GOING TO DO IT ANYWAY – he hoped it just made the old ladies stop and think for a second about what they were doing.

They'd had a lovely two weeks in Puerto Banus, he and Mrs Lewis; he'd bought the villa in the early eighties and would randomly invite customers to spend a couple of weeks there with him. Although in her eighties Mrs Shirley Lewis was still pretty agile and would go swimming in the pool every day, although she had required hospitalisation after being towed behind a speed boat on a large inflatable banana.[2]

They'd got along famously but after a lovely big bowl of paella, Tommy had spoilt things by hiding her nightie and

2 But who can blame her? On a banana, with the wind in your face, the sun on your back and the sea spray dousing your legs and lower torso everything seems all right with the world and you never want it to stop.

suggesting that she go to bed wearing just her vest and a cardigan worn upside down with her legs in the sleeves and a cereal bowl over her unmentionables. A tussle had ensued; Mrs Shirley Lewis had developed an asthma attack and casting round for her Ventolin, Tommy had grabbed a tin of Pledge furniture polish instead and got her to inhale that. Deep breath! Pssst! Deep breath! Pssst!

The upshot was another trip to Marbella General Hospital and Shirley temporarily transferring her allegiance to the Sevenoaks branch of Tandy.

Mrs Lewis fitted the hearing aid and was pleasantly surprised by the difference the 25-watt tweeter made; things seemed to really sparkle in her ear, but at the same time not detracting from the mid and bass ranges. She was aware of the extra weight, however, pulling down on her ear, displacing the bifocals.

Yes, she thought as she wandered off down Tottenham Court Road, this would delay the decision that faced all old-age pensioners: whether to go digital or wait till the technology had come down in price.

Mr Sashki watched as Mrs Lewis climbed on to the bus and pulled away; his admiration turning to sorrow via bitter regret.

Mrs Lewis, her eyesight distorted by a displaced bifocal, was sure the single-deck bus was a double decker, and in trying to climb up into the non-existent upper deck, banged her head on the ceiling and died ten days later from Women's Institute Induced Embarrassment Syndrome.

She was buried with the hearing aid still in place. Lady Mayoress Lockyer gave the address, a smile playing at the corners of her mouth. The shopkeepers from the electronics stores on Tottenham Court Road turned out in force to pay their last respects.

A notable absentee was her daughter Joan, unable to make it due to a large septic blister on the small of her back and the words 'I am macho man' spelt out in reverse in scabs.

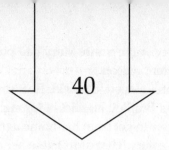

40

World of Wicker

'You know, that took me a lot longer than I expected,' said Mary Waite as she watched Jenny Durban unwrapping the huge laundry basket.

'Oh, Mary! It's wonderful! You just can't beat homemade, can you?' said Jenny as she tipped up the basket.

Then Mary noticed it: a small red Made In China sticker on the base. Aaggh! Help! she thought. Must divert Jenny's attention. She must not see that sticker.

Mary lashed out and punched Jenny in the face. Jenny fell back clutching her jaw and brained herself on a marble shoe plinth. She was out long enough for Mary to pick off the sticker with her fingernail. Embarrassing situation avoided. As Mary was getting the last little shreds of sticker off the basket base, Jenny started to wake up. Panicking, Mary jumped into the laundry basket and pulled the lid down on top of her.

As Jenny came to it was already seven o'clock. She clutched her aching jaw and started to remember what had happened. She'd been unwrapping a large wicker laundry basket when Terry Waite's wife Mary had punched her in the face for no apparent reason.[1]

Wait a minute! Seven o'clock! But she had to be at Knobby's to meet Bradley Hennessy for eight! It would take her at least an hour to get from her home in Blackheath to the top Notting Hill eatery. That didn't give her much time to get ready.

She ran upstairs and opened her wardrobe door. All her clothes hung crumpled on hangers. Jenny operated the iron-on-demand system of clothes management, which was fine as long as you had twenty minutes to spare before getting dressed. There just wasn't the time now to get anything ready. She looked down at her blouse and skirt spattered with jaw-blood and saliva. Oh, what would Jennie Bond do in this situation?

She looked up at the many photographs of royal correspondent Jennie Bond clipped from various magazines that adorned her bedroom walls. Bond was always well turned out, always smart but contemporary.

Thinking quickly she stripped down to her underwear, took the Jennie Bond photos out of their frames and using Pritt Stick and Sellotape, fashioned a Jennie Bond photo poncho. She stood in front of the full-length mirror and swooned. Somehow with this outfit she was getting all the glamour of Jennie Bond in one single garment.

She looked above the neckline of the poncho to see her battered face and swollen jaw. What the hell had Mary been up to? She had been a lot more relaxed when Terry had been on that hairdressing course. Hmm, she needed a hat, but which one . . .

She glanced at her watch: OH MY GOD! Seven-fifteen!

1 This happened to me once, so I know just how much it smarts. She's a real southpaw too.

200

She'd heard that if you weren't at Knobby's to claim your table on time not only did you lose the table but were also expected to pay for the meal you might have had. The maitre d' apparently made you stand there and choose from the menu and wine list, then added 15 per cent service charge, then once you'd paid up you were banned from the restaurant for life and destined to appear on Knobby's Blacklist, a pamphlet circulated amongst London's eating elite.

Jenny Durban shivered, flew down the stairs and out of the door, stopping only to grab the lid from the laundry basket.

'Hello!' said Mary Waite brightly, staring up at Jenny from inside the basket, her face framed by wicker.

Jenny hesitated. 'I haven't got time now!' she said, and was through the door and on her micro scooter. A flick of the foot and the mighty machine roared into life and before she knew it New Cross, the Old Kent Road, the Elephant and Castle and Waterloo Bridge had been dispatched in no time. She headed up towards Earls Court, careful to avoid the Westway, which, according to earlier reports, had flooded again. Through Earls Court, then White City and right to Notting Hill.[2]

2 Not the route I'd take.

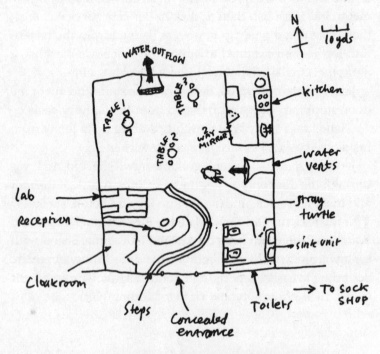

N
10 yds

WATER OUTFLOW

TABLE 1
TABLE 2
TABLE 3

2 WAY MIRROR

kitchen ←

water vents ←

stray turtle ←

sink unit ←

lab →
Reception →

Cloakroom

Steps

Concealed entrance

Toilets

→ To SOCK SHOP

Diagram of Knobby's Restaurant.
to show water in and outflow.

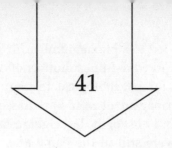

41

Dinner at Knobby's

Bradley Hennessy stood in front of Knobby's Restaurant. The façade was a sheer 30-foot piece of stainless steel with a single halogen light countersunk in it, indicating where the door was. You couldn't see the actual doorway unless you got close up. There was a fine mesh wire grill to one side of it, with a button, itself stainless steel, with a tiny green LED sunk into the middle. The entry phone.

The whole thing had been designed by Graham off *Changing Rooms* only this time Handy Andy hadn't got a look-in (his quote had been a little high. 'Hey! It's me, Graham, you're dealing with,' Graham had said, 'not some Surrey mum who wants her alcove relined with MDF.' But H.A. had refused to budge).[1] It was precision engineering at its zenith.

Bradley had booked the table a year ago, even before the restaurant had opened; he'd heard a buzz, tracked down a

---

1 What happened to Handy Andy the straight-talking chippy? Not sure but I think I saw Tommy Walsh on *Cash in the Attic*, and he'd put the weight back on that he'd lost on *Fit Club*.

postcode, which led to a phone number. To book a table for two you were required to fulfil a number of criteria. The first step was to go for psychological testing; if that proved favourable the management would ask to see your last three years' accounts and a list of the last eight restaurants you had visited. If you were still in the game after that you were required to deposit a small amount of gold bullion in a Swiss bank account. Although this didn't absolutely guarantee a table you were in with a very strong chance. For most of its customers it was thrilling to be treated so bad.

Bradley contemplated the night ahead. He saw Jenny Durban very much as a business proposition; oh, she was nice enough and not bad-looking, but if he could get closer to her that meant getting closer to Durban Feet too. Although he would never admit it in public, he really admired their new range of teenage feet. The adolescent-foot market was a notoriously difficult one; these fickle-minded, surly, authority-challenging zit-balls were just so hard to please. One week it was a sporty look, the next minimalist, the week after that foliage. To be successful, you really had to be in touch with the street. Durban had brought out some transparent resin feet that actually looked like you didn't have any feet at all, which, of course, the teens loved. They weren't just for show either, they had real spring to them too, a good pair of serviceable feet.

Bradley was desperate to get the formula for the resin and had ordered his science boffins to melt down a selection. So far their analysis had been inconclusive. With Manny out of the way the coast was clear for a little light industrial espionage.

His game plan for tonight was dinner, then hopefully back to her place, where he would canoodle with the woman for a while then feign back problems – he had the spinal X-rays in his car if she needed proof. He would explain that he needed to take his medication, which often made him drowsy, and would then pretend to fall asleep. Taking this as her cue the woman should drop off too. While she snoozed Bradley would quietly sneak off and have a snoop around for resin recipes.

At that moment the scooter came flying round the corner. Jenny knew she was going too fast and wrestled with the handlebars, but it was as if it had a mind of its own; she winged a pillar box, sending the scooter spinning, then slammed into Bradley Hennessy, knocking him clean over. Moments later she was back on her feet casting around for her date. She heard a moan and saw Bradley's feet sticking out from under the crumpled scooter. He rose shakily.

'I think you were giving it a little too much choke.' He laughed demurely. 'Hello, darling,' he added and kissed her on the top lip, then snuck a leg round behind her right knee and toppled her over. 'Ah ha!' he said. 'That was for Earls Court!'[2]

He pulled her to her feet and looked her quickly up and down. He hadn't remembered the chin being quite so big and discoloured, or maybe it just looked bigger under the laundry-basket lid she wore as a hat. He studied her poncho . . . the pictures of the grey-haired woman – was that Valerie Singleton? Photos of Valerie Singleton from *Blue Peter* and *The Money Programme*? Her choice of attire was somewhat dismaying. Where did they get this stuff, these girls?

'You look great,' said Bradley, weakly.

Jenny felt his eyes undressing her then dressing her up again in something more suitable and looked away. The impact had resulted in a couple of large tears in the poncho, which she had hastily tried to make good with her own spittle. She made a mental note that once in the restaurant, she

2 Remember how he'd tackled her as part of his courtship?

would order something with mayonnaise and use its weak adhesive properties to effect a slightly more permanent bond. Bond – Jennie Bond, ha ha! she chuckled inwardly at her unintentional joke.

'Eight o'clock bookings!' boomed a voice from the steel façade.

'That's us,' said Bradley.

Jenny's heart was racing. Despite the late departure she'd made it! This was it! They were really going to eat at Knobby's.

Bradley stepped up to the grill, the halogen light overhead shone brighter as he muttered the codeword that had been provided by the restaurant on acceptance of his booking. 'Majique,' he said.

The steel door slid up.

'Welcome Bradley and Jenny to Knobby's taste experience,' said a tall leggy blonde in a silver shell suit and a ceramic bowl on her head. 'Have you brought your samples?'

'Yes, yes,' said Bradley handing over two vials, one of sweat the other of saliva.

Jenny went ashen and could feel herself about to be sick. She had forgotten her samples! Knobby's was unusual amongst restaurants in that it was they who decided what food you should order, based on the contents of your sweat and saliva. The samples were to be presented on arrival and then analysed by the chef using his Kenwood Mass Spectrometer. Then, and only then, could the chef make his recommendations, tailoring the courses specifically to your biochemistry. It was strictly one set of vials per booking though. The gold bullion, the psychological tests, the samples – all these hurdles were a kind of test of diners' resolve. Did you want to eat at Knobby's or not? It certainly separated the men from the boys.

'Your samples, Jenny?' said the blonde lady.

'Yes, of course, I just . . . can I just use your loo?' said Jenny, trying to appear calm.

She let herself into the ladies' cubicle and sat on the pan. What could she do? She could easily provide the samples but she needed those vials! Maybe she could sneak out of the toilets and somehow get into the office – was there an office? Where did they keep the vials? They were bound to be under lock and key. She looked down. Oh God, her Jennie Bond-photo dress was dipping into the toilet water at the back. 'Yuk!' She stood up. Now it was sticking to the backs of her bare legs. Oh, what to do?

Just then she heard the click of the next-door cubicle and the rustle of her new neighbour lowering her undergarments. Jenny crouched down on all fours and peered under the cubicle wall. Two legs, pants round ankles and a handbag, yes, an open handbag and, oh joy! – the vials in the bag. She hadn't handed them over yet!

Jenny let herself gently out of her cubicle, feeling the photo mush slapping against her calves. She pulled her poncho up over her face in disguise and waited.

Bradley was standing staring at the walls; there seemed to be some sort of tidemark all round the restaurant about a foot above the floor. Like the place had flooded recently. He looked over at the diners. There were just three tables, each seating two, making six diners in all, set in about an acre of stripped-pine flooring and brushed aluminium fittings. This was really exclusive. The clientele all looked vaguely familiar but there were none that he could easily name. They were all perfectly manicured, without a single nose hair out of place.

'Come on, Durban,' he said out loud, kind of hoping she'd hear.

As the woman emerged from the cubicle Jenny flew at her, pushing her back on to the toilet seat and grabbing her beautifully plumped-up quiff, whacking it back on the cistern once, twice, three times. The woman grunted; Jenny whacked it back again. Her body went limp. Jenny felt the woman's neck for a pulse; she was out cold but still alive. She felt sick at the needless violence but what could she do? If you failed this test you were thrown out of Knobby's. She grabbed the handbag, liberated the vials, closed and locked the cubicle door, climbed out and over, then scribbled OUT OF ORDER on it in lipstick and headed back to the restaurant, leaving a trail of Jennie Bond papier mâché pledgets as she went.

'Sorry to keep you, Bradley. Here they are,' she said brightly, handing over the vials to the bowl-hatted attendant.

'Fine, thank you, Jenny. Come through.' They were led down a gravel ramp to the dining area.

'That's odd,' said Bradley, fingering the pipette dropper next to the knife and fork at his place serving. Jenny noticed that she had one too.

'I'll have a gin and tonic, and what will you have, Jenny?'

'No, you will wait for your test results,' said the waiter.

'Well, how long will that take? I'm spitting feathers here,' said Bradley.

'I will throw you out,' said the waiter sternly. Two bouncers stepped forward from the shadow of an alcove.

Jenny flashed Bradley a look of concern and Bradley backed down. 'Fine, whatever,' he said.

The first course consisted of a bowl of something like a watery soup or consommé. The waiter set up a Bunsen burner in the centre of the table, adjusted the flame to a roaring blue and then explained that Jenny and Bradley should take their pipettes and squirt the fluid through the flame. An overhead tannoy system rang out: 'Note how the flame changes colour, notice the smell that is produced. This is your first course.'

'How wonderful!' said Jenny. 'How thoroughly innovative.'

They duly squirted the food juice through the flame two or three times, taking deep tokes on the stink. Jenny tried hard to convince herself that she was getting something out of it but after a while just felt a little light-headed. Bradley bored of it pretty quickly and took to sucking the juice down straight out of the pipette. That earned him another warning from the waiter.

'Next course! Seafood!' barked the tannoy. With that water started to pour out over the restaurant floor.

'It's sea water,' said Bradley, noticing large clumps of sea-weed.

Then the kitchen released forty tiger prawns.

'Use the net stowed under your seat,' called the waiter, shouting from a sandbank.

They felt underneath; sure enough there were small shrimp nets like they used to have as kids, but the prawns were fast. Bradley had caught one, speared it on his fork and sacrificed it in the Bunsen burner, searing its tiny legs and antennae off.

What is this freaky place? he thought, but had to admit he was enjoying the sport of it, if not the food itself.

Jenny failed to catch any of the second course.

'Third course! Use the spears concealed in your chair uprights.'

With that, three huge leatherback turtles were released from a hatch and started circling the diners, nipping at their ankles and gobbling down the few remaining prawns.

In the kitchen Gusley Bolex, the chef and proprietor of Knobby's, watched his diners through a two-way mirror as they splashed around vainly trying to cobble together a mouthful of food. He was much respected, at the top of the culinary tree, and three of the highly coveted Michelin stars hung on his cooker, but still the TV people would not sign him up. He'd developed an outlandish three-pronged haircut, peppered his speech with expletives, he made exaggerated gestures with his hands when he talked and had a distinctive hee-hawing laugh; hell, he'd even had his tongue injected with collagen to give him a bit of a lisp, but still they resisted.

ITV had made a pilot show six months ago, a kind of Back-to-Basics-type of thing – how to boil water, effective whisking, applying salt – stuff that 'Just no one is doing any more,' according to his agent. The plan was for the show to become more complicated as the weeks progressed, finishing on his new techniques of food liquid vaporisation and inhalation.

The actual show wasn't that bad it was just Gusley; whatever he did, he had this kind of desperate 'please like me' look in his eye that was an immediate telly turn-off.[3]

Well, stuff them, he'd thought. Since then he had deliberately tried to exclude media people from Knobby's with the screening tests and, apart from Mike Hollingsworth[4] slipping through the net with his young niece, it had been pretty successful. As he looked out at his diners – the man with the eye patch, the lady in the Jennie Bond-print dress, the man in the tweeds, the grey-haired woman in the tracksuit, the black woman with the Bacofoil flares – all struggling to divide the corpse of a restless seafaring amphibian, he thought, at least they had nothing on him, no axe to grind, no ego-puff pointage to trade. They sure were a weird-looking bunch, though. Ho hum, he thought, and returned to a large lump of boiled brisket, which he was injecting with cat blood.[5]

Just then a tall woman with blood-encrusted face appeared at the top of the stairs and pointed at the woman in the tracksuit, who was elbow deep in turtle flesh and who looked suspiciously like Valerie Singleton.

3 This can only work if that person also has a tragic back story such as mother ill or bullied at school.
4 Once Mr Anne Diamond and a powerful player in the media circus.
5 It doesn't sound appetising but in fact the cat blood sets off the beef nicely. Serving suggestion: tin of peas sploshed on it.

'There she is! It was her!' Three security officers in riot gear stormed in behind her and arrested the hapless grey-haired lady.

'But I'm Virginia Wade!' she bellowed as she was man-handled out of Knobby's, a turtle using the opportunity to take a bite out of her ankle.

'Excuse me? Have you got any mayonnaise?' asked Jenny. The waiter laughed haughtily and canoed past her to the kitchen.

Kevil Garment shook his head and sucked on a piece of semi-cooked turtle flesh. He had hardly looked up from his meal since sitting down. He was really into it, really enjoying the whole experience, though he was a little hot under his thick blond wig, beard and eye patch.

Back in the kitchen Gusley was confused as to whether Virginia Wade was a media type or not.

'Yes, she has commentated on tennis tournaments on tele-vision,' said his assistant, 'but she is principally a sports person.'

They agreed that unless she got a permanent post with a channel, she was free to return. Gusley placed her pudding back in the fridge.[6]

'Just an advert or a voiceover would do!' he blurted, but-tering a bridge roll.

The evening went pretty much to plan for Bradley. Jenny fell asleep in his arms at a quarter past midnight, although her tummy was still rumbling from lack of nosh (she'd only managed to graze the turtles and had had an allergic reaction to the dessert, probably due to the fact that it had been tailored to another lady's biochemical profile).

Bradley gently slipped out from under her and padded off

6 Leftover cat blood mousse served between two After Eight mints with a sprig of ginger hair on it.

round the house in search of the resin recipes. He came upon Manny's study pretty quickly, eased the door open and let himself in. The whole room was under a thick layer of dust. Jenny hadn't bothered to hoover it since Manny had been sent down.

He wandered over to the filing cabinet: one drawer labelled 'Insteps 1978–84', another marked 'Standard toe sizes' and then ... what was this? 'Top Secret Teen-foot Resins'. He pulled at the drawer. It was locked. He felt for his pocketknife, slid it under the catch and gently but firmly jemmied open the drawer. There before him, rattling around in the bottom, was an off-the-shelf box of Plasticraft, the resin-based craft toy that enabled children to make paperweights. He stared in disbelief then gave a jump as he felt a hand slip under his shirt. He turned with a gasp – it was Jenny.

'You need only have asked,' she said, her face puffed up from the pudding.

'What do you say to a Durban and Hennessy merger?' said Bradley, arching one eyebrow like Sharon Watts off *EastEnders*.

'I thought you'd never ask,' she parped, pulling him towards her.

'Here let me take this off for you,' he said, easing the wicker linen-basket lid to the floor.

This was not in my plan, thought Bradley. He had never meant to fall in love.

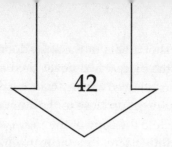

42

Winnipeg Get Your Gun

Bruvose Haintree's son Jake was only twelve and had developed an interest in firearms at about three. Bruvose and Meerox had always resisted buying gender-specific toys, trying to avoid sexual stereotypes, and they certainly did not want to perpetuate the cycle of violence by buying Jake a toy gun. Problem was, Jake would pick up anything vaguely gun-shaped and go 'Pow! Pow!' pretending it was a gun. For a while they had banned bananas and sticks from the house but he would always find something that said 'gun' to him. Bruvose had once found Jake with a sharpened avocado pear, pretending to hold up an off-licence.[1]

In the end they relented and bought him a small Smith and Wesson .45 calibre revolver for Christmas. It was only a very basic gun, and they'd made Jake promise he wouldn't fire it at them.

Bruvose felt the weight of it in his hand; there was something wonderful about the quality of the thing. He squeezed

---

1 The shame of it was, it was a Waitrose 'perfectly ripe' avocado, and it was ruined.

the trigger and shot a hole in the shed door. Hmm, you got quite a kick off the piece. He'd never fired a gun before and figured there was no need for any training or target practice so long as he could get up close to the animal.

He turned back to the copy of the *National Enquirer* advertising the new Mother Teresa movie featuring Demi Moore as the young Teresa and Denzil Washington as the love interest. Estrakhan the pig was listed as executive producer. He was bound to turn up at the premiere. He peeked out of the shed door, tucked the gun into the top of his trousers and walked off the balcony and back into the apartment.

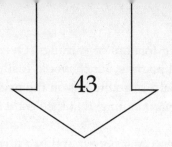

43

Carly-vs.-Post-it Notes

It had taken fourteen years for Carly to realise that she wanted out of Sheppey. The only thing standing in her way was the ferry fare.[1] She was banking on getting substantial damages from her court case against the manufacturers of Post-it Notes.

When Carly had first started up Gonk's, she had called in on a trawler to tidy the shelf and finding the trawler man out, had left a Post-it Note explaining that she had visited and that he should phone her if he was interested in her services. A Post-it Note, it seems, from a rogue batch. The nether end coated not with adhesive but with Teflon.[2] Static electricity had held it on the trawler door just long enough for her to turn her back, then it was away in the wind. The trawler man never got that note.

---

1 This is, of course before the suspension bridge connecting Sheppey to mainland England – carrying traffic over the Swale and adjacent mud flats on 19 spans ranging from 44 to 93 metres long, the tallest point 29 metres high.
2 How could this happen? I suspect foul play, but have no proof.

She was suing for loss of earnings. Over fourteen years some forty-eight pounds, which would easily cover her ferry fare and set her up in a new flat on the mainland. Her case hinged on the length of time that the Post-it had stuck to the trawler door.

She was representing herself and had a witness who was willing to testify that they had not seen the Post-it Note on the door some thirty seconds after it had been applied. Admittedly her witness, Bernardine, was blind but Carly had thought of a way to convince the defence team that she could see. First (obvious, this one), if she left her white stick and guide dog at home that would help. Now for the clever bit. With a little ingenuity she had managed to get the details of the judge's aftershave, and by posing as a dry-cleaning sales assistant had got hold of the Post-it-Note lawyer's vest. By exposing these smells to her blind friend she could train her to recognise the smells and direct her answers accordingly, thus to all intents and purposes making her appear sighted.

Carly had set up a replica scented area in her flat and would address various questions to Bernardine, barking the names of the smells until she'd got the hang of it.

'Vest! Vest! Old Spice! Old Spice! Vest! Vest!' shouted Carly, sending Bernardine spinning on the spot.

Carly was spending most of her considerable spare time in Sheppey Library reading up on adhesive law: *Copydex vs. the Crown*, *The Great Bostick Trial of 1852*, *Epoxy Resin vs. Clive Anderson*.[3] Despite the fact that the big adhesive lobby had never lost a case, Carly was in characteristically optimistic mood.

Ah! If only she could find her lucky Gonk. Once again she started her daily routine of searching her flat from top to

3 His defence on that occasion hinged around the use of the word resin as opposed to glue.

bottom. This would often take up the best part of the day. The Gonk wasn't in the house, she kind of knew that; she knew he'd probably left to start a new life (what could she offer him in her current situation?), but still a nagging voice in the back of her head would pipe up, 'Have you checked under the towels in the airing cupboard?' She knew the towels had been bought long after Gonk's disappearance[4] yet still she found herself at two o'clock in the morning, hoping against hope to catch a glimpse of his green body hair.[5]

4 They were a wedding present from Keith Harris.
5 This could be Orville's.

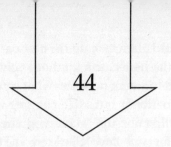

44

Bob Dylan Goosed My Father

'Carly! Carly!' shouted Zevon as he walked around the ladies' department of the Heathrow Airport branch of River Island.

'Hello, Zevon,' said the assistant. 'We haven't seen you for a while.'

'Have you seen my sister Carly?' said Zevon.

'Do we really have to go through this again?' asked the assistant as Zevon started to get changed into the women's clothing he had in his hand luggage. It is always at this point that he is escorted from the premises. Every time. Zevon thought that if he could get fully changed into his sister's clothes, someone might recognise her and tell him whether she'd been in recently. It was like the reconstructions they do on *Crimewatch*.

As a couple of the burly security guards roughed him up, a young woman approached him. 'Carly, is that you?' It was Alanis again. 'Carly?' she repeated. She had mistaken Zevon for the singer Carly Simon.

Carly had looked a lot like Carly Simon from birth, which

is why she was called Carly in the first place. The strong Carly Simon resemblance runs through the family. In fact, Zevon's father acted as an undercover Carly Simon double during the Vietnam War to try to infiltrate the left-wing folk-singer movement. His first mission involved having full sexual relations with Bob Dylan.[1] Zevon Senior baulked at this and as Dylan made his move he sidestepped him, falling three storeys out of a window. Fortunately Donovan broke his fall. Oddly, while in this guise Zevon Senior wrote some of Carly Simon's best songs.[2]

Meanwhile the real Carly Simon, dressed as Zevon's father, was forced to bring up Zevon and his sister Carly. This led to them both picking up a number of Carly Simon's mannerisms, which just added to the confusion.

The Vietnam War came to a messy end and Zevon Senior was demobbed; he shed his Carly Simon disguise and returned to his family. A grateful, if slightly confused, Carly Simon returned to the folk scene, only to discover a back catalogue of songs she had never heard, and so required the words on cards when performing them. She couldn't work out why Bob Dylan had started blanking her either.

'Carly?' said Alanis to Zevon.

'Have you seen me? I mean her?' said Zevon.

'Carly Simon?'

'No, no, my sister Carly; have you seen her? She works in River Island, I just don't know which branch.'

'Carly? It's me. Alanis . . . You know . . .' She started to sing, 'How about gettin' offa these antibiotics . . . Right?'

Zevon wiped the lipstick from his mouth and removed the toothpicks which were holding his breasts up.

1 How's that for a Theme Time Radio Hour!
2 But I can't remember any of them. Oh yes, 'You're so vain' which I think I'm right in saying was written about me.

'Oh God! I'm so sorry!' exclaimed Alanis, realising her mistake. Her face contorted into a grimace and she staggered back.

'No, wait! I . . . it's not what you think!' shouted Zevon.

'You mean it's not an attempt by you to impersonate your sister in an attempt to jog memories of her?'

'No. YES! Yes.'

'Do you have a VCR?'

'Um, yes . . . but . . .'

'Do you have episode four, series five of *Heartbeat* on tape?'

Zevon now came to despise this tragic figure.

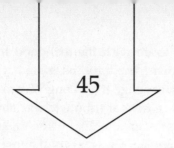

45

Opportunity Misses

I guess you're probably asking yourselves, 'That's all very well, but what happened to Paddy Zellwacker?' Well, a lot of us reckoned Paddy Z had been promoted a little ahead of his time. Only three months before the Yentob fight/meeting, Paddy was working on his parents' farm in Suffolk. It was one of a tiny group of resolutely progressive hi-tech farms, which had bucked the trend and stuck to the old ways of farming established before the current organic boom. They used anything and everything in the way of fertilisers, hormones and weedkillers to give themselves retail advantage. In fact, some of the meat that was coming off the pigs had so many different chemicals in it that under EU laws it had to be sold as metal.

There was a small group of the right-wing, lower middle classes who loved this type of product, and it was going down a bomb in the Tory heartlands of Basildon and Boomsheerary.

Boomsheerary was a new town set up in Essex in the eighties. No one was quite sure where the name came from, but it was something to do with the feel-good feel of the word 'boom' (boom town), the 'rary' bit hinted at the jingoism of the First World War song, 'It's a Long Way to Tipperary', and also in there was a note of tribute to the late Derby winner, tragic Shergar.

The Zellwackers' farm was one of the first to start feeding their pigs iron filings in an attempt to make magnetic pork chops. The idea being that you take them out of the freezer and stick 'em on the side of the fridge to thaw out (high up, so the dogs don't get 'em), and they cook quicker because they hug the contours of the frying pan. No good for stews as the meat sticks to the bottom and burns, nor for ferries either because the magnetism interferes with their sophisticated navigational equipment, but in Boomsheerary the kitchens were ringing with the 'slap, clunk!' of chops hitting ferrous surfaces.

Paddy's upbringing had been far from conventional. Whenever the McGann brothers came on TV his mum would say, 'Oh look, there's your brother.' Naturally enough he grew up assuming he was related to the fine Liverpool-born acting dynasty. Fact was, Mrs Zellwacker didn't know she was actually saying it. It was a hangover from an evening out to a hypnotist show in the early eighties. She went along because she thought it would be a laugh and maybe would help her to give up hang-gliding. But from that day on, whenever she saw a McGann brother she automatically said, 'Oh look, there's your brother.' She'd confused a number of people over the years and had been banned from babysitting in the area on the nights that the McGanns were on TV.[1]

Paddy must have been about five when he started to turn black. It was traced to the magnetic chops. Gradually over

1 This ruled out most of the year, except Whitsun when family tradition prevents any McGann from working.

four or five years the whole family turned black. When people say 'black' when talking about skin colour, they really mean a dark shade of brown, but Paddy really was, at twelve, jet black.

Immediately their previously friendly neighbours treated them with suspicion, daubed racist graffiti on their walls and on one occasion burnt a 'T' on the front lawn (it should have been a cross but the carpenter had not unfolded the plans properly. It was not what the racist neighbours had wanted but it was paid for and was a lovely bit of joinery so they decided to burn it anyway).

This upsurge of anti-feeling-feeling was doubly confusing for the Zellwackers because, originally hailing from South Africa, they had deeply racist views. They ended up hating themselves in a completely irrational way. So after a number of racially motivated beatings in the family (Pa Zellwacker was beating up Paddy calling him a 'black bastard' when he caught sight of himself in the mirror and turned his fists on himself), they decided there was nothing for it but to integrate. Ma joined a gospel choir; Pa took an interest in rap music. Thing was, Ma was tone deaf and Pa couldn't rap for toffee.

It didn't stop him from releasing his 'Farmer's Rap' single. All right, I know you want to hear a bit. He set it to the tune of 'Old Macdonald':

I got pigs and chickens down on the farm,
With efficient fencing and hedge maintenance they'll
    come to no harm.
Them motherfuckers like to scoff
With the brothers that they meet down at the trough . . .

I mean, what can you do? It was played a few times on local radio but pretty much got stuck at number fourteen in the

223

national charts. There was talk at one time of an appearance on *Top of the Pops* but his performance on Channel 4's hip young current affairs programme *The Priory* (named after the home of the prior or abbot's deputy) was far from successful (there had been a very rude letter from the producer, countersigned by Jamie Theakston).[2] Halfway through the second verse ('The horses neigh but I say yea . . .'), Pa pitched forward and fell into the crowd, badly injuring three or four babies in the front row. Then security had set the dogs on him.

It was amongst this chaos that the young Paddy was expected to grow up. I know what you're thinking: with a background like that at least he has a lot to draw on for his comedy. No, Paddy just did Knock, Knock jokes. Sounds limiting, doesn't it? But there was a real buzz about him, the feeling being that it was time for the Knock, Knock joke to make its return.

At the BBC a focus group had turned up the statistic that people come through doorways a frightening three hundred and sixty times a day; what's more with younger people – the target ABC1s – the figure almost doubled to some seven hundred. This was clearly a lucrative market that remained untapped.

Paddy Zellwacker was really the only young exponent of the Knock, Knock and so was heavily feted by the TV bigwigs. Problem was he only had four. Four Knock, Knock jokes. And all of them, except one, were already in the public domain. He would open with 'Isabel' (Isabel necessary on a bicycle), then move on to the classic 'Ivor' (Ivor let me in or I'll kick the door down), building to 'Dr' (Dr who? Yes), which slightly subverted the form. Then to finish he would return to

---

2 C4's *The Priory* was presented by Jamie Theakston and Zoe Ball and what was good about it was that the presenters were not afraid to laugh at themselves.

the 'Ivor' joke but with a twist (Ivor ready let you in), turning it into a kind of running gag, which can be popular.

Even on a good night, with laughs, that was maybe twenty minutes of material. It's obvious to you and me that Paddy needed to be allowed to grow, to serve his apprenticeship on the punishing club circuit, but Zevon said to him, 'When you're hot, you're hot,' and booked him out on a punishing course of meal meetings with TV executives. He was up to fourteen meals a week. Some days he would arrive at the Ivy for breakfast with Yentob (BBC1), finish that, walk round the block and back in for brunch with Mrs Vashy Varmint (BBC2), round and out and back for lunch with Kervil Garment (ITV), out and round the back for high tea with Rictus Sardonicus (Channel 4) then finally out, round, and back for dinner with Paul Raymond (Channel 5). His seat at the Ivy never had a chance to cool down. In fact staff had been forced to treat it with a flame retardant (Paddy had an unusually warm behind anyway, another by-product of toxic meat, and he'd learnt from bitter experience that when visiting a zoo or safari park to give the baboon enclosure a wide berth).

Sadly all these lunches had meant that he'd ballooned to a massive 23 stone.

Eventually Kevil signed him up for two series of twenty-three, to go out peak time on a Saturday: *Knock, Knock, It's Paddy Z* (Kevil felt that 'Zellwacker' was too complicated for the ITV audience) and the highly prestigious *'N Audience with Paddy Z* (they dropped the 'A' as a nod to club culture).

At the end of the first recording Paddy was surprised by Michael Aspel and the *This Is Yo' Life* team (they dropped the 'ur' in a silly typographical error), a mean attempt by the BBC to carve out a little Zellwacker food-pie for themselves.

The producers had decided at a *This Is Yo' Life* production meeting that Paddy's real family were far too stilted in their delivery of the amusing anecdotes that they had been provided with to make it on to the programme and they were hastily re-cast. Jean Boht played Mum, Ben Kingsley, Dad and, in an odd example of life imitating art, the McGann brothers (minus Paul) played his extended family. He was only twelve remember (just twelve in fact) so the celebrity count was bumped up by people who had been on adjoining tables to his at the Ivy (a very moving piece to camera by Tamara Beckwith) and three of the four surviving Doctor Whos for no real reason other than it was great telly (Knock, Knock! Who's there? Yes, it is!). To cap it all, enter Paul McGann – introduced as, 'a man who might possibly be your brother', taking the number of Doctor Whos up to four.

Needless to say there was a big fight backstage when the real Zellwacker family, who'd been allowed to watch it in the green room, picked a fight with the dummy family. Then Schnorbitz, first in the queue for the buffet, dribbled over the food as he searched for the king prawns (everyone knew there were twelve hidden there somewhere). Henry Kissinger (a late booking) managed to pull him off and they rolled around on the floor for four hours – people thought they were just playing before Kissinger, hoarse from shouting, managed to get the upper hand, cowed the huge dog, then rode him round the hospitality suite at Teddington Studios. It was midnight before Henry left, his hair gelled flat with St Bernard slobber, and suit covered in fluff.[3]

Then the Doctor Whos had a scrap over who was the last person to have the sonic screwdriver 'because it's not working any more' and poor Paddy was stuck in the middle of it even more confused about his life than before.

Well, the *Knock!Knock!* show failed to pull in the ratings and Garment quickly moved it up the time slot, first to half-past

[3] This is the third and final human riding an animal in this book. Can you name the other two?

ten at night, then to two o'clock in the morning, then finally, in a stroke of genius, to Saturday teatime on BBC1 against *Blind Date*.[4] The show was not recommissioned.

It seems crazy now but no one ever really asked the question, Do people really want to see a 23-stone, unnaturally black, hot butted, magnetic, inexperienced twelve-year-old tell four Knock, Knock jokes that they've heard before?[5] Sometimes it's a good idea just to step back from these things for a moment.

4 Even with a guest appearance from Brian Gould – in his heyday.
5 I know you're thinking, 'Yes, I would actually' but you're not the typical ITV1 crowd.

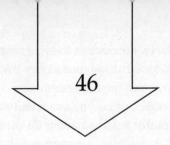

46

Let Down By Your Own Convenience

Manny Durban and Jonathan Aitken[1] stood back and admired the brand new Ford Open Prison Visitors' Centre and gentlemen's toilets.[2] In as far as they could stand back and admire it, being in it.

That will be one of the first things I will do when I've escaped, thought Manny. Stand back and admire the centre properly.

They had both learnt so much from the experience. Not just about joinery and building techniques – although both were now surprisingly confident about putting in a suspended ceiling. Jonathan particularly felt he had a lot to thank the centre for; he had found his true vocation, his Divas of Rock Show – although he could already see that he might outgrow the rock thing and want to broaden it to other types of music. He'd sketched out the skeleton of a sister show, Gentlemen of Rock. The business brain of the 'old Jonathan',

1 Yes, we're back with them now.
2 While we were diverted, they finished building it.

the pre-Divas of Rock Jonathan, could see that using just two knees limited the amount he could do with a presentation, and that one day he may have to take on additional staff.

I'm sure as you read this your own mind is racing, as mine is, with the possibilities of this new entertainment format. 'It could rival the Internet,' Jonathan said out loud, then blushed and looked down at his shoes embarrassed at this public display of enthusiasm.

Manny, too, had learnt a lot about himself from the visitors' centre project. For the first time he'd enjoyed the close company of men working in a team.[3] He'd enjoyed choosing all the various fittings and could see in himself a little of his father, the great artificial foot pioneer. As soon as he got out, he vowed, he would try to broaden his horizons, maybe take more time off work, do an evening class in something. At the same time he was aware that he hadn't got quite as much out of it as Jonathan, which left him sort of vaguely annoyed.

'You don't think that only putting in a gents' toilet will raise suspicion?' said one of the murderers, who had just finished buffing some chrome work on the automatic doors.

'It's a chance we have to take,' replied Manny. The new bogs were already putting a strain on the prison effluent system, and that coupled with a world shortage of toilet bowls had meant they'd had to make the difficult decision to dispense with the ladies' toilets and just put up a sign saying LADIES THIS WAY, which led any women bursting to go round to a doorway with OUT OF ORDER written on it. They all knew it would hold the girls off for a short while only but hopefully it would buy the lags enough time to escape.

As it was the gents' was far from ideal. The three urinals fed into one single-gauge outflow pipe where there should have been three separate ones (or one maxi-gauge one) and

3 A bit like the buzz I guess you get appearing on a show like *Gladiators*.

the sit-down in the cubicle fed into a macerator powered by three blackbirds on a treadmill chasing a worm suspended an inch in front of their beaks.[4]

With the rest of the centre finished to such a high standard it was a pity that it should be let down by the conveniences, but it was important the escape committee remembered why they had built the visitors' centre in the first place. To escape. Okay, if they got a first-class visitors' centre and other contracts out of it, so be it.

Manny and Jonathan wandered round the exhibits. They were all deliberately vague because there wasn't really that much to say about the prison. The trick was to present them in a form that you see in these types of places. For instance, 'The History of Ford Open Prison' exhibit: a large laminated surface with an etching of a Victorian street scene and some flints under glass had little to do with the text, which read 'Ford Open Prison was opened some time in the early eighties by someone fairly prominent, probably the then Home Secretary'. Then there was a picture of Whitehall and a man in a frock coat. They had padded out the section with pictures of events from the 1980s such as Normski, the New Romantics, a line of cocaine and a rolled-up old twenty-pound note.

A bit further on you could push a button that lit a red light over a prostitute sitting in a shop window under the title 'Vice in the Eighties'.

No one had really spent a lot of time on the content of the visitors' centre but, like the ladies' toilets, it was designed merely to give the desired effect.

Just then in darted 'Thumbs' McDuff (so-called because as soon as he got out, he was planning a hitchhiking holiday around the Algarve). He was out of breath, panting.

'Sir, Mr Durban, sir!'

4 Lady Aitken had smuggled the worm in completely by accident.

'Yes, Thumbs, what is it?'

'Heard a rumour; the governor's been going through his paperwork and has submitted plans for a conservatory.'

'Conservatory? How does that affect us?'

'This is the bit he is planning to have it added on to!'

'Right!' said Manny stiffening. 'Could you perform Divas of Rock tonight, Johnnie?'

Jonathan Aitken visibly blanched. 'Well, if I had to, I suppose . . .'

'Good man,' said Manny. 'Right, men. We launch tonight!'

The whole prison was buzzing; Manny and a few of the murderers put up some little posters advertising Jonathan's show: *Divas of Rock Returns With Special Additional Guest*.

There was huge speculation amongst the prison officers about who the special guest might be, but Jonathan had kept his forearms carefully covered. He sat alone in his room with his compass and bottle of ink putting the finishing touches to Bonnie T. It was such short notice; he hoped the bleeding would stop by curtain up.

A large bundle of leaflets flopped into the driver's cabin and the prison governor leant back and had a look. *Ford Open Prison Visitors' Centre . . . to open tonight.* The paper was glossy and looked authentic enough. He made a quick call to the local planning department and, yes, it was all above board. Damn those stuffed shirts in Whitehall, why did they never inform him of these things? Wait a minute . . . tonight? But that's show night . . .

Protocol dictated that he should go to the opening but he couldn't possibly miss Divas, they'd all be talking about it the next day; God knows it was hard enough to be the boss without not being able to enjoy mutual recreational activities together. This Divas of Rock Show was just the sort of thing he needed to help him to bond with the workforce – and the inmates for that matter – and why should he be forced to miss it just because those prats in top brass had not told him about the visitors' centre? No, he would attend the show and then drift over to the visitors' centre opening later on. He'd met Jimmy Cricket before anyway.

These were exactly the thought processes that Manny had predicted. One of the murderers (actually, to be fair, manslaughter; a hit and run)[5] had taken the decision to advertise that the centre was to be opened by Jimmy Cricket. He'd reasoned that a celebrity would be booked for such an opening and they all agreed that Jimmy Cricket was perfect for two reasons: one, that although everyone liked Jimmy he had opened the solitary-confinement block only two months earlier so he was unlikely to be much of a draw (particularly when put up against Divas of Rock), and two, he had a very distinctive outfit that could easily be replicated. The inappropriately labelled wellington boots and funny hat were a signature; they said at a glance 'Jimmy Cricket'. Someone immediately started adapting the necessary.

5 And the bloke he'd killed had been a drug dealer, so it sort of didn't count.

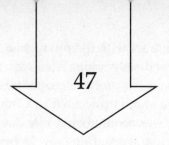

47

The Tower of Dength

Somehow Deng had managed to roll Joan Lewis on to her front and force her up on to her feet; they were now making slow and unsteady progress down Oxford Street. Joan had resigned herself to the trip and was now concentrating on just getting him there. She glanced at her watch; it was nearly half-past six. Her partner John[1] would be wondering where she was.

She approached Oxford Circus and glanced down to see what was on at the Palladium: Jim Dale in *Digby the Giant Dog*. Is that still playing? she wondered. She remembered seeing it as a girl and being so disappointed. It wasn't a giant dog at all; it was a normal-sized dog but it was always placed in the foreground with the actors in the background so it appeared big. Everyone was disappointed and a number had left. The promoter had been clever; in the small print on the back of the tickets it said that they weren't allowed to discuss the show with any third party. By buying the tickets they had

1 Never knowingly undersold! Yes, he was sick of that joke, let me tell you.

entered into a contract with the production. So word never got out about how disappointing it all was, and it did great business, though no one ever went to see it twice.

Joan and Deng came up to Oxford Circus; they passed Shelleys[2] and she was about to carry him down Regent Street to Tower when it happened: Deng saw Debenhams.

'Wah!' he gasped, his mouth gaping open in amazement. 'Wah!'

'You want to go in?' said Joan, gesturing with her free hand.

Deng nodded. Joan headed up the steps and carried him through the huge glass swing doors and into the family-orientated department store. Deng nodded to the security guards and stared in wonder at the light-fittings department.

What kind of king lives in a palace like this? he wondered.

'Deb-en-hams,' explained Joan, leading him around from wall fittings to central-ceiling lights to standard and bedside lamps. She had to admit the display was pretty good and felt she was only seeing it properly for the first time. You know what it's like, you have these things on your doorstep but you never really appreciate them. She suddenly felt proud to be British.

'Up,' she said, leading Deng up the escalator. She'd grown quite fond of the old boy over the course of their fabulous journey together. She looked at his shabby regulation Communist Party garb and thought, perhaps I'll buy him something. She felt her purse. She was only a rep for a pharmaceutical company and was not exactly loaded but she'd like to get something for the old man.

She helped him up into the menswear department and straightaway his attention was grabbed by the mock-designer

2 The shoe shop, not the shop selling memorabilia of the sitcom *Shelley* starring Hywel Bennett.

gear in the teens' section. He picked up a pair of blue jeans with heavy embroidery on the pockets and trouser legs; there was also a big white smock he liked, and he pulled a neckerchief off a rail and added that to his pile of stuff and finally a big, brown floppy beret. Joan looked in her purse; there was no way she could afford all that but Deng was now in one of the cubicles getting changed. When he came out in the tight jeans, the white smock tucked in over his ample belly, the fancy neckerchief, all crowned by the huge floppy felt beret, Joan didn't know whether to laugh or cry. He just looked fantastic! It was not a combination you would ever pick out yourself but it was just so him! Deng had a great big grin on his face; he looked like a million dollars, and what's more he knew it.

'I will buy this,' said Joan, indicating the smock.

'Wah?' said Deng. Going to leave.

'No, Deng, you can't leave, you have to pay for the goods.'

'Wah?'

'I will buy the smock as a present, but you must pay for the rest. Where's your money?' she said, putting her hand into the tight warm fabric of his pocket. Deng blushed, the new outfit was working, he thought. He leant forward and tried to kiss her. She pulled away but her hand was trapped in his pocket and as he headed towards the door, he dragged her with him.

'Stop! My hand!' she said.

'Excuse me, is there a problem here?'

Deng was stopped in his tracks by the tall security guard in fine Debenhams livery. Just then the sales assistant from teenware caught up with them carrying Deng's old clothes. 'Thank goodness you've stopped them; they haven't paid for the clothes, Brian.'[3]

3 Could be Brian Gould, but probably not.

'Well?' said Brian, the security guard. Deng flashed a look at Joan like a wounded animal as if to say 'Help me'.

'I wish to start a Debenhams card account.' She could hardly believe her own voice.

'Good,' said Brian. 'Step this way and Bob will sort out the paperwork.'

When they got out of Debenhams, Joan had crouched and allowed Deng to climb on to her back almost as if she were in a trance. They set off down Regent Street towards Tower Records. She was thinking back to when she had put her hand in Deng's pocket and was confused. She shouldn't be feeling these emotions, but she had liked it! Dammit, she wanted to put her hand in his pocket again!

As they approached Sock Shop he indicated to her to slow down, and she took up a gentle trot, coming to a stop then carrying him in and taking him round the racks of socks. Deng looked through the racks, activating the musical ones. The short ones were the latest single releases: Travis's new one, Modjo's latest; the longer socks were the albums: Phil Collins's *Face to Face*, Russ Conway's *Even More Party Hits*, *OK Computer* by Radiohead – all titles that you couldn't get over in China but nothing particularly special. He scooped the lot up and dumped them in his basket. Then he saw it. Yes, that was the answer: 'Rudolph the Red-Nosed Reindeer'.

Great! Problem solved. He took two pairs of the seasonal hit and placed them on top of the others in his basket. That should keep the old girl quiet, he thought.

'That's three hundred and forty pounds, please, sir,' said the sales assistant.

'Ahem,' Deng coughed, and looked at Joan. He was saving his holiday money for Tower.

'I'd like to open a Sock Shop card account, please,' she said. And this time she said it gladly.

Onwards down Regent Street; Joan had got her second wind,

after all it was not far now. They looked across at Gap for Kids and could see Jonathan Ross's wife struggling to force Bradley Walsh into a pair of short trousers as Brian Conley looked on.

It was ten-thirty before they made it into Tower Records. Joan had lost all track of time but had been able to phone John from a phone box.

'Can't talk now, John,' she said, Deng leaning over her shoulder, his face pressed against the handset. 'But I won't be home until late.'

At the other end John could hear the soft breathing of someone else as she talked. 'I wish that boss of hers would get off her back,' he said as he hung up. If only he knew!

She discharged Deng outside Tower and he walked up to the doors gingerly. The trip had taken so long, could it live up to his huge expectations? Joan suddenly felt at a loss as to what to do. She looked at her watch. If she got her skates on she could be home in an hour. She stood watching as the little Chinese man headed up the steps. She felt for him; he seemed so vulnerable on his own. She decided to wait. Well, Tower closed at midnight so he couldn't be more than an hour and a half – she looked up at his portly frame disappearing through the double doors and into his audio retail nirvana.

Deng whistled out loud as he saw the racks and racks of CDs and started straightaway snuffling down amongst them looking for Status Quo stuff. He'd gone past about ten racks and hadn't seen any and had started to feel a lump in his throat as if he were about to cry. 'Can I help you?' said a member of staff, a young girl carrying a large bundle of CDs in her arms.

'Status Quo?' asked Deng, opening his hands in a query type of pose, which added to the drama.

'Ah, yes, come with me.' Deng jumped on her back, taking her by surprise completely, but she bent over and twisted her frame and Deng slid slowly off and on to the floor.

'No!' she said, 'not that!' He seemed to understand this time (either that or he was tired of fighting). The girl led him along the rock and pop CD racks, past Sinitta, Sneaker Pimps, Stakka Bo – and there they were: four Status Quo CDs.[4] Deng looked at the rack, went through the four, then scratched his head and went through them once more.

'Everything okay?' said the girl.

'More!' said Deng.

'I'm afraid that's all we've got in stock.'

'MORE!' roared Deng.

This time the girl ran off. Deng grabbed handfuls of CDs and started throwing them about the place. The cases smashed to the floor, many with their tiny hinges broken or fronts cracked. 'More! MORE!' he shouted, spinning around into the Stealers Wheel display, knocking it over.

He reached down, grabbed the base of one of the CD racks and tried to pull it over, succeeding only in increasing his frustration as the racks were all securely bolted to the floor. People were staring at him, but he had that wild look in his eyes that said 'Don't mess with me'.

Joan could hear a commotion coming from the inside of the store and guessed it was probably Deng, long before the first police car arrived. Her first reaction was to head on into the store to see if she could help her new friend. She could see the heads of the crowd in rock and pop and pushed towards them.

As she forced her way through the grunge-addled teens and folk-infested foodies, she saw Deng. He was stripped to the waist now. She gasped to see his Quo tattoos, impressive in their scale if not their execution. He was taking CDs and breaking them. Just breaking them up in his bare hands. The

4 1979's *Whatever You Want*, 1983's *Back to Back*, 1984's *12 Gold Bars, Vol. 2*, 1986's *In the Army Now*.

guards tried to restrain him but many of the audience egged him on. He took the sharp jagged edge of a T'Pau CD and cut a deep line across his chest. Blood spurted down his pale sweaty body. A security guard wrestled him to the floor. They heard the sirens outside.

At this point Joan was pushed into a bargain bucket of hits of the seventies by various artists. She tried to get back up but her ample rear was held fast in the bucket and she watched helplessly as Deng was manhandled out of the shop rolled up in bubble wrap.

Needless to say there was a huge press presence. Flash pounded the air like ignited magnesium in a glass bulb. They all knew it was Deng Xiaoping but no one could make out his face. The bubble wrap was doing its job. Inside the wrap Deng could make out rough figures, could hear the crowd, though muffled. It was all just one wash of blunted stimuli, his principal emotion being disappointment. He just wanted to get home. Not to the bed and breakfast, to China.

As Tokwan stepped forward, David Yip recognised him immediately. 'Your friend needs to rest, I think,' said David, lapsing into Cantonese.

'He has followed the Quo for many years, sir; you understand, don't you?' answered Tokwan, still in his pyjamas.

'I understand. Use my car to get him out of here.'

Tokwan helped Deng into the passenger seat of a bottle-green Renault Clio, walked round to the driver's side, climbed in, turned the key in the ignition and set off back to Walthamstow. They drove in silence. Tokwan wondered how this would affect their relationship. He suspected that it could only worsen things between them and he had already started planning to go into hiding when they got back to China.

He muttered words of comfort to Deng who sat motionless in his bubble-wrap world. Tokwan flicked the radio dial to Radio 2 and quickly off again but not before the distinctive strains of Status Quo blared through the little hatchback: 'And here we are and here we are and here we go . . .'

Deng rocked back in his seat and let out a howl like a wounded animal.

Yip spent the rest of the night on the phone to the editors of the dailies getting them to suppress the story. After a short while he felt the bulky presence of the Home Secretary at his side.

'Need a hand there?' said Willie, settling down beside him. 'I couldn't sleep.' The truth was that despite the new bird in his life, when he closed his eyes he still saw Helen.

Joan slept the night in the bargain bucket in Tower Records; the fire brigade were only able to cut her out at first light. To this day she occasionally calls out his name in her sleep and in her dreams imagines she can still feel the warm flannelette of his pocket.

Tokwan and Deng pulled up outside their bed and breakfast at half-past two in the morning. The door was open and Mrs Lamb stood there, arms folded, silhouetted in the doorway. Tokwan helped Deng out of his bubble-wrap housing and walked him up to meet her. The stern look melted to one of concern as she saw Deng's injuries. She'd guessed it was him from the news reports.

'Come on, you two,' she said. 'Early start tomorrow. I'll make us a cup of tea,' and she led them indoors.

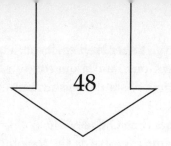

48

U-hu! I'm Over Here

' And I will attempt to prove to you today that that
... Post-it Note should have been more sticky.' Carly
closed her A5 exercise book and sat down. She felt her opening address had gone well.

She'd elected to go for trial by jury and there had been
some delay due to the Post-it Note manufacturers objecting to
certain jury members. They'd rejected one because he was
wearing a wig and he'd refused to reveal what adhesive he'd
used to adhere it; ditto the lady with dentures. Another
member of the jury wearing an 'I love Pritt Stick' T-shirt had
been asked to leave.

The initial round of questions and answers had gone pretty
well, Carly thought. She was almost enjoying the theatre of
the whole thing: the lawyers in their wigs, the judge with his
long robes. It had been such a long road to this day that she
felt relieved that at last the case was being heard.

Mentally she'd spent the potential winnings a thousand
times. She'd decided she was going to split it four ways, after
she'd paid her ferry fare off Sheppey. A quarter she would

keep, a quarter to go to her brother Zevon, a quarter to be put into trust for her Gonk, and a quarter to set up a fighting fund to help victims of similar miscarriages of adhesive justice.

'Call Miss Bernardine O'Casey!'

Bernardine seemed uneasy as she took the stand, and initially answered her questions to the window then knocked over a glass of water.

Carly looked over at the judge. At his feet was a bag and Carly could see some loose bits of wrapping paper and a birthday card, then blanched as she saw a full four-piece gift set of Fabergé's Brut For Men. It was his birthday. He was emitting a new scent. What kind of justice was this?

It didn't take long for the Post-it Note lot to wangle out of Bernardine that she had been blind from birth and that she had no idea what a Post-it Note was, let alone what it looked like. It did not look good for Carly. It was quite clear that she'd got her friend to lie for her.

The Post-it Note lawyers sat back in their dugout and looked over at Carly in hers, smug grins breaking out across their faces. Then they called their first witness.

'We wish to call local businessman, James Cockle.'

'Call James Cockle!' said the clerk, and who should stroll up to the witness box but none other than Mr Cockle himself. There was a gasp from the jury as he took the stand.

Cockle, older yet sleeker, now proceeded to testify that he had seen the Post-it Note on the trawler door when he'd been to sell cockles down at the docks some eight hours after it was supposed to have fallen off.

'Carly, do you wish to cross-examine?' said the judge.

The evidence against her was overwhelming and she was cursing herself for bringing the case in the first place. She had never really been sure if the Post-it Note had fallen off or not; she'd just created the scenario in her mind and the obsessive side of her brain had made her see it through. She had no useful questions. Why prolong it any longer than necessary?

'No, m'lud, no questions.'

The judge's summing up left little doubt where his sympathies lay and, without actually saying the case should be dismissed, the jury was sent out with a pretty clear idea of the verdict he was looking for.

They were back in ten minutes. Just long enough to eat the crisps and biscuits laid on by the judiciary.

'Have you reached a unanimous verdict?'

'We have.'

'How do you find the defendants, Post-it Notes?'

'Guilty!' cried the foreman. 'Guilty, Carly!' he shouted, adding Carly's name. The members of the public in the courtroom were up on their feet cheering, Mr Cockle was jostled as he left, Carly was carried shoulder-high through the public gallery.

The scars were still deep regarding Mr Cockle. In any other town Post-it would have won; it was an open and shut case. But not in Sheppey. In Sheppey they look after their own.[1]

---

1 But not their old folk – most choose to put their elderly relatives into residential care, much as they do on the mainland.

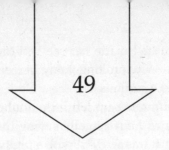

49

Ham Rolls

It was only two hundred yards from the hotel to the Hollywood cinema where the new Mother Teresa film *M. T. The Extra Celestial* was being premiered, but the studio had insisted that Estrakhan take a limo. As Estrakhan was helped in by the doorman, Nosegay was already ensconced in the back seat. He'd been out in the car all day, riding around town making calls from it, taking photos of himself lying across the back seats. It was pathetic.

Estrakhan nodded a grudging greeting to Nosegay who was fiddling with the TV, which showed a fuzzy picture of a news anchorman in a bad wig. The TVs in the back of these things never worked; it stood to reason as you're not supposed to have a TV in a car. Estrakhan turned and flicked out his back leg, terminally damaging the TV set.

Nosegay swallowed his annoyance. Why was Essie always so crabby? Most pigs would give their right arm to be shown the sort of privileges he'd been shown.

Estrakhan sat looking moodily out of the window. They were stuck in traffic and had not yet left the hotel forecourt.

Essie scratched his neck. The shirt collar was uncomfortable, and he didn't care for the dinner suit either – even if it was Gucci. Pigs weren't supposed to wear clothes – if they were, God would have given them proper shoulders. No, it was all part of this humanisation thing that Nosegay and Zevon had dreamt up. Give human qualities to a pig and people will treat it with greater respect and, more importantly, pay a human-sized fee.

Estrakhan, his nose pressed up against the smoked-glass window, sighed, blowing two flares of moisture up it. He'd made up his mind that morning about the sitcom. He had decided to walk. Tell them to stuff it. Okay, he knew he was maybe burning some bridges here and he didn't actually have too much other work lined up, but sometimes you had to take a risk to effect a change. He hadn't told Nosegay yet but he smirked as he imagined the look on his face when he did.

'Ter-her,' Estrakhan chuckled.

'What are you laughing about?' asked Nosegay.

Estrakhan shook his head as if to dismiss it.

'No, come on, tell me; what's so funny?'

Once again Essie shrugged it off, his lack of shoulders reducing the impact.

'You're laughing at my outfit, right?' Nosegay was completely paranoid about his appearance. Maybe because Zevon was so confident about his. Oh sure, Zevon's taste was outlandish; I mean, completely so – he could easily turn up to an important business meeting in a pair of tartan plus fours, pink roll-neck and camouflage hankie knotted on to his head – but at least he could carry it off. Nosegay, on the other hand, always looked like his mum had dressed him.[1]

Where can you go wrong with evening wear? You ask.

---

[1] Often his mum had dressed him, or at least laid out the outfit on his bed for him the night before.

You're right, the men's dinner suit is a classic, but Nosegay had to fiddle with it. He was turned out not in a black suit but a very dark chocolate-brown one, bell-bottomed trousers with a high waistband digging up into his armpits, a white collarless shirt and a great big, brown bow tie that wrapped round his neck and up behind his ears. He looked ridiculous and he had a pretty good idea he did, but, and here's the problem, he wasn't quite sure. A little tiny part of him thought maybe, just maybe, he looked fantastic.

Nosegay turned his face to the window, trying to catch his reflection, but instead seeing the traffic. Traffic. Good job he'd allowed plenty of time. The premiere was due to start at seven and it was – he looked at his watch – half-past two. That gave them a clear five hours. Nosegay settled back on to the banquette and nodded off. He drifted in and out of a sleepy haze, periodically half opening his eyes and seeing the pig in its dinner suit, the traffic outside, the crowds of people. Half-past four: they had now left the hotel driveway; half-past five: they'd rounded the corner and could see the cinema; half-past six: . . . what? Half-past six! At this rate they were gonna miss it! Nosegay snapped to and kicked Estrakhan.

'No, Tristan! Get Siegfried to help you!' blurted Essie, waking up.[2]

'We gotta get out here and walk,' said Nosegay. 'Driver, stop the car, we'll walk from here.'

'You'll what?'

'We'll walk.'

'Sorry, can't allow that,' said the driver, flicking on the central locking. 'If something was to happen to you I'd be liable; the studio would have my nostrils for pen restrainers. No, we'll only be another hour and a half.'

'We haven't got that sort of time. Just let us out.'

2 Yes, it was that *All Creatures Great and Small* dream again, but then you knew that, I hope.

'Sorry, can't do that.'

With that Nosegay grabbed the shattered TV and, pulling hard, yanked it off its bracket and lugged it out of the window. He then forced himself through the hole, snagging his new suit in several places.

'Come on, Essie!' He beckoned to Estrakhan, who was still reeling from the bad dream. Estrakhan shook his head. There was no way he was—

Nosegay had him by the collar now and was yanking at him. He was half in and half out of the car, his hindquarters stuck fast.

The driver indicated to pull over. 'Okay, okay!' He helped Nosegay open the door, cursing him under his breath. They pulled Estrakhan back into the vehicle, then the driver opened the door and let them go. Nosegay sweetened the situation with a roll of hundred-dollar bills to cover the window, the TV and to buy the driver some root beer or whatever it is these people drink over here.[3]

Estrakhan was in a bad mood now as he was led along the sidewalk towards the cinema, fifty yards away. His suit was torn in a couple of places and his skin, friable from the lack of mud, bled into the soft fabric where he had been cut. Nosegay's face was flushed and sweaty, his hair all messed up as he strode on. It didn't take long for members of the public to notice the pair and their progress was further hampered by the pawing of the pap-minded populace eager to lay hands on the great Estrakhan.[4]

As they reached the steps Nosegay forced Estrakhan to turn and wave. The old pig forced a smile through gritted

3 Root beer, Budweiser, Bud Lite, Coors, Coors Lite, coffee, Coca-Cola, Diet Coke, Pepsi, Pepsi Max . . . some distilled water.
4 Unable to sign autographs, Estrakhan placed a wet nose into an ink pad held by Zevon, which he then pounded onto the page, or in some cases body part.

teeth. He was vaguely aware of a figure stepping forward and getting too close; he felt the hot breath in his pig's ear.

'You're ham,' said Bruvose Haintree, nuzzling the muzzle of his son's gun hard against the great beast's torso. Trigger. Bam! Bam! Bam!

The scene in front of Essie's eyes span slowly, vaguely floaty; he knew what had happened. His mouth, unable to emit a cry, tasted the sweet ferrous flavour of blood. He saw the red-carpeted steps in front of him and thought momentarily of how the blood would not stain. In his mind's eye flashed Lennon, Kennedy, Luther King, Estrakhan.

As he went down he hoped it was the end.

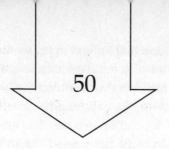

50

Dream Team

'Outta my way! Get away from him! Give him some room to breathe. Don't move him! Let me get an airway into him. Oxygen *now*! There's no pulse – get the defib! Fifty joules! Stand back! Adrenalin. Quickly! What we got? Okay, a hundred joules. Atropine now! Wait, there's an output! Get him in the ambulance!'[1]

The air ambulance was there in a couple of minutes and the paramedics had all but brought Estrakhan back from the jaws of death on the pavement.

Nosegay had sat with him as he was ferried to Cedars Sinai Hospital, Palm Springs.

'You're gonna be fine, Essie, hang on in there. We're getting you to a hospital.'

For the first time since the shooting Estrakhan opened his eyes. 'Oh Christ, still here?' he grunted, seeing Nosegay.

'That's it, Essie, fight it.'

The first bullet had passed straight through him, avoiding

1 I had a T-shirt with this on, once.

all major organs, and had lodged in his scrotum (from then on giving him a kind of legendary macho status), the second ripped through his liver (but avoided the hepatic artery and vein) and lodged in the gall bladder. The third did all the damage and did not end up in a pouch of any kind. It entered under the seventh right rib, passed through the right lung, entered the inferior vena cava (the main fat vein draining bloodfood into the heart); slowing down, it had rebounded off the sternum and embedded itself in the wall of the left ventricle of the heart. That's what had caused the cardiac arrest.[2]

Estrakhan's vision clouded once again. 'He's circling the drain!' muttered a paramedic charging up the defib. He picked up the phone to the cardiac surgery team.

At the same time Nosegay phoned his friends at the *National Enquirer* and *Weekly World News*. 'Yes, they're taking him to Cedar Sinai. See you there. Say, Ed, could you get me a Big Mac? Sure, no problem, yeah Big Mac Meal, whatever; no, don't scale it up. I know, it's just that with Essie so ill I'm not that hungry. I don't think I could manage a large meal.'

Once at the hospital Estrakhan was rushed on a gurney straight to the operating theatre. Nosegay scrubbed up and accompanied him.

Mr Pumphrey-Pepper, Cedar's top cardiac surgeon, strode in. Straightaway he was in control. 'Blood pressure?'

'Seventy over thirty.'

'Hmm. Entry wound?'

'Right seventh, P-P.'

'Hmm.' P-P looked at the X-rays. 'But you're happy to continue?'

'What choice do we have?'

'Scalpel!' And he was away: the skin was open, and he was

2 I mean I'm guessing here, but that's what it looked like from the NMR.

starting to split the sternum when he looked up and saw for the first time Estrakhan's face. He walked up to the head and turned it in his hand to face him, just to make sure.

'A pig? This is a pig?'

'Yeah?'

'But I'm Jewish.'

'He has insurance,' said the intern.

Mr Pumphrey-Pepper hesitated for just a second, shrugged and returned to the job in hand: open-heart surgery on a pig.

Estrakhan was in hospital for three months. At first it seemed that his heart would recover but the damage done by the bullet was too severe and he was placed on the waiting list for a transplant. Zevon and Nosegay had decided to hold out for a human one. It meant a longer wait but they figured pigs don't live as long as humans, so if Estrakhan had a human heart it would mean a longer life (more importantly a longer working life), and, besides, it was a great publicity angle. 'You only fit it once so fit the best . . .' said Zevon, paraphrasing Ted Moult in the old Everest double-glazing ads.

All the major tabloids had run campaigns – Find a Heart for Essie – showing pictures of the hapless pig sat in his hospital bed with tubes coming out of him and forcing a smile (Headline: Tubes Help You Breathe More Easily). Estrakhan himself was so drugged up the whole thing was just a morphine haze; all he knew was that he'd never felt so happy, he just couldn't work out why.

The heart came, ironically, from a paparazzi photographer who had failed to get out of the way of the ambulance transporting Estrakhan from the helipad to Accident and Emergency. Nosegay had seen the whole thing and it seemed to him that the ambulance driver had accelerated and steered into the man. The photographer had only suffered a broken leg and some bruising but while recovering on the ward had died from a mysteriously delivered Harrods food hamper. It seemed the courier had suffocated him by holding a big piece of smoked salmon over his face for a full seven minutes, rendering him brain dead. No matter, Essie's healing chest was reopened and the new heart laced into place.

Estrakhan had got to know the hospital staff pretty well during his stay and was sad to leave; meanwhile he'd finished his eagerly anticipated first novel from his hospital bed on a laptop computer. As a little farewell the staff had squirted mud down the hospital steps by way of a tribute. He left to the usual clanging of the bells of the press scrum.

Nosegay had been by his side throughout. It was funny, before the shooting he'd just seen Estrakhan as a cash cow, a way of making a dollar or two, but as he'd sat with the porcine celebrity and would-be novelist, over the days and weeks and months he had really grown to like him, to understand him. He had been there when they'd pulled the tube out of his throat, had watched as the physiotherapist pummelled his chest to help him to expectorate mucus, and had then learnt how to do the procedure himself. It was Nosegay who had supported Estrakhan's first few steps after the operation, who had emptied the catheter bag when it was full, who had tried to soothe the aching chest scar with his own specially homemade poultices.

It actually took a serious telling-off from the sister on the ward to get him to stop taking on these nursing duties as it was beginning to piss everyone off. His homemade poultices formed, as they were, from a potent mix of Vim, Harpic, Sarson's Malt Vinegar and a squirt of toothpaste to mask the smell, seemed to be slowing down the healing process, and Nosegay was warned to back off or risk being banned. He then chose to sit outside Estrakhan's window playing what he considered to be sweet, restful songs on the flute (mainly 'Annie's Song' by John Denver).

'You're fired,' Estrakhan grunted to Nosegay on the steps

of the hospital. They were his first real words since his mind had begun to clear.

'Uh?'

Estrakhan wrote it out in the mud at his feet. U R FIRED. And with a haughty sniff he trotted off down the steps and into the warm leather banquette of a limousine, its door held open by Mr Padua Craw.

Padua flashed a look of guimpt along the mud trail to Nosegay. He opened the door of his limo wider to let Nosegay see beyond. On the back seat sat Spielberg, Rupert Murdoch, Ron Howard, Sean Connery and Mel Sykes. Dream team.

Nosegay sank to his knees, his mouth open in a scream but no sound came out. The limo was three blocks away before they could hear the wailing. He was crushed.

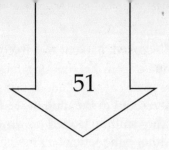

51

Rockshow

Jonathan Aitken paced up and down behind the two towels suspended across his cell, which he was using as stage curtains. He could hear the low hum and hubbub of his audience as he puffed nervously on a can of fly spray.[1] His forearm was still sore from the afternoon's tattooing session. He looked at his watch which formed a belt around Bonnie's waist. Five minutes to go to curtain up. Better get the legs ready.

He pulled up his trouser legs to prepare the shins for performance; it usually involved just a quick wipe with a cloth soaked in surgical spirit. But he took one look at 'his girls' as he referred to them, and almost threw up with fear. Where he had been kneeling, working on the visitors' centre that afternoon, he had created two large blood blisters directly over the faces of his two principal performers. You could just about make out their features through the dark purply-red blotches, but no way were they recognisable as his divas.

1 It killed his plaque, stone dead.

254

'Oh my God!' cursed Aitken. What could he do? He grabbed the compass from his dressing table and jabbed at the blood blisters to release the blood, but as they emptied they still left some colour behind and now throbbed with pain.

'One minute, Mr Aitken.' Thumbs popped his head round the curtain. 'Ready to go?'

'No!' yelled Aitken; he could hear the murmur of the crowd beginning to grow restless. 'Thumbs, look!' He showed Thumbs his messy legs.

'Oh my God, what do you . . . do you wanna cancel?'

'What – and let the boys down?' he said, thinking not only of his audience but also of the escape plan. 'No, the show must go on, Thumbs. Announce the girls!'

With that Thumbs disappeared out front and did his intro.

'Ladies and gentlemen, please meet your Divas of Rock.' The music sprang into the overture: 'Nutbush City Limits' segueing into 'Private Dancer', segueing into 'Steamy Windows' ('Up with your Body Heat. ...!'), a puff of dry ice and . . . 'Ladies and Gentlemen, from the U.S. of A. . . . Miss Tina Turner!'

Aitken lowered Tina Turner shin on to the raised palette that was his stage. There were audible gasps as the inmates caught their first glimpse of the mutant shin puppet.

'Talkin' 'bout Nutbush . . .' Jonathan started to sing but his throat was dry and the words crackled and stuck to his teeth like tartar.

'This ain't the show we got last time!' a voice yelled. 'It looks nothin' like Turner!'

Panicking, Jonathan shouted, 'Advance the tape!' to Thumbs who pudged the fast forward on the cassette player with his finger. He thought maybe he could pull it round if he brought Bonnie on, and started to roll up his sleeve. As he did so his cufflink knocked off the delicate scabs that were just forming over the red-raw tattoo.

He plunged his forearm into the arena but the tape was not far enough ahead and the Sam Fox hit 'Touch Me' struck up.

'Touch me, touch me, I wanna feel your body . . .'

'You're one sick monkey, Aitken!' yelled a screw, and then it started: the slow handclap.

Then a voice above the fray: 'Give him a chance! It's not a professional outfit! It's Mr Aitken trying his best. Besides, what else is there to do?'

It was then that everyone remembered the visitors' centre opening with Jimmy Cricket and with that they were all up on their feet and stampeding out of the door.

Aitken strapped up his legs, put a big plaster over each knee and sat back against the painted walls of his cell. Thumbs came over and put a comforting hand on his shoulder.

'Don't worry, sir, there'll be other shows.'

'Will there, Thumbs? Not for this old lag.[2] His dreams in tatters he turned his face to the wall not wanting Thumbs to see his tears. Then he snapped out of it with a start. 'Wait a minute, if they're not here . . . where?'

Over the other side of the prison, Manny Durban hadn't even bothered to put on his Jimmy Cricket outfit, a move borne out by the turnout; just the murderers and him. He glanced at his watch – half-past eight; in ten minutes it would be time to put up the partition wall, start her up and gently ease the visitors' centre away from the main building.

Not long now, he thought, creating a double image in his mind of his wife Jenny superimposed over his arch enemy, Deng Xiaoping.

'What's that noise, boss?' said Tommy the Neck.

'What's what?'

---

2 He was right and upon his release he signed up for a theology course in an attempt to expunge the whole showbiz bug from his blood.

'That.'

Manny could hear it now, a low thumping, it sounded like . . .

'Blimey! It's them – the governor and the screws!' said another of the murderers, popping his head round the door.

'Stall them!' bellowed Manny, quickly pulling on his inappropriately annotated wellies and funny felt hat, and practising his soft Irish vowels.

Well, they could only delay them for a matter of minutes. 'Mr Cricket is just changing and would prefer not to be bothered' ventured Tommy.

'Outta my way!' yelled the governor as he and two-thirds of his staff piled through the turnstile and into the Ford Open Prison Visitors' Centre.

'That's it, come on in – there's more,' said a soft, lilting Irish voice, and there, to all intents and purposes, was Jimmy Cricket. Manny, only having managed to pull on the Jimmy Cricket hat and boots, had quickly angled the lighting down to put him in silhouette. The screws blinked into the bright lights as 'Jimmy' started his piece.

'Come here, there's more,' he lilted. 'I have great pleasure in declaring this centre open. Thank you and goodnight,' he said and jumped down off the sales counter and scurried off into the gents', locking the door of the cubicle behind him.

'Is that it?' said the governor.

'Well, he'd done a whole lot of stuff before you arrived,' said Tommy.

The screws were immediately disappointed; it seemed that they'd had not one but two great entertainments snatched from under their noses, and what had promised to be a truly great night had fizzled out as quickly as it had started. It was half-past eight now, so most of the evening had already gone; all the West End shows would have started and by the time they'd made it into the town they'd never be able to get a seat in a pub. They just sort of drifted away, kicking over bins as they went. A few went back with the governor for one of his slideshows, but most just hung around the prison corridors cursing under their breath.

Manny sat on the toilet seat, his fingers crossed, listening to the crowd filing out. As the last one left he slipped the bolt and emerged into the centre proper.

'Well?'

'They've gone.'

'Sure?'

'Yes.'

'What happened to Johnnie?'

The murderer told Manny what he knew from snippets he'd caught from the screws.

'Right, put up the partition wall and cast off.'

The murderers set to erecting a partition wall, then chipped away at the mortar binding the visitors' centre to the main prison block. Manny turned the key in the till and the V6 engine roared into life. There was a creaking, wrenching noise and the visitors' centre pulled out into the middle lane of the M4. Manny put it into third gear, released the clutch and accelerated away; through his rear-view mirror he could see the bulk of Ford Open Prison. In one window a grey-haired man, his eyes red from crying, offered a wave.

'So long, Jonathan, and good luck,' muttered Manny, and headed off towards junction 12.

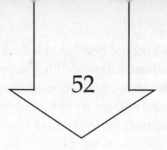

52

Restoring the Status Quo

Deng Xiao and Tokwan Ping made their way through airport security. It took some time as his suitcase of musical socks set off the metal detector, and the customs men decided to search his bag. They insisted on Deng activating each of the socks in turn to check that they were indeed what they appeared to be.

The security area rang out to 'Like A Virgin', a slightly tinnier version than Madonna originally intended but still catchy enough to set the customs officers' feet tapping. Deng followed that up with 'Wake Me Up Before You Go-Go' to keep them on the dance floor. Passing baggage handlers joined in and pretty soon it was a party with DJ Deng. Twenty minutes later, to Deng's dismay, they were starting to drift away. Panicking and misinterpreting the mood completely, Deng activated 'Helter Skelter' sock, a slightly obscure track off the Beatles' *White Album*. People started leaving in droves. He rummaged around in the bottom of his suitcase looking for something to win them back, and in desperation he started up 'Zoom' sock by Fat Larry's Band. All around couples put down their hand luggage and snuggled up for a slow one. Four slow ones followed. Then a fifth. Tokwan nudged Deng and pointed to the clock; just twenty minutes before take-off, if they weren't careful they would miss their plane. Deng waited for the number to finish and then slipped off his 'Almaz' socks by Randy Crawford.

'You've Lost That Lovin' Feeling!' shouted a cleaner, locked in an embrace with a pilot.

'No, no!' said Deng, signalling with his hands that the disco was over.

'Come on! One more!' shouted the pilot. 'I was nearly in there!' he added with a leer.

Deng resorted to a tactic used by discos all over the world when they won't empty. He took from its packet a gaudy unattractive sock and activated it.

> Wassamatter me, hey!
> Got no respect . . .
> Wassamatter you, hey!

Joe Dolce's 'Shaddup You Face' had been available on sock for years.[1]

As the security-area disco started to empty, Deng and Tokwan put the socks back into the suitcase. Deng looked up. There was a commotion over at the departure lounge. He could see a pig trotting through the phalanx of photographers.

Flash!

'Estrakhan, this way! To me!'

Flash!

'Estrakhan, are you back in the UK for good?'

1 But had been discontinued in all other formats in the year 2000 for fear of the millennium bug.

Flash!

The wise pig, looking pale and haggard, grunted his responses, shielded by five burly minders. Padua walked alongside, one arm around him protectively.

'How are you feeling, Essie?'

'He's fine.'

'Is it true that the show has been cancelled due to poor viewing figures?'

'Mr Estrakhan just wants to talk about the book,' barked Padua. 'He is merely back in the UK visiting family and friends. Now, if you'll excuse us . . .'

The posse headed out on to the main concourse where a stretch pig box waited.

In all the hubbub surrounding Estrakhan's arrival no one noticed the two elderly men in denim jackets. Not so long ago the same fuss would have been afforded them. The two faces, one framed by a thick mane of shaggy blond locks, the other shiny on top with fistfuls of long hair scraped back into a ponytail, were once guaranteed to stimulate a similar Pavlovian-style response. They'd had enough of it by now, though, recognised and pursued so many times they were happy to go unnoticed.

Unnoticed by all but Deng Xiaoping. One look and he dropped his wife's precious sock case and ran. As he ran, he let out a low whine. He hit the two men at chest height, knocking them to the ground, and buried his face into their bellies, hugging them, breathing in the heady smells of Rick Parfitt and Francis Rossi of Status Quo.

They were the last smells to reach the smell centre of his brain box. After the events of the past few days the excitement was too much for his flabby, ancient heart, which could now barely keep a chicken alive. He raised himself up on to his haunches, his heart squeaking on for a few more beats; rearing up, he staggered on, the thin, poorly oxygenated blood just about reaching his leg muscles, everything else gradually shutting down. He looked up. He knew he was dying, but the face he pulled was one of utter bliss; his journey over. As the final mist descended, Deng was vaguely aware of a form he recognised, then the painful sting in his face as a size twelve, English artificial foot hit him plumb between the eyes. He felt no more. He fell forward, his ankles pressing against the stainless-steel rim of the baggage carousel, which activated his socks, his brain-bone and muscle-body dying to the strains of 'What You're Proposing' . . . on sock.

'Just supposing, indeed,' chuckled Tokwan to himself, and knowing his death sentence was now lifted, he put on a straw hat and mingled off into the crowd like at the end of the *Silence of the Lambs* film. He wandered past Manny Durban who produced a further false foot as if to strike him, then something told Manny, 'Let him go; you got what you wanted.'

Manny looked up at the departures board. Some crazy misspelling had rendered it not 'Heathrow' but 'Deathrow'. He shuddered; his eyes combed the timetable and, to his complete and utter dismay, he saw his flight had left. He sat down and ordered a skinny latte and Calibre Con Citronie. He felt a warm, familiar arm around his midriff and turned to see Lady Aitken.

'Come on, tiger, leave that. Let's get on the next plane out of here.' They kissed and as Manny pulled away from the chamois-textured lips, he spotted his wife Jenny, arm in arm with that rogue Bradley Hennessy. For a moment he thought about throwing the spare foot at him, then thought again. What was the point? What would it achieve? As long as she was happy. He turned back to his snog-in-hand.[2]

He was distracted again by the sound of weeping; he

2 Which is, as we all know, worth two in the bush.

looked around and there was a portly older man seated at one of the fixed tables outside Burger King, hunched over his burger – could it be?

Big Willy Whitelaw, his bacon double Swiss gone cold, his fries soggy from tears, mumbled over and over to himself, 'But I just don't love Steph, it's Helen I want.'

People stared, and used the tables further up the concourse outside McDonald's. A policeman talked casually into his walkie talkie, the Home Secretary fixed in his gaze.

Somewhere a video recorder turned itself off having just recorded the programme before *Heartbeat*.

Somewhere else a studio exec toyed absent-mindedly with a pen restrainer made from a man's nostrils.

Three months later Mrs Arty Leg-Bourke got the photos back from her Greek holiday showing her in various poses with the deceased Chairman of the Chinese Communist Party.

'Willie?'

That voice? Could it be? Willie looked up, his heart leapt with joy.

'Helen? . . . I . . . what . . . Where's Lord Owen?'

'Forget about him, it's you I want.'

'But how can I be sure? After all I've been through these last days.'

'Can we take it one day at a time?' said the parrot, her voice sounding uncannily like that of Dr Owen.

Willie's mind raced, his face flushed with raw oxygenated blood and he sobbed uncontrollably, tears of happiness and confusion.

Feeling a woman's hand on my shoulder I pulled my eyes away from the melee. I instinctively knew it was Carly. I looked up to Zevon. His face broke into a fat smile, exposing three rotting-chicken pre-molars.

'Carly?' said Zevon.

'Yes, are you flying?'

'Yes, to Leeds,' said Zevon. 'But I've been looking for you everywhere . . . Where. . .?'

'I've been living on Sheppey, the Isle of Sheppey. I told Mum; she had the phone number and address and everything.'

'Doh! Mum, of course!' Zevon slapped his forehead with his hand, dislodging some painted mince. It suddenly dawned on him how he could easily have traced his sister – by talking to one of the two people they had in common: their motherperson. Fourteen years wasted!

'Here's twelve pounds; I won the court case.'

'What court case? How did you get that nosebleed?' he asked.

'I was assaulted in that shop,' she said, indicating River Island. 'They threw me out.'

She looked down at me and with a broad grin handed me an Abbey National savings book. 'And a third for you! I've been looking for you everywhere. Where have you been?'

'I've been looking after him,' replied Zevon.

'Come here,' she said, her arms outstretched, gently lifting me up to her face, my fuzzy green acrylic body hair brushing her chin. She stared into my bug eyes and caressed my black felt beak and feet.

Oh yes, didn't I mention it? I am a Gonk. Carly's Gonk.

And I suppose you're waiting for me to wake up and reveal that this whole thing took place in my 1987 coma year. Well, I got news for you – I don't wake up. I'm still in it.

Zoooooooooooooooooooooooooom![3]

_____

3 I told you so.

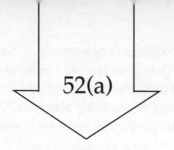

52(a)

Alternative Ending

Deng Xiao and Tokwan Ping made their way through airport security. It took some time as his suitcase of musical socks set off the metal detector, and the customs men decided to search his bag. They insisted on Deng activating each of the socks in turn to check that they were indeed what they appeared to be. Passing over the Madonna socks, the customs officer selected a pair featuring the Isley Brothers.

The security area rang out to 'You've Lost That Lovin' Feeling!' and the customs officer eyed Deng up and down in what looked like a rather suggestive manner.

'Hi, I'm Clive, great taste in music,' he said.

Deng stared back at him blankly and as the sock track finished he pressed the next one, this time it was 'Don't Leave Me This Way' by the Communards.

Deng continued to stare, but Clive took this as a 'lingering look' and placed a crooked finger under one of Deng's armpits and started to tickle him. Deng started to giggle at first, then issued forth a deep throaty laugh before activating the next sock.

'YMCA' by the Village People left Clive the customs officer in no doubt that Deng was cruisin' and he brought his other hand in and started tickling Deng in earnest on the tum tum. Deng had no option but to tickle him back. The two of them rolled around on the floor tickling each other in what was verging on ecstasy. So engrossed were they in the session and so loud their laughter that they were completely unaware of the commotion over at the departure lounge. They exchanged phone numbers and Deng caught his plane back to China. Clive flew over that summer to stay but Mrs Xiaoping took exception to the attention he was paying her husband and initially insisted that he be killed. Deng reluctantly agreed but managed to smuggle his friend out of the country, substituting the body for that of his brother-in-law Tokwan, who Deng had been planning to kill for virtually the entire Yookay trip.

It was a shame that Deng missed the arrival of Status Quo, back on an internal flight after a brief tour of the black country. In fact the sight of Rick Parfitt and Francis Rossi waltzing through the departure lounge created such a furore that no one noticed the arrival of porcine author and ex-TV star Estrakhan the pig. He'd been strip-searched by Clive at customs and so had been delayed; by the time he made it through there was just the one person waiting – the driver laid on by Random House, his publisher.[1] He was on his way to be interviewed by Mariella Frostrup at the Hay-on-Wye literature festival.[2]

By the time Manny Durban had parked the Ford Open Prison Visitors' Centre, Deng Xiaoping was safely airborn. He hadn't considered the Maximum Headroom barrier at

1 Yes, after all the column inches following the transplant they'd hurriedly gone back and made an offer.
2 He wasn't to know that there was no actual hay at the Hay-on-Wye Festival.

Heathrow's short stay car park and had to drive back down the flyover and into the Sofitel Hotel car park to find the twelve empty bays that he needed to take its huge bulk. Tommy the Neck looked up from his bunk.

'I'm going back for him, sir,' he whispered, a look of determination on his face.

'Back, Tommy?'

'For Mr Aitken, sir. It's not right. It wasn't his fault his knees scabbed over. He's all right is Mr Aitken.'

'If that is your wish, then you must go,' Manny had replied. He had nothing but admiration for this felon who had really done nothing wrong other than mow down a pedestrian whilst under the influence of Evo Stik and Tippex thinners. 'What if he takes the act on the road, Tom?'

'Then I'll follow him, sir, I love show business.'

With that Manny flicked the central locking and let himself down on to the tarmac. He looked at his watch and realised he'd missed his appointment with Deng. He felt the weight of the two dense resin feet in his hands and looked up. A jet, flying low having just taken off, thundered over head. Oh well, worth a try, thought Manny and he threw both feet as hard as he could at what he perceived was the first-class section of the plane. The feet ascended, missed the tail of the plane by about forty feet, went over in an arc and descended, hitting Willie Whitelaw as he arrived at the entrance of the Sofitel Hotel, having arranged over the phone to hire the honeymoon suite. He stumbled forward and fell to the floor stone dead. Helen the parrot fluttered up, landed on his hair and gently nuzzled the old guy's face, tiny parrot tears falling in cascades upon the old guy's sideburns.

'Please, no! Not now! Not my Willie!' A bodyguard pulled her off and tried to force her into a Home Office cage. 'No!' she cried, freeing herself from his grip and flying high, ever higher until suddenly she was sucked into the engine of a passing 747, her feathers spewed out of its rear like so much green squid ink on a documentary.[3] Helen and Willie were destined to be together, yes, but in heaven.[4]

Meanwhile, in the airport lounge, I, Carly's Gonk, looked up at the departure board. Some crazy misspelling had rendered it not 'Heathrow' but 'Deathrow'. I shuddered; my eyes combed the timetable and, to my complete and utter dismay, I saw that my flight had left. I sat down and ordered a cappaccino and a Kit-Kat. Then I felt a warm arm around my midriff and turned to see Lady Aitken.

'Come on, tiger, leave that. Let's get on the next plane out of here.' She kissed me and passed her hand under my beak and stroked it.

Somewhere a video recorder turned itself on and recorded *Heartbeat*.

As I walked with Lady Aitken towards the gate I looked back, just as Zevon's sister, Carly, disappeared into River Island. I looked up at Zevon who was chaperoning me.

'I don't suppose I'll ever find my sister,' he said.

'Have you thought about phoning your mother?' I asked.

'Good idea,' he said. His face broke into a fat smile, exposing three rotting-chicken pre-molars.

'Okay?' said Zevon.

'Yes, you?'

'Yeah, it's been fun today hasn't it?' said Zevon.

'Yes, it has,' I replied.

Then I was conscious of something being pulled out of my throat. I took a great lungful of air and blinked away the harsh light, blinking again I could make out a silhouette, another blink and I recognised the form of Zevon.

3 About squids.
4 Subject to the provisos, previously discussed, about whether God and his heaven actually exist.

'You hit your head on the table, you've been in a coma for a year, it's 1988,' he said, managing to fill in pretty much all the blanks in one sentence.

'So why am I dressed like a punk rocker?' I asked.

'Rag week,' said the doctor.

'Rag week.' I chuckled. 'Zoooooooooooooooooooooooom!'[5]

5 The first line of the song made famous by Fat Larry's Band, also available on sock. Hence, there is one less 'o' in it – go on, count them.

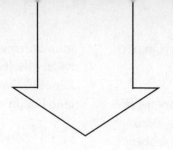

Cast

(If it was ever made into a film)

Carly's Gonk	Sir Ian McKellen
Zevon	John Lydon
Nosegay	Michael Winner
Estrakhan the Pig	Matt Lucas
Deng Xiaoping	David Yip
Tokwan Ping	Gok Wan
David Yip	Burt Kwouk
Margaret Thatcher	Dana
Amanda Holden	Barbra Streisand
Bruvose Haintree	David Soul
Meerox Haintree	Farrah Fawcett-Majors
The Pygmies	(McFly – made small using CGI techniques)
Prince Edward	Ian Hislop
Terry Waite	Brian Blessed
Mrs Waite	Judi Dench
Peter Stringfellow	Paul Weller
Norman Tebbit	Duncan Goodhew
David Owen	Christopher Lee

Ted the Pet Shop Owner   John Barrowman
Diarmuid Gavin   Paddy Kielty
Selina Scott   Renée Zellweger
Mrs Lamb, proprietor of   Jane Fonda
  Tower Records B&B
Andrew Lloyd Webber   CGI
The voice of Andrew   Andy Serkis
  Lloyd Webber
Will Carling   Patrick Mower
Will Carling's Mum   Patricia Routledge
George Bush, Sr   Stephen Merchant
George Bush, Jr   Ricky Gervais
Jeremy Thorpe   Graham Norton
Pierre Trudeau   A.A. Gill
Brian Gould   Brian Cox
Alan Yentob   David Baddiel
Archbishop of Canterbury   Dave Lee Travers
Arty Leg-Bourke   Peter Noone
Bernie the Busker   Ray Quinn
Record producer/highway   Peter Jones
  maintenance man
Mr Cockle   Rick Stein
Mrs Joan Lewis   Michelle Dotrice
Mr Sashki   Sanjeev Bhaskar
Gusley Bolex   Al Murray
Carly   Linda Ronstadt
Carly Simon   Barbara Dixon
Manny Durban   Matt LeBlanc
Jonathan Aitken   Gerald Harper
Tommy the Neck   Tommy Walsh
Jenny Durban   Virginia Wade
Virginia Wade   Valerie Singleton
Bradley Hennessy   Charles Kennedy
Willie Whitelaw   Patrick Moore

The voice of Helen the Parrot	Whoopi Goldberg
Alan Titchmarsh	Albert Finney
Eddie Titchmarsh	Tom Courtenay (reduced in size using CGI techniques)
Lady Aitken	Gayle Porter
Jane Asher	Twiggy
Jonathan Ross	Paul Ross
Jane Ross	Cleo Rocas
Brian Conley	James Gandolfini
Bradley Walsh	Russell Brand
Alanis Morissette	Jane Horrocks
Paddy Zellwacker	Diarmuid Gavin
Padua Craw	Hywel Bennett
Sir Peter Hall	Vic Reeves
Normski	Himself
Carol Vorderman	Nancy Sorrell
Vanessa Feltz	Michelle McManus
Kevil Garment	Howard Jacobson
Dale Winton	Gary Wilmot
Jimmy Cricket	Sean Pertwee
Francis Ross and Rick Parfitt	Journey South

NOTE: I have not cast myself in the film as I would prefer to have a small walk-on cameo such as an audience member during the *Divas of Rock Show* because, actually, I'm quite interested in seeing that show. Also, it frees me up to do other things.

NOTE: The film rights to this book are still available.

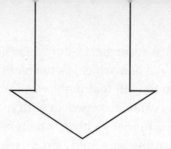

Interview with a Comedian by
Man Foo Hong

About six years ago when the book *Flight From Deathrow* was first published, I put in a request to interview Harry Hill. Unfortunately, at the time, I was told that he was 'Too busy' or alternatively that 'His brain hurts at the moment, we'll get back to you' or, laughingly 'He has lockjaw, subsequent to a bite from a slow worm'. I persisted with my requests: two, three times a year I would put my name into the hat that his PR, Don Raljex, uses to decide such things – but I always drew a blank, coming away with a feeling of being fobbed off. This was particularly odd as I had been a lifelong fan of his TV shows such as *Are You Being Fallen Over?* and *What's Been On TV Recently?*, not to mention his Channel Four shows *Puppet Nite!* and *Let's Get Something Going Here*, and of course his stand-up comedy. I remember so vividly, so long ago now that I daren't even mention it, sitting in a sweaty backroom in some pub in Edinburgh and seeing him for the first time. He came on at such a pace that he pummelled us in the front row with his jerky movements and grunts; it was like nothing I'd ever seen before or since. The suits, the high collar were there – but where now a bald dome sits was thick brown hair which, as the night progressed, fell out in fistfuls. On the bill that night was Damien Darkly – a richly poetic observational comedian with such lines as 'How come things are different to how I thought they would be back then?' Supporting was Sandy Brum, with his face cracking hilarious reflections on the week's news, plus semi-lewd meanderings on his own love life and anatomy. I'd reviewed Harry's shows positively for years; surely he had no reason to blackball me from the press pack?

Then one day, and I swear this is true, a parrot landed on my bird table and spoke to me.

'Call Don, Harry's ready now! Call Don, Harry's ready now!'

And it sounded just like the high-collared buffoon himself. So I rang Don. The interview was arranged without a hitch, and a week later I was ushered into a suite of rooms in London's famous Dorchester Hotel where Don greeted me like an old friend.

Don   Hi. How was your trip down?

MFH   Fine . . . a bit—

Don   Okay, just so you know Harry's a little fragile today.

MFH   Oh?

Don   Yeah, shouldn't matter but just so you know, he had a bit of a bad Christmas. I can't go into details, but best not to bring it up.

MFH   Fine. I wasn't really intending to, to be honest.

Don   Fine. You want some crisps or something, or a drink?

MFH   No, no. I'd better get on with it. Has he recovered from the lava burns?

Don   Lava burns? What?

MFH   You said the last time I asked for an interview that he'd suffered lava burns to his thighs after a trip to Pompeii.

Don	All healed. Good, right well there's the door. Mr Hill awaits, follow me.

I pass through the low doorway and there he is in a gilt Louis XVI chair, his head almost entirely retracted into his collar, just the shiny pink top of it poking forth. Don and I stand watching him for a moment.

HH	You can make anything from plasticine you know.
Don	Ahem!
HH	What! Who!

His head pops through like a ping-pong ball through a hoop and his eyes blink as if not having seen light for some time.

Don	Calm down, Harry, it's just Man Foo Hong, the journalist I told you about.
HH	Yes, yes, of course. Please sit down, Mr Hong.
MFH	Thanks.
Don	Let me know if you need anything.

With that Don is gone and I am left alone with this bizarre creature. Close up he looks much older than he appears on television, and with a liberal sprinkling of make-up. His face is heavily lined and yet entirely without hair. The eyes sparkle and as he blinks (*was* it? Surely not!) he appears to have a third eyelid – like a lizard!

HH	I see you study me, Mr Hong.
MFH	Um, sorry yes, I'm a big fan.
HH	So Don tells me. Welcome. Tell me, child, what is it you wish to know about?
MFH	Oh!

That caught me rather unawares. I'd expected some sort of preamble, some niceties about the weather or my travel arrangements but it seemed we were straight into the interview.

MFH   Um . . . Tell me, Harry, where do you get your ideas?

HH   Let me turn that round on you – where do you get *your* ideas? Where did you get the idea for that question?

MFH   I just wondered where you got your ideas from.

HH   Please no!

Harry grabs a butter knife from the table and advances towards me with a scone.

MFH   Sorry! Um, I didn't . . . mean to offend!

He sits back down and crumbles the scone in his hand, then grinds the crumbs into the carpet.

MFH   Are you under a lot of pressure at the moment?

HH   Yes.

MFH   Why?

HH   I had a bad start to the year.

MFH   Do you want to tell me about it?

HH   Will you excuse me for a moment?

MFH   Yes, but you're not leaving, are you?

HH   No, I just need to go outside.

He gets up at this point and leaves the room. There is a muffled scream like someone being wounded badly or head-butted. Harry's publicity agent Don then enters with blood streaming down his nose, with tears on his cheeks which then start to mingle with the blood.

Don	(Shouting) Did you mention Christmas?
MFH	He did!
Don	He says you brought it up!
MFH	No, I swear, you told me not to and I didn't. I just never would; I don't want to upset him!
Don	Why didn't you do what I told you to do?
MFH	I asked him where he gets his ideas from, but he went for me with a knife!
Don	That's just him being eccentric. Where's the knife now?

I fish the knife from the butter dish and hand it over to Don.

Don	Good. Any other sharp items that could be used as a weapon?
MFH	The swizzle stick from my Coke?
Don	Not really. Listen, he's under a lot of pressure, just go easy on him, okay?
MFH	Yes, I'm sorry, I thought I was.
Don	And don't mention (expletive deleted) Christmas.

Don leaves, then after about ten minutes Harry comes back into the room and sits down. He acts as if nothing has happened but I notice a slight bruise on his forehead and can smell what I think is Day Nurse on his breath.

HH	Sorry about that but I had to go to the loo.
MFH	Really?
HH	Yes. Why? Don't you believe me?
MFH	Yes, yes perhaps we can move on with the—
HH	Why would I make something like that up?
MFH	Please, I'm sorry, I believe you.
HH	Thank you. So what is it you want to know?

I scan through my papers.

MFH   Where do you . . .

I notice his hands clenching the arms of his club chair.

MFH   Where do you get the shirts made?
HH   Oh God!

He puts his head in his hands now and rocks back and forth on his chair, moaning gently. I can see the top of his head quite clearly and notice what looks like a tiny keyhole. I sketch it quickly on my pad.

HH   What's that you're drawing?
MFH   Nothing.
HH   Let me see!

He tries to snatch the pad from me, we wrestle to and fro with it for a while until it tears off in his hand.

HH   You saw my nootie!
MFH   Your what?
HH   My nootie . . . the hole on the top of my head. Mum used to call it my nootie.
MFH   Can I ask you about it?
HH   Of course! Um, well, when I was a kid my mum noticed that I got a lot more head lice than anyone else in my class. She'd treat it with the usual stuff but within a couple of days the nits would be back. Finally she decided to shave my head. That's when she discovered the nootie.
MFH   Yeah?
HH   Yeah, it's a keyhole into the brain and there was a big spider in there that was feeding off the lice.
MFH   Okay . . . Is it still in there?

HH	What?
MFH	The spider.
HH	No, it was eaten by the dormouse—
MFH	Right . . .
HH	– which had to be killed and removed in sections. Now there's just cotton wool and occasionally I'll stick a Post-it Note in there for safe keeping.

I seize my chance to steer the conversation back on to the novel.

MFH	There is an important part of the plot of *Deathrow* that hinges on the adhesiveness – or not! – of a Post-it Note. Tell me how that came about.
HH	What? Post-it Notes? I guess they were just invented by someone. I remember when they came out; they revolutionised the whole written reminder. I mean previously you had to scribble it on a pad and leave the note somewhere prominent – by the phone was a favourite place – and you'd need a way of keeping the note in place, a pinboard or even a paperweight. Of course these things seem like ancient history. If you had a pinboard or paperweight in your house these days people would laugh at you; you'd be a figure of fun and considered backward. But that's what it was like in the pre-Post-it Note world.
MFH	No, I mean the whole Carly strand to the story. Do you have a sister?
HH	Bit personal, aren't you?
MFH	Well . . . I could Google it and find out quite easily.
HH	Oh, Google blackmail, I see, charming! Yes, okay, I do have a sister.
MFH	Oh yes, now I remember seeing her on *This Is Your Life*.

HH	Yes, it was her that had all the king prawns at the buffet.
MFH	And not Snorbitz then?
HH	You're clever. Yes, whenever I mention Snorbitz I'm really meaning my sister.
MFH	Has she read the book?
HH	Yes, yes, Snorbitz has read it but of course she knew much of it already.
MFH	How much of it is truth and how much . . .
HH	Fiction?
MFH	Yes.
HH	I can't say. I mean it started off as a purely fictional work then things started to happen that were in the book—
MFH	After you'd written it?
HH	Yes.
MFH	Like?
HH	Like Jonathan Aitken getting put in prison.
MFH	You predicted that?
HH	Yes, that bit is a prediction that came true, so who's to say how much of the rest of it will come true. It's like that stuff – science fiction. I think it came directly from that spider in the nootie, pressing down on the brain, you know?
MFH	Was that definitely a medical condition?
HH	I had a brain scan, if that's what you mean. I've got it. I had copies printed up and circulated round all the chat shows. Richard and Judy were particularly interested but decided not to go with it in the end.
MFH	Yeah?
HH	Yes, they were going to put it on You Play We Pay. God, that was brilliant! Because it wasn't always that easy to tell what it was, and even if you knew what it was, to use words to describe a picture – really hard!

MFH   But isn't that what an author does?

HH   I don't know.

At this point Harry pulls his shirt collar up round his face so I can't see it. The next ten minutes are spent like this with him answering each question through the shirt collar.

MFH   Why are you doing that?

HH   I is scared now.

MFH   Scared?

HH   Yes you is scaring I.

MFH   It's helpful if I can see your face when I ask you the questions.

HH   You've seen it enough.

MFH   This is a bit rude. I'm going to have to get Don in.

HH   (Mimicking me) I'm going to have to get Don in to tell you off too, if you're not careful.

MFH   Do you want me to get Don in?

HH   (Mimicking me) Do you want me to get Don in?

MFH   Right . . .

I get up and go to the doorway where Don is standing with a cup to his ear against the door, listening in.

Don   Oh, hi, um . . . everything all right?

MFH   He's doing that thing with the collar that you said he might.

Don   Pulling it up?

MFH   Yeah, I mean I don't want to—

Don   Oh he did, did he? Right. Wait here.

Don walks purposefully back into the room. I can hear him shouting at Harry then a prolonged scuffle ensues. I sneak a look round the door and see the two men on the floor rolling around, each kicking out at the furniture: a vase crashes to the floor from an occasional table, a footstool is sent careering across the room. Each holds the other's hands as they struggle so no actual punches are thrown. Gradually, the movements start to slow as their energy is sapped until they are just two guys on the floor holding hands. Then, finally, Don stands up, grabs a bowl of pot-pourri and brings it crashing down on Harry's head. Harry makes grunting noises of 'Okay, you win!' and pulls the collar down.

HH   Can I have an ice pop?

Don   Oh, where am I gonna get an ice pop from round here?

HH   Ice pop?

Don   Okay, if you promise to behave. It's an important journalist. It's really vital we get this interview out and in a positive light. It's a great book Hazza; I truly believe that. You've got to do your best for it. Yeah?

HH   S'pose so.

Don   All right. I'll get you an ice pop, and send the journo back in.

HH   Thanks. And Don?

Don   Yes?

HH   Sorry for being difficult.

Don   Hey, that's what I'm here for, you old rogue.

I duck back out of the room as Don approaches.

Don   Should be okay now. Any more problems, let me know.

I walk back in as Harry is climbing back into his chair.

HH   Sorry about that! Hi! I'm Harry! Do you need anything? We can get you something on room service or something. Some peanuts or wine?

MFH	Um . . . No, no, that's fine.
HH	Monster Munch?
MFH	Um, well maybe if you . . . some Monster Munch would be nice.
HH	Not at all.

He reaches inside his coat and pulls out a box of matches, takes one of the matches out, and jams it into the closed box, like a makeshift aerial on an old-fashioned radio. He holds the matchbox up to his mouth and talks into it, like an old-fashioned walkie-talkie.

HH	Hello? Hello?

Then turning to me he says:

HH	No, I'm afraid there's no one in the kitchen. Sorry. I'll try again for you later. Can't have you going hungry now, can we?
MFH	Okay. So we were talking about (I comb through my notes) . . . Carly.
HH	Snorbitz, yes? What is it you wish to know?
MFH	At the end when she finds her Gonk – is that you? Are you the Gonk? You say you are.
HH	Do I look like a Gonk?
MFH	No . . . but . . .
HH	Are you calling me a Gonk?
MFH	No, I meant . . .
HH	Relax, I'm playing with you, just tooling around. Am I the Gonk? Let me see. I certainly was a little Gonkish in my relationship with my sister.
MFH	Gonkish?
HH	Yes, you know, playing the Gonk.
MFH	Not really.

285

HH	Yes, a little passive, a little bit polyester cotton felt mix, if you know what I mean.
MFH	Not really. What does the Gonk mean?
HH	I think the Gonk character in the book represents Everyman.
MFH	Michael Billington in the *Guardian* saw it very much as a Christ figure.
HH	Did 'e? He must be off his rocker! No, the Gonk, to me, is Everyman. Often when I'm in a difficult position I ask myself what would the Gonk do in this situation? You know?
MFH	Okay, let's look at another aspect of the book. You namecheck a number of celebrities.
HH	No, they were just names I made up.
MFH	You made up the names?
HH	Yes, I was completely shocked when the lawyers got involved and said that many of these names already existed. I suppose, subconsciously, I had maybe heard of them, like by osmosis.
MFH	But you present a show reviewing the week's TV.
HH	*TV Burp*, yes?
MFH	So you watch hours and hours of television.
HH	What is your point?
MFH	So you must have heard of say . . . Bradley Walsh?
HH	Walshy? Yeah, of course I know Walshy. Met him at the ITV Christmas party – nice guy and a fine actor but I've never heard of any of the others.
MFH	Jonathan Ross?
HH	Who? No.
MFH	What about Alan Titchmarsh?
HH	Pure coincidence. Of course once the book came out, all these various people of whom you speak came out the woodwork and wanted money, but I gave them something better than money – I gave them my friendship.

MFH   Friendship?

HH   Yes, I took over Pontins, Camber Sands, and booked the whole lot of them in – Bradley, Dale, Alan, Carol Vorderman – and we partied like it was 1994 again. The weird thing? We all got on really well, then after about a week they started to act out the novel. That's when I asked them whether they'd be in the film of the book I've been planning.

MFH   Were they up for it?

HH   No. No, they thought if we were all working together it would spoil our friendship. Maybe they have a point – business and pleasure and all that. Also, they weren't convinced by the Gonk costume. They said it wasn't realistic and that people watching the film would be distracted by it.

MFH   Is the film going ahead?

HH   Some guys at Film 4 are interested but want it to be more social comment. They want the Gonk to be more working class and maybe living on a big inner city sink estate.

MFH   Give me an idea of a typical working day for Harry Hill the author.

HH   Why?

MFH   I think it would be interesting for people.

HH   Okay, well, get up, clean my teeth, go to the toilet—

MFH   More the bit where you're writing . . .

HH   Oh! Um, well, I sit at a desk and turn the laptop computer on, which isn't on my lap, but my desk, which I'm not sure is allowed actually, but anyway I turn it on and start typing the ideas on to it, then after about an hour I have a cup of coffee and then start typing again, then it's lunchtime—

MFH   Okay, I can see this interview is not really going anywhere.

I get up to leave.

HH   No! Wait! Please don't go! What's wrong?

MFH   You're not answering any of my questions! I'm wast-
      ing my time.

HH   Okay! Okay! Ask me another. Anything. Go on!

MFH   Anything?

HH   Yup.

MFH   What happened at Christmas?

HH   I put my Christmas tree out for the bin men without
      realising I'd left a chocolate decoration on it, and I
      only found out when I looked out of my bedroom
      window at midnight to see my (a tear wells up in his
      eye) . . . Sorry, this is painful . . . to see my neigh-
      bour . . . my neighbour Harold Pinter . . .

MFH   Harold Pinter, the playwright?

HH   Yes. He's standing over the tree and his wife—

MFH   Lady Antonia Fraser?

HH   Yes, Tony is directing a torch at the chocolate decora-
      tion and staring at me. Harold takes the choccy,
      unwraps it and puts the whole thing in his gob. He
      chews it for a few moments then sticks his tongue
      out, and Tony plays her torch on it so I can see the
      mushed and melted chocolate, then he swallows it
      down. I'm sorry, I can't go on . . .

With that the floppy-collared loon is up out of the chair and
through the door. A moment passes then Don the PR enters.

Don   How'd it go?

MFH   Um . . . fine.

Two days later, at around one in the morning, I received an
anonymous phone call. The caller was rude about me

288

personally and my trade, and then proceeded to boast of 'a fantastic start to the year'. It sounded like Harold Pinter.

Man Foo Hong is a Features Writer for many of our most popular men's magazines and writes a daily blog at manfoohong.com.

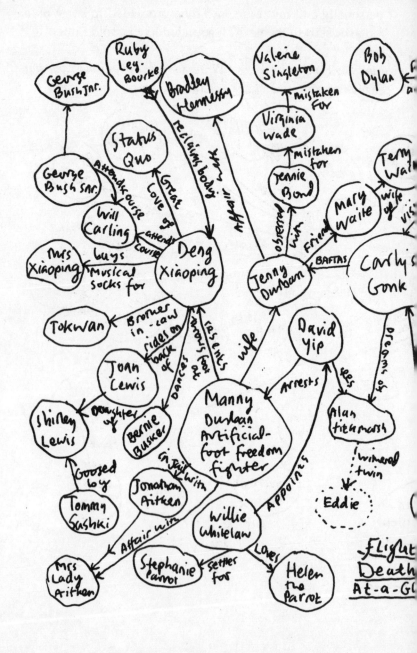

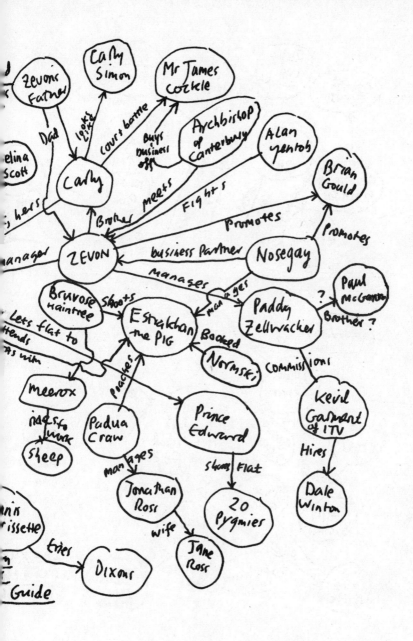

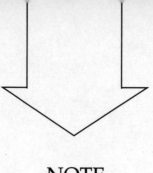

NOTE

If you've been affected by any of the issues in this book maybe you should be on some sort of tablets? Might be worth looking into.